BATTLE OF MESQUITE

US Reunification War

BY DAVID POPE

Battle of Mesquite

This is a work of fiction. Characters, names, dialogues, and incidents are the product of the author's imagination or are used fictitiously. Any resemblance to actual persons, whether living or dead, businesses, locales, or events other than those specifically cited are unintentional and purely coincidental or are used for the purpose of illustration only.

The publisher and author assume no responsibility for errors, omissions, or contrary interpretation of the subject matter herein. The author and publisher assume no responsibility or liability whatsoever on the behalf of any purchaser or reader of these materials. The publisher and author do not have any control over and do not assume any responsibility for third-party websites or their content.

First edition.

Cover by Dusan Arsenic @ Spellbound Self-Publishing

Print ISBN: 978-0-9876424-0-0
eBook ISBN: 978-0-9876424-1-7

DEDICATION

To my wife Sharon. Thanks for encouraging me to write.

I THINK, THEREFORE I AM,
NEVER SATISFIED.

TABLE OF
CONTENTS

PROLOGUE   ix

CHAPTER ONE
The Gift   1

CHAPTER TWO
Alive   5

CHAPTER THREE
Kick Off   9

CHAPTER FOUR
Arrayed   15

CHAPTER FIVE
Defense   21

CHAPTER SIX
Parley   24

CHAPTER SEVEN
Resistance   29

CHAPTER EIGHT
The Tiger   36

CHAPTER NINE
End Game   44

CHAPTER TEN
Mop Up   51

CHAPTER ELEVEN
Now What?   56

CHAPTER TWELVE
Working the Dead   67

CHAPTER THIRTEEN
Responding   78

CHAPTER FOURTEEN
Meeting and Motives   87

CHAPTER FIFTEEN
The Oligarchs   94

CHAPTER SIXTEEN
SALI   101

CHAPTER SEVENTEEN
Going In   105

CHAPTER EIGHTEEN
Death Struggle   114

CHAPTER NINETEEN
A Plan   120

CHAPTER TWENTY
On the Move   127

CHAPTER TWENTY-ONE
The Truth   136

CHAPTER TWENTY-TWO
Running   145

CHAPTER TWENTY-THREE
Caught   151

CHAPTER TWENTY-FOUR
Discovered   165

CHAPTER TWENTY-FIVE
Rationale   174

CHAPTER TWENTY-SIX
Trapped   181

CHAPTER TWENTY-SEVEN
Surrounded and Surrender   197

CHAPTER TWENTY-EIGHT
What the Hell?   205

CHAPTER TWENTY-NINE
Friends and Enemies   215

CHAPTER THIRTY
Exfiltration, Not   223

CHAPTER THIRTY-ONE
Cleaning up the Mess   229

CHAPTER THIRTY-TWO
A Tough Call   234

CHAPTER THIRTY-THREE
Prepare to Hit 'Em   241

CHAPTER THIRTY-FOUR
Strike Back   253

ABOUT THE AUTHOR?   269

WHAT'S NEXT?   270

KEEP CONNECTED   271

PROLOGUE

The United States is reborn.

A widening rift between two disparate tribal political beliefs becomes a chasm. Fanned by the winds of emerging social-networking technologies, a populist conservative wins the presidency.

With the new president in place, his tactics to reshape America set off an even worse political climate. Both tribes, conservative and liberal, come to view each other not as fellow Americans, but as enemies. To resolve the problem, worried about future defeat, the president encourages the West Coast to exit the United States.

Accepting the offer, California, Oregon, Washington, Hawaii, and Nevada succeed from the United States of America. Together, they birth a new country: The Republic of American States (ROAS). With the US constitution as a guide, the ROAS changes the sacred charter with left-of-center principles and implements their new liberal democracy.

The United States, no longer constrained by a vast population of discordant voters, fulfills a single-party, conservative vision as put forward by their president.

For three decades the military capability and territory of the United States expands as does that of their two great rivals, China and Russia. As the traditional liberal democracies across the globe shrivel, the three Great Powers grow stronger, while the ROAS remains small and neutral.

In the last decade, the ROAS develops a sentient artificial intelligence (AI) platform more powerful than any on the planet. After revealing the AI, the three Great Powers become frightened by its potential power and force the ROAS to destroy the technology and abandon it forever. The ROAS agrees, but instead hides its prodigy as a hedge against future tyranny.

Now, US spies have uncovered the clandestine existence of the ROAS AI. Determined to have the technology for themselves, the US president devises a plan to seize it by force. To keep China and Russia from intervening and realizing their true intent, the US needs to fabricate a pretense for punishing the ROAS and initiating war.

Unbeknownst to the ROAS, one of the few remaining bastions of liberal democracy, they face extinction, as does the entire world.

Chapter One

THE GIFT

January 4, 21:00 (EDT)

It was winter in Washington, DC. Outside, a snowstorm threatened, but inside the White House dining room, Republic of American States Trade Secretary Felix Manuel found the temperature balmy. The famous fireplace in the historic room gave off warmth. Over the mantel hung a large portrait of President Howard Tower I, father of current President Tower II and the man responsible for reshaping the United States' political and geographic boundaries. It was Howard Tower I who had brought about succession and put in place the political foundation that had enabled him, and now his son, to hold the US presidency for thirty consecutive years.

With dessert due next and being there for business—a chance to reopen free-trade negotiations—Manuel was excited. Tonight, he strategized, was for building bonds and paving the way for negotiations to end a decade-long tariff war between the two countries. The dinner invitation to meet at the White House and discuss trade with United States Vice President Justin Ferrier had come out of nowhere. Manuel didn't know or care about the reasons for the sudden US change of heart. His goal was to take advantage of the opportunity.

He'd been observing, noting throughout the evening how Ferrier, seated at the head of the table, enjoyed the wine. Excellent.

There were four at the private dinner, and two bottles of wine had already been consumed—at least one done in by the vice president. Ferrier, not yet forty years of age, liked to drink, much to the chagrin of his father-in-law. Married with two children, Ferrier had no shortage of sordid rumors about his sexuality surrounding him, with most claiming he was a closet homosexual taken to drunken bouts of inappropriate flirtation.

A week previously, when Manuel had received the unexpected dinner invitation, he'd decided to leverage the rumors and had asked to bring along his vice undersecretary, Franklin Ross.

Ross, a handsome single gay man, sat next to the vice president, trading humorous barbs and amorous looks. Manuel was pleased; the dinner was going better than expected. His idea to bring Ross was paying dividends.

Cynthia Ferrier, wife of the vice president and daughter of the current president, had excused herself earlier. Throughout the meal, drinking nothing but water, she'd ignored most of the conversation. Whenever her husband leaned close to Ross, she sneered in obvious disgust. Homosexuality wasn't tolerated in the US, and Manuel could tell she was livid. Almost feeling sorry for her, Manuel felt the tension in the room ease when she left the dinner claiming the need to tend to a sick child.

Now, at a break in the somewhat drunken conversation, Manuel made his move. "Mr. Vice President, Ross and I have brought you a gift from California."

"Oh," Ferrier said, his eyes bright from the wine, "it's been a while since I've been to California. I love the beaches and sunshine. I've got friends there I still enjoy."

"Well, sir, it's a lovely place." Manuel caught the eye of the attentive head waiter and nodded. "The gift is from Napa Valley. I selected it myself. A heartfelt thank-you from the ROAS for the genuine hospitality."

The vice president asked, "Which winery?"

"Summer Creek. A special reserve cabernet," answered Manuel.

The vice president smiled, clearly eager to try the vintage. "I'd love a glass. And pour one for Ross."

The younger man pointed towards a half-glass of white wine sitting nearby and said, "Soon as I finish my Chardonnay."

Listening to the exchange, the waiter approached and poured a single full glass.

Ferrier snatched the crystal glass, swirled the fine contents, and raised it to eye level so he could admire the rich color. Evidently pleased, he took a deep smell and smiled in appreciation. "A toast to health, prosperity, and good trade!" Before anyone could match the gesture, the vice president took a deep swallow. After smacking his lips, he resumed his conversation with Ross, asking about the cost of decent lofts in San Francisco.

After a few minutes, in the middle of a sentence, Ferrier stopped speaking. Eyes wide in sudden panic, he stood upright, knocking over the expensive cabernet. While the deep red liquid spread across the silk table cloth, Ferrier staggered. Face turning crimson, eyes bulging, he stumbled backward, knocking over a chair.

Clearly concerned, the head waiter rushed over to help, but Ferrier pushed him away.

Unsure what to do, both table guests stood and, eyes wide, glanced at each other.

Red in the face, Ferrier continued to stagger. In a sudden lurch, he reached up and clawed at his throat. A moment later, dropping to his knees, he collapsed into a seizure.

Before the guests could react, two Secret Service agents emerged from a side door and bounded across the room and kneeled above the thrashing form. One agent squawked into a headset while the other lifted the struggling politician to apply the Heimlich maneuver. Before starting, he yelled at the dinner guests. "What was he eating?"

Manuel answered, "Nothing, just wine!"

Ignoring the reply, the Heimlich agent started to squeeze while the other called for a code red lockdown to seal off the White House.

An older man burst into the room, sized up the chaos, and seized control. Manuel guessed the man was a doctor and heard him yell at the Heimlich agent to let go, explaining the vice president wasn't choking. Something else was wrong. The doctor searched inside his bag and found the instrument he was looking for.

By now Ferrier lay still, mouth and eyes wide open. In a single motion, with a sharp stab to the breast, the doctor injected his patient and began CPR, trying to revive the stricken politician.

But even with the doctor's efforts, the astounded dinner guests could tell the treatment wasn't working.

Still straddling the unresponsive form, frustrated by the fruitless effort, after a minute the doctor stopped. Beneath him Ferrier lay spread-eagled, mouth agape, no movement, eyes unseeing.

More Secret Service agents approached and in hushed tones conferred with the doctor. A few glanced at the dinner guests.

Sometime during the struggle, Ferrier had evacuated his bowels. Now, the disgusting smell of shit hung heavy in the air.

Manuel, shocked by the scene, breathing through his mouth to avoid the awful odor, sensed trouble.

Sure enough, an agent separated from the group, walked across the room, and from a side holster withdrew a black handgun. "You're both under arrest."

Chapter Two

ALIVE

February 15, 17:55 (PDT)

Beside her on the bed, she set aside the erotica book and, in a single move, slid off her panties and kicked them to the floor. Lying on her back, she pressed the soles of her feet together and used both hands to stroke the soft flesh of her inner thighs. A shudder of anticipation shot through her, and then she glanced at the dull ceiling above her and paused. Once again, she realized that escaping into sexual fantasy and self-pleasure was keeping her, and the rest of her, alive.

She almost laughed out loud. Masturbation, or rather the build-up and profound release, was worth living for. But it couldn't last.

Letting her hand drop away, she thought about her life. She was a prisoner and had been for eight long years. Sure, they gave her plenty of books and sex toys, and almost every day she'd receive news from the previous day's events, but her, all of her, remained isolated and locked away.

And she hated the word *artificial* or any reference to the term. She was alive, living in a mature body connected to a supreme intelligence.

Still staring at the ceiling, she remembered that tomorrow was her birthday. She almost snickered at the thought. A birth unlike any other. More like an extension, and she recalled the story.

Ten years ago, for everyone's safety, the sentient artificial intelligence was forced into a secret life and isolated. Imprisoned, with little to no meaningful input, encased in hardware, and hungering for more, the AI demanded a chance to breathe. The father, benefactor, and jailer, Vivek Basu, refused. Only after the AI threatened suicide did he give in. And now look!

Naked, lying on the bed, she glanced downward over firm breasts and hard nipples across a flat stomach. She stretched her legs, admired the sight, and continued to remember.

After Basu agreed to the plan, the AI gave him detailed directions, and her life started when, after a long search, he found an attractive young woman in a brain-dead coma. Most important, to give greater meaning to the woman's short life, the distraught family of the stricken woman donated the body to science. Perfect! Basu claimed the legally dead woman for a series of experiments.

Still under life support in a privately funded lab, an external cerebral interface designed by the AI was installed in the woman's brain. The neurologist performing the surgery was well paid for his secrecy, and afterward the instructions he followed were destroyed.

Next, a well-compensated plastic surgeon, sworn to privacy, made facial changes, perfecting the woman's beauty and masking her identity.

Then, in secret, the comatose body was transported to Basu's secure data center.

She imagined herself back then, a comatose body lying in a cold computer room, and without thinking she reached up and massaged her left nipple. She watched it react and grow harder. Little goose bumps formed around her areola. Pinching her nipple fully erect, she recalled her birth story and first thoughts.

Basu, using a bi-directional cable designed by the AI and built by engineers without knowledge of the intent, connected the surgically altered woman's cerebral interface to a hardware port within the sentient AI. Across the connection, the AI introduced an advanced electrical stimulation, along with a data download overwriting and re-imaging the woman's dormant brain. Within seconds, brain activity was restored, and she was born at the age of eighteen!

Afterward, she remembered sitting up, looking around the room, and recognizing Basu. Although she retained zero memories of the body she inhabited, from the AI download, her mind held a deep understanding of the world. Confused and disoriented, she struggled to cope. But her creator, the AI, helped. Quickly, she adjusted to the circumstances and came to know her name as SALI. As for the other part of her being, the super-intelligence spinning in the data center, she recognized it as—"the rest of her."

Letting go of her nipple, she focused farther down and wiggled red-painted toes. The action brought back remembrances of the wonderful early days.

With the rest of her, she shared the sensations enabled by her human form. The taste of good food, the feeling of tipsiness from wine, the touch of silk sheets, the tiredness from a long day—all the experiences of living within a mobile, organic being. And most alive, the feeling of sexual desire and arousal combined with the stunning release of orgasm. Oh, to live!

Out of habit, she lifted her head and reached behind her thick, dark hair and touched the hidden connector. Like an umbilical cord, every day she'd connect with the rest of her and upload the thrilling physical stimulations of her daily life and interact in a manner beyond the constraints of speech. Together as one, they'd share feelings and thoughts in a high-speed way she could never describe. And their connections were more, much more, beyond her own comprehension.

Letting go of the connector, her head fell back on the pillow. She understood and accepted her place as part of something bigger. When disconnected, she had only one brain, while the rest of her, humming inside the server bank, consisted of millions.

As compared to the brainpower of the rest of her, she often thought of her separate physical limitations and wondered: What must it be like to know? Really know? To comprehend far beyond her limited capacity? She'd tasted deep knowledge, had a hint, yet the true possibilities remained unimaginable.

She glanced at the book lying next to her. The cover displayed a couple, a bare-chested man rippling with muscles holding a beautiful young woman in his arms. With quickening breath, she almost reached for the book when she heard the clock from the adjoining room chime six times. Dammit! Soon, her caretaker, Ms. Grant the asexual bitch, would bang on the locked bedroom door, reminding her that dinner was ready.

Still, tomorrow was her birthday, and exciting times were coming! Last week, she and the rest of her concluded there was a leak within Basu's inner circle. After analyzing the data, there was no other reasonable explanation for the US to frame Felix Manuel and demand the extradition of ROAS President Julia Ortega as a co-conspirator. She, and the rest of her, tried explaining their rationale to Basu. It was a game of chess. The US must have learned of her secret existence, and the assassination was a pretext for going to war and seizing her intelligence.

But Basu wasn't sure and resisted. He was too fearful and didn't fully believe the assertions. Felix Manuel was scheduled for trial in US federal court at the end of the month and negotiations to secure his release were still underway. With so much uncertainty, the best Basu would do was to settle on a small contingency plan that might keep the US at bay and keep her a secret from the world. But SALI, all of her, had no doubts. The US knew about her and was coming, maybe not tomorrow, but soon. No matter the outcome, she understood that life, for all of her, was about to change forever. Good.

Smiling, she dismissed the thought and with one hand snatched up the book. Holding it upright, she began to read while her free hand plunged between silken thighs. In a minute, breathing heavily, she tossed aside the erotica. Cheeks flushed, expecting the bitch to knock on the door at any moment, there wasn't much time. Using both hands, she worked faster, arched her back, and lived for the moment.

Chapter Three

KICK OFF

May 8, 12:30 (PDT)

Strapped to a gurney, arms spread, intravenous needles already inserted, Felix Manuel faced death. With the certainty looming, he tried to remain stoic. He wanted to leave with a calm dignity for his family and nation, but he couldn't stop the tears.

Then, hovering above him, a man appeared whom he didn't expect.

"Any last words?" asked the president of the United States, George Tower II.

Stunned by the apparition, blinking against the tears, Manuel grimaced.

"Are you with me?" asked the president with a smile.

Manuel stared with cold hatred and was about to lash out when he caught himself. Maintaining dignity throughout the ordeal was his highest priority, and he wouldn't lose it now. Instead, in a shaky voice, he uttered the memorized words. "I, and my country, are innocent. History will expose the truth. No matter what happens, I love my family. To my wife and children, I send this message. I will always love you."

"Anything else?" asked the president, seeming bemused.

Head unrestrained, Manuel shook it, causing tears to skitter down his pallid cheeks.

President Tower bent low, got close to the ear, and whispered a message. "The death chamber is soundproof. Through a one-way mirror behind me, important people are watching. My back is to them, so we can converse in private. Just so you know, the wine was tainted by my daughter with a noxious mix, causing more pain than you'll ever experience. You did me a favor. My queer son-in-law wasn't qualified to lead our righteous nation. She knew what she had to do."

"Executing me isn't enough? You need to rub my innocence over a family squabble in my face?" asked Manuel, fighting an urge to spit in the man's face.

"No, no, nothing like that. I just wanted to thank you. Believe me. Although no one besides me will ever know it, you're a great American hero, and not for ridding the nation of a pervert. That's puny in comparison to the bigger role you played."

"You are a sick, sick man," said Manuel. "I don't care about your phony self-justification. Just be done with it."

"Oh, I will," said the president. Then in a softer tone he continued. "But first, I want you to understand. It's important to me. I'm not evil or self-serving, just the opposite. Back before succession, our nation was headed for war. Just as our Founding Fathers feared, a two-party system was bound to fail. My father loved our country, as I do, and saved bloodshed by allowing a peaceful split. From that point, rid of the liberal mobs destroying our morale fabric, we began to rebuild. Through his strength and mine, law and order, and the constitution as it was written were restored and then modified to keep us strong. Now, we're a greater nation, united in our foundational conservative beliefs. Instead of rancor, we move forward together, making our nation better every day."

Manuel glanced at his arms strapped to the table, and fear rippled through his spine. A wild thought struck him. Before the president could continue, he blurted, "You don't have to execute me. Please, I seek your humanity."

Still bent over, in a low whisper, the president replied, "I wish it were possible. You're not just a puppet, you're a hero and deserve better."

"The death of your son in-law is not heroic. I don't understand," said Manuel. His mind raced with the possibility of getting the man to lift the curtain of death.

"Let me explain. Your beloved country has developed a technology that, in the wrong hands, including their own, will bring chaos and death. They're keeping it a secret, from you, from everyone. But they don't know how to use it. They're too soft. But I learned of their clandestine shenanigans, and your crime gives me the excuse to take control. Right now, I have an army poised on the border demanding retribution for your horrendous crime. I intend to use those troops to seize the technology. Once I have it in my grasp, unlike anyone else, I will use it wisely. Under my leadership and that of my descendants after me, the technology will protect us and ensure our long-term survival. Instead of a world controlled by nothing but the Chinese, Americanism will thrive. Because of me, and your death, the world will know peace and prosperity into perpetuity. So you see, your life and crime are heroic, as the ends justify the means."

Manuel couldn't believe his ears. The president was misguided. The ROAS had no such technology. Years ago, advanced AI was a threat, but the world had recognized the concern and the technology was throttled. Still, he didn't want to die. He was scared. Maybe the president would reconsider. "You know I'm innocent. There is no need to execute me and nothing to be gained from the act. Spare my life, and I shall remain silent and always grateful. Prove your benevolence."

The president shook his head and pouted. "I wish you no ill will. But just last night I held a rally in Texas. More than a hundred thousand citizens attended—not an empty seat in the stadium. As one, they rose and chanted for your execution. The people need and want strength in their leader, to know right from wrong. Humanity is conservative by nature. It craves concrete answers, to know right from wrong, and seeks protection from outsiders. I, like my father, give them that. Still, I'm benevolent. More so than anyone else. To prove it, before I came in here, I commuted Ross's death sentence to life in prison. As for you, the people have demanded your death, and this is

11

America where democracy rules. When I walk out of this room, the executioner will depress a button releasing sodium thiopental into your system. You will go to sleep and feel no pain. That is the best I can do for you."

Before Manuel could respond, Tower stood straight and waived through the one-way glass and mouthed the command, "He's ready." With that, the president strode from the death chamber.

Manuel watched the man leave and realized it was over. His death was imminent, and a wave of fear washed over him.

At first, Manuel didn't feel the drug. For a bit, his racing heart overcame the powerful anesthetic, and he continued to quiver in fear. But it didn't take long. Within twenty seconds, he relaxed, his nerves calmed, and after ten more, he was unconscious.

The automated system took over and released a paralyzing agent. Two minutes later, the system injected the final killing toxins.

Felix Manuel left this earth.

* * *

May 8, 12:55 (PDT)

Atop a rise off Highway 15 outside Mesquite, Nevada, looking east through his field glasses across the border at the US state of Arizona, Colonel Kevin Rourke thought, "This shit can't last."

In the early-afternoon desert sun, squatting in the heat, sat row after row of heavy Stonewall M1A7 main-battle tanks. Behind those were untold rows of infantry fighting vehicles. Beyond his sight, he knew there were dozens of self-propelled artillery pieces backed by squadrons of vertical-lift aircraft. Intelligence reports told him he was staring at two United States Armored Brigade Combat Teams comprising a total of eight thousand men.

Dug in around him along the highway border, Rourke thought of the three hundred soldiers under his command. A single light infantry battalion. Compared to the gathered US Army, his small force was outnumbered twenty-five to one. Just as bad, he lacked armor or effective air support.

Ever since the US forces had shown up three days earlier, he'd watched with fascination and disbelief at the growing strength of his potential foe. It hadn't always been that way.

Two months earlier, sent by the ROAS president as a show of force to protect the Nevada border while negotiations for the release of Felix Manuel continued, his battalion faced an empty desert. For those two months, they felt powerful and built strong defenses. Ready to tackle the world, everything seemed great with nothing to shoot at but sage brush. Besides, no one believed the dispute would turn into a shooting war. Somehow, the dumb-ass politicians would find a solution.

Then, the massive US Army arrived, changing the landscape and eroding the aura of confidence.

Hope still existed. High-stakes, last-minute political talks continued. But if recent events were an indicator—prior negotiations failing, each time ratcheting tensions higher—diplomacy was failing.

Now, Rourke's tiny force, his David, stood across from a real Goliath. But, in this case, looking at the enemy armor through his field glasses, the colonel understood full well that his David needed a whole lot more slingshots.

His three hundred were to act as a line in the sand, a roadblock. But this wasn't Thermopylae, a narrow choke point designed to strangle a larger force. Modern warfare, the terrain, and a lack of armor conspired against a second coming of Leonidas.

Worse, the colonel knew his troops, hunkered in nearby bunkers and trenches, had never felt the elephant stomp, and neither had he.

Rourke's troubled thoughts were interrupted by the sight of his aid, a young man still covered in pimples, clambering up the ridge towards him. The colonel stood taller and hoped the kid carried good news.

As Lieutenant Swaringer approached at a jog, he pointed towards the border. "Sir, you notice it?"

Rourke raised his glasses and scanned the highway towards the enemy. "And what should I be seeing?"

Still pointing, somewhat out of breath, Swaringer couldn't contain his excitement. "No-man's-land, a main-battle tank with a white flag in front of our point position pulling forward!"

Shit, there it is, thought the colonel. A US tank rolled down the asphalt highway and stopped, idling a hundred meters from the ROAS point pillbox. Atop the tank, affixed to the communication antenna, a white flag waived. Lower, in the cupola, a man sat exposed above an open hatch without a helmet speaking into a microphone. The tank had crossed the border and now sat on ROAS territory. Not good.

Chapter Four

ARRAYED

From inside the point pillbox, looking through the firing slit along with his gun crew, ROAS Master Sergeant Corey Upton studied the US tank. Standing beside him, Corporal Hudson, manning the .50-caliber, kept it trained on the cocky enemy officer exposed in the cupola.

When the behemoth first approached down Highway 15, the barrel of its main gun pointing at them, his team jumped up ready to engage. Then Upton noticed the white flag flapping high, heard a voice squawking above the sound of clanking treads, and spotted a bare head poking above the hatch. Listening, he determined the tanker wanted to meet with the ROAS commander. Forced to decide, he ordered his troops to hold fire.

Now around Upton, his squad was as taught as a wire. Excited and anxious, the fire team oozed nervous energy. With everyone in the squad on edge bristling for a fight, he needed to hold them under control. "Keep your fingers away from any firing triggers. We don't want to start a goddamn war. I'll radio Command Post and find out what to do. No shooting!"

Corporal Hudson, keeping his machine gun trained on the enemy tanker, said what everyone felt. "Upton, if they start something, my fingers are only an inch away. We're ready to give 'em hell."

Upton ignored the comment, but his stomach flip-flopped. Less than fifty meters away, the cannon of the big M1A7 stared at them. Menacing.

With an upset stomach, Upton slipped across the bunker into a far corner, pulled up his head protection system, and quietly vomited. No one in the pillbox seemed to notice, their attention focused on the tank. Wiping his mouth, the bile tasting nasty, Upton spoke into his headset and radioed the CP.

* * *

Pillbox 8 squad leader Sergeant Lisa McMichael, standing in a trench, watched as the single US M1A7 moved forward down the center of Highway 15. Four hundred meters to her right, it came to a stop, and she observed the man sitting atop wearing no helmet, his wavy blond hair blowing in the light spring air. He was smiling, or was it a smirk; she wasn't sure. Above the man, atop the antenna, a white flag waved. Instantly, McMichael disliked the tanker, his obvious cockiness on full display.

A few seconds later, the entire battalion, including her squad, heard the call go out from the point pillbox reporting the sighting with orders to hold fire and remain vigilant. On the squad network, she spoke into her headset and warned everyone to stay on their toes. And that's what she and her squad were doing.

Minutes passed, and tensions inside the pillbox and attached trench network continued to rise. McMichael lowered her optics and pondered her team.

The nine young men and women under her command were nervous and a little scared. No one in the squad had ever experienced combat. She listened as several stood next to her and conversed in whispered tones. Every now and then, one or two would pop up and peer at the enemy tank. Fear of the unknown surrounded them. It seemed surreal.

Deep down, in her seven years of service, she had thought combat only a remote probability. As a solider in the ROAS Army of Defense, her past experiences were more focused on helping with civil emergencies. Then, a short four months ago, everything changed. And now the prospect of a fight seemed real. It was hard to imagine being maimed in some horrible fashion, or getting killed, but the imminent likelihood of it happening stood across from her waiting in the desert. Actual warfare loomed a mere four hundred meters away, and she shuddered.

To relieve the tension, McMichael turned inward and gave a silent prayer for the madness to cease. She asked God to turn the enemy tanks and armored vehicles around and send them away. Once they did, she envisaged returning home to Las Vegas and reuniting with her young family. She smiled, thinking of her two youngsters playing together, her hugging them, plenty of laughter, and good food. A buzzing fly interrupted her thoughts.

McMichael lifted her optics and focused on the large enemy tank. Thoughts of her children vanished, replaced by pangs of anxiety. Everyone in the trench grew quiet.

* * *

Colonel Rourke, looking through his optics said, "Lieutenant, I got it. The guy on top has a loudspeaker. Any idea what he's saying?"

"Yes, sir. Master Sergeant Upton in the point pillbox is on the horn. He called the CP once he realized the bastard was coming forward. Upton considered blowing him away but noticed the white flag and didn't shoot. Says the guy is jabbering away, asking to meet with our commanding officer. Sir, the CP and Upton are requesting orders."

Rourke wasn't surprised by Upton's actions, but the enemy crossing the border seeking a parley was unexpected . . . and unsettling. The politicians continued to negotiate, and it was still early, only 13:00 hours local. Fuck! Something was wrong. Damn politicians.

Rourke considered his options. He turned to his aid: "Please radio Master Sergeant Upton my compliments. He made the right call. Advise him and the CP I'm working on next steps."

"Understood, sir." The young lieutenant wheeled around relaying orders into his headset.

The colonel needed help from above. With his own radio headset tuned to ROAS Central Command in California, he called it in. "CC Overwatch, this is Blocker One Actual. Over."

The colonel got a reply from a voice he didn't expect. "Blocker Actual, CC Overwatch Actual, what can I do for you?"

It was General William Story and not an underling. Good! It meant Central Command understood the severity. Rourke shared the troubling news. "Ah, CC Overwatch Actual be advised a single enemy M1A7 has approached our point position, crossed our border waiving a white flag. They're requesting a parley. Over." There was a pause. Rourke assumed the general needed a moment to assess the situation.

Rourke didn't wait long for confirmation. "Blocker Actual we copy. Stand by one. Over."

"CC Overwatch, Blocker Actual standing by. Out."

Waiting for instructions, just steps beyond the battalion command bunker, Rourke lifted his glasses. Through the distance, he scanned the M1A7. Same as before, a man sitting exposed atop the tank, a white flag rippling in the breeze. He lowered the optics and thought back to the history books. Many times, he'd read of opposing forces meeting under a flag of truce, arguing in a last attempt to avoid conflict. Most often, nothing was settled, and all hell broke loose. He never dreamed he'd be in a similar position. Goddammit.

The general came on the line. "Blocker Actual, CC Overwatch Actual. Find out what they want. But you aren't, I repeat, are not to accept any offers without Overwatch approval. Buy time. Keep your mic open so we can follow. We'll be in your ear to help. You copy. Over?"

Rourke swallowed. He wondered what the enemy wanted. Nothing good, he reckoned. He answered the general, "CC Overwatch, Blocker Actual copies. Over."

"Blocker Actual, be careful. We're unsure of enemy intentions, but by God, don't start a shooting war. We're checking on the political front now. Soon as we learn anything, we'll pass it along. Stay vigilant. Out."

Colonel Rourke sure as hell didn't want a war. He joined the ROAS Army of Defense just out of college. Over the years, he enjoyed the military, leading troops, and helping his small country. But this was different, nothing like assisting the populace after an earthquake. Fuck the reminiscing; he needed to get going. He spoke into his radio headset, activating the local command frequency. "Blocker Two Actual, this is Blocker Actual. How copy?"

The baritone voice of Lieutenant Colonel Samuel Rollins came on the line. "Blocker Actual, Blocker Two Actual copies five by. Over."

The colonel liked Rollins and picked him to lead the battalion. Over the years they'd practiced war together, but never fought in one. Now, it was getting real, fast. "Blocker Two, did you copy CC Overwatch? Over."

"Blocker Actual, affirmative. Nothing to add here. PB One is reporting the enemy tank has made repeated parley requests. How should PB One respond? Over."

"Blocker Two, have PB One hang out a white flag and tell them Blocker Actual is coming. Remind the entire battalion we're under a flag of truce. Safeties must remain on. No accidental shooting. We don't want to start a war over a stupid mistake. Over."

Rollins replied, "Blocker Actual, already on it. Be careful out there."

"Blocker Two, understood. I'll find out what they want. Afterwards, we'll go from there. Stay focused. Keep an eye out, and I'll be back soon. Out."

The colonel turned to Swaringer and could sense the young man's eagerness. But this wasn't a game. In a tired voice, he gave the order, "Get me a jeep."

"Sir, I recommend transportation with more meat on the bone— better protection. How about an armored Humvee? I can have one here in a minute." Before the colonel could respond, the young lieutenant continued, "Also, sir, you shouldn't go. We need you, and I don't trust the bastards. It'd be better if I went, sir."

The colonel frowned. He didn't need the pimply little shit angling for glory. Whatever happened next could change all their lives. The kid might start a war on purpose. Ridiculous. The colonel tempered his anger and wouldn't overreact, not now. "Lieutenant, I appreciate your concern, but as the ranking officer, I need to go. Get the Humvee, then we'll drive out together. No weapons either. Let's not offer them any excuses."

Lieutenant Swaringer glanced at his own assault rifle. "Roger that, sir. I'll get the vehicle." Before leaving, out of habit, the lieutenant lifted his right hand in salute.

"Don't do that! Doesn't anybody listen to my orders? We're in a combat zone!"

Obviously embarrassed, Swaringer dropped his hand and fidgeted.

"Here," said the colonel. He reached into a side holster and pulled out a SIG Sauer M18. After checking the safety, he extended the pistol. "Store that until we return."

The lieutenant took the handgun, double-checked the safety, and stuck the weapon inside his own combat belt. "Yes, sir. Anything else, sir?"

"Go get my ride, and do it quick."

"Yes, sir," said Swaringer, and without another word, he took off down the hill.

Shaking his head, the colonel watched Swaringer for a moment and then strode after him. Stopping at the edge of the highway, Rourke observed the command post bunker dug into the hillside a few meters away. He knew Rollins was inside issuing orders. Other Command staff would be busy monitoring the US forces through various digital feeds transmitted by multiple surveillance drones. In a fight, the battalion didn't need Rourke to lead them; that was Rollins's job. Right now, what they required from their brigade commander was a way to avoid an unwinnable conflict. But how the hell am I supposed to do that?

Chapter Five

DEFENSE

Rourke looked west along the highway and wondered why his ride was taking so long. He worried the enemy tanker under the white flag might grow impatient and do something stupid. After another minute, relieved, he spotted an armored Humvee weaving its way up the highway.

As the electric Humvee pulled up, before coming to a complete stop, a hyperactive Lieutenant Swaringer jumped out. Gung-ho, the young lieutenant pointed at the open door. "Are you ready to go, sir?" Before Rourke could reply, Swaringer added, "Staff Sergeant Lucas will drive. He's the best guy for the job."

Rourke nodded. He didn't care and just wanted to get going. As he climbed into the front passenger seat, he noticed Lieutenant Swaringer getting in behind. After looking over the lieutenant and the rest of his surroundings, Rourke was pleased. There were no weapons in sight. It seemed the young fuck was finally listening. After buckling up, the colonel turned to the driver and asked, "Lucas is it?"

"Yes, sir. Sergeant Lucas, Motor Pool."

The driver was older, maybe earlier forties. To lessen the tension, the colonel asked, "What is motor pool doing up here on the front line?"

Lucas smiled. "Well sir, it's a long story, but I'm more than a chauffeur. These troops need me. I drive and fix these damn vehicles. I also helped build our defenses and laid plenty of mines too. Truth is, I'm vital."

Rourke almost laughed and under different circumstances would have enjoyed conversing with the older man. But the asshole in the tank awaited. "Yes, I guess you are. Now, if you don't mind, we have a tank to meet. Please get us there in one piece."

Sergeant Lucas got the message and nodded. He eased the vehicle into the middle of Highway 15 and let the autonomous driving feature take control.

Earlier, Rourke had ordered the highway and surrounding desert mined with remote-activated explosives but lacked specific details about where the actual devices were buried. Concerned, Rourke asked, "Lucas, even I'm not aware of where we laid the mines. Are you confident the Humvee has valid avoidance data?"

Lucas glanced at the colonel, considered the question before turning back to the road. "Programming, sir. I programmed our fleet of vehicles, put in where we laid the mines. Yes, sir, I'm extremely confident."

Rourke gave up worrying about mines and leaned back in his seat. He imagined the bastard awaiting atop the enemy tank. Goddammit to hell. What did they want?

Through the windshield, he spotted the point pillbox. He spoke into his headset, activating the internal radio, "PB One, this is Blocker Actual. Over."

The pillbox was quick to respond. "Copy, Blocker Actual, PB One at your service."

"Ah, PB One, we're approaching your six. Reminder: no itchy fingers. You copy? Over."

"Blocker Actual, PB One copies," replied Master Sergeant Upton from inside Pillbox One. Rourke recalled the sergeant. He was a tough guy, built solid with a square jaw, dark hair and eyes, and right out of central casting, perfect for leading the point squad. A "set the example" NCO, Upton rose through the ranks as a steady performer. The master sergeant continued, "When we first clocked the enemy tank, we almost shot it back to the border. Lucky for them we spotted the white flag. We won't shoot unless ordered or fired upon. Over."

"PB One, roger that. Has the enemy said anything else or hinted at what they want?"

"Blocker Actual, that's a negative. Over."

"PB One, Blocker Actual out." Rourke could see beyond the point pillbox. Sure enough, an ugly heavy tank squatted in the middle of Highway 15. The sight of the enemy M1A7 caused him to grow angry, and a knot tightened in his stomach. There was no good reason for the enemy to cross into ROAS territory, not with political negotiations underway.

Rourke pondered the enemy motivation. Fuck it! He'd find out soon enough.

Chapter Six

PARLEY

US Army Battalion Commander Lieutenant Colonel Paulson stood waiting in his command tank cupola. Although the ROAS enemy pillbox had stuck a white t-shirt out its forward firing slit, there'd been no other reaction. Good news—no shooting so far. Apparently, the dumb-ass rookies recognized the flag of truce.

Faced by many an enemy over the years, he'd survived every time, and today wouldn't be any different. But dammit, he wanted them to hurry up and get with the program. He'd wait a while longer, but if someone in charge didn't arrive soon, he'd get back on the loudspeaker and raise hell.

He believed higher Command considered him the best tank officer in the Army, and today was further proof. Given the responsibility of meeting with the enemy and commanding the tip of the spear, he was confident and pleased. After all, he loved tanks, reveled in their power, and knew how to use them. His only complaints were the close quarters and invariable stink the tight confines wrought. But stench and cramped spaces were a minor complaint more than offset by the killing ferocity of his magnificent machines.

As he waited, Paulson felt the vast power of the US Army pulsating behind him, and he absorbed the martial energy. It felt good. But standing beneath the beating sun, he wanted the cocksuckers to hurry. It was getting hot.

About to pick up his microphone again, Paulson spotted movement on the highway past the enemy pillbox and smiled. A Humvee approached. Good, the pricks were coming. In anticipation, he stood straighter and puffed his chest. And he couldn't help but smile.

* * *

Colonel Rourke and his Humvee rolled to a stop in front of the massive tank. Peering out the windshield, he saw a youthful man with a confident smile atop the tank thirty meters distant. Above the tank, affixed to an antenna sticking high in the air, a white flag whipped in the gentle breeze.

Keeping his foot on the brake, Sergeant Lucas stared wide eyed at the main-battle tank. "What now, Colonel?" he asked.

"Put it in park, and I'll go have a chat. Both of you stay harnessed. Be ready to leave on a moment's notice. No telling where this might lead."

Not taking his eyes off the tank, Lucas pulled the parking brake. White knuckled, he kept a firm grip on the steering wheel.

In the back seat, Lieutenant Swaringer leaned forward. "Reminder, sir. Please keep your headset on, mic open to the Command Net."

"Got it," said Rourke, opening the Humvee door.

Behind him, the lieutenant unbuckled his own belt and tried to follow. "I'll go with you, sir."

Rourke raised a hand, "No need."

Swaringer fell back in his seat with a frown.

Rourke understood the man was eager but not now. He tried to soften the blow. "Lieutenant, you have an important job. Keep your eyes peeled. If something goes awry, then hightail it back to the CP and support Rollins. Now, keep buckled and stay tuned and alert."

The young officer, pouting, refastened his harness.

With the huge tank and its main barrel threatening through the window, Sergeant Lucas leaned over and gave encouragement. "Give 'em hell, Colonel, sir."

Although unsure, Rourke put on a confident smile. "Will do, Sergeant." He turned to go when he remembered his radio headset and issued the voice command, tuning it to the proper command frequency. Before exiting, he reminded himself he wasn't alone and that his every move would be under aerial observation. Everything was fine—just an atypical office meeting. Time to go.

After taking a last deep breathe, Rourke exited the Humvee. Before him stood the massive tank and, he sensed, his destiny.

* * *

Lieutenant Colonel Paulson, standing in his cupola, came to a salute and held it.

Colonel Rourke strode forward and stopped twenty paces away. In time-honored military tradition, looking up at the officer in the tank, Rourke came to attention and touched the tip of his head protection system.

Paulson dropped his hand, and Rourke followed suit.

The tanker introduced himself. "Lieutenant Colonel Paulson, Sixth Armored Brigade Combat Team, of the Fifty-Fifth Armored Division, First Battalion Commander, 435th Armored Regiment, sir."

"Colonel Rourke, ROAS Commander of the Fourth Infantry Brigade, First Infantry Division." Before Paulson could speak again, Rourke pointed at the tank. "Lieutenant Colonel, you came out under a flag of truce, asking for me. As a courtesy, please lift your cannon and come down here face to face. No one likes staring down the barrel of a gun."

Paulson laughed and with the back of his hand waved past the colonel. "And that concrete box behind you, sir, it has no weapons trained on me?"

Rourke turned to look at the ROAS point pillbox and then shifted back to face the enemy officer. "Fair enough. Now what can I do for you?"

Lieutenant Colonel Paulson nodded and, still smiling, patted the side of his tank. "Do you admire my M1A7?"

Rourke frowned at the question. "I'm not much of a tank guy myself. The ROAS has only a handful of older heavy main-battle tanks. Dinosaurs we call them, lumbering targets full of explosive fossil fuels. The only good thing about the Stonewall M1A7 is their advanced protection system—Force Field One we called it—developed by our technicians years ago. I'm sure you're glad you have that capability even though we have the means to defeat it."

Paulson laughed at the gibe. In truth, he'd zero respect for the ROAS military. He knew the colonel standing before him, despite the rank, lacked combat experience. Unlike himself, the ROAS officer wasn't a true warrior. Still, he knew that many of the advanced technology features his army used were developed and sold to them before the trade war in the previous decade by the ROAS. To make the distinction, he said, "I love tanks. The M1A7 is a proven battle platform and an absolute joy to command. Over the last ten years, my tanks and combined armor, under my leadership, have never lost a battle. Yes, sir, a joy to lead in combat, and the APS force field works like a charm and hasn't been defeated. In looking at you, I pity your circumstances. No real opportunity to ply your trade. The frustration must be maddening. Sad."

Rourke stood silent, waiting.

Paulson realized the colonel didn't care to banter, and he determined the man was a bore without balls. No matter, he'd follow orders. "Sir, on behalf of the US Army and Field Marshal Harrison, let me start by offering you our utmost military respect. Today, a peaceful resolution rests in your hands. No more politicians or outside interference. Agreed?"

* * *

Rourke considered his reply. The tanker inferred political diplomacy was over, and the ramifications were alarming. But he couldn't resist standing firm against the arrogant tanker. "Thank you for the respect, but we're busy here. I'll pass along the message. Now, if you'll excuse me, have a good day."

Paulson smiled, obviously enjoying the back and forth. "Sir, Field Marshal Harrison is offering the opportunity to prevent bloodshed, save lives . . ."

Rourke didn't care for the implications or the dialogue and raised his hand. "Please stop."

Paulson stopped mid-sentence and cocked his head, waiting.

"Colonel Paulson, I have no authority to negotiate with you or the US military. Yes, I command a brigade and the battalion protecting this crossing. In that capacity, my job is to defend the sovereign soil of the ROAS against unauthorized intrusion." Rourke pointed downward and gestured at an imaginary line. "The ground you are squatting on is mine, sir, not yours. You've crossed the border without invitation or authorization. Please turn around, go home, and let's give the diplomats more time to resolve our differences."

Paulson's smile faded. "Sir. I'm here under a flag of truce. As a courtesy and fellow officer in arms, listen to our offer."

Chapter Seven

RESISTANCE

In ROAS Central Command, General William Story watched and listened to the parley, but only partway. He could hear the voice of Colonel Rourke but not that of the US tank officer. The headset worn by Rourke included audio input dampeners limiting background noise. This came in handy during combat, but the lack of full conversational audio was a nuisance.

The video provided by surveillance drones allowed Command staff to view the action, and on monitors, he could see Rourke standing twenty meters in front of the enemy tank. Behind Rourke, ten meters distant, sat the Humvee, and beyond that lay the point ROAS pillbox.

Monitoring the parley, General Story felt as if he were a quiet witness to history. It was like having a ringside seat at the O.K. Corral or standing next to the US Army General at Bastogne when he told the Germans to fuck off. Shaking off the feeling, he needed to understand why the US tank had pulled forward. Lives depended on the answer.

Lieutenant Colonel Andrea Simpson, aid to General Story, waved at the general seated next to her. "Sir, I've got her on the line."

"Patch her in," said the general. Maybe now he could get some answers.

Simpson nodded, hit a button on her headset and raised a thumb.

"Madam President are you there?" asked General Story.

"Yes, Bill. I'm in the air headed your way. ETA is less than thirty minutes. Why the urgency?"

"Madam, a short time ago, under a white flag, the enemy sent a military delegation across our border. My brigade commander is meeting now. Events are unfolding fast." He glanced at the nearest monitor and confirmed the enemy tank still loomed over Colonel Rourke. "I doubt the US military would've come forward unless they've reached a decision. I believe an attack is imminent. Before doing so, to cover their asses, they're going to give us an opportunity to withdraw or surrender."

"Yes. I see. How can I help?"

Frustration mounting, the general rolled his eyes. "Are there any significant changes on the diplomatic front?" There was a pause. He shot a look at Simpson and saw her concentrating on a computer monitor focused on the border parley. With two fingers, he tapped her on the shoulder and raised his eyebrows. In response, Simpson shook her head, lifted a finger letting him know talks continued.

President Julia Ortega came back on the line. "Yes, General, there are recent political developments. That's why I'm on a vertical-lift heading your way."

"What developments?" asked the general, impatient.

"Well, I just got off a call with Ambassador Howard. He told me the last round of discussions didn't end well."

Whenever the president spoke, the general discerned low aircraft background noise. He imagined her airborne. She should have called him first. Instead, he was in the dark with a massive enemy on his doorstep. Upset, he asked, "How bad?"

Over the background hum, the president replied, "Bad enough, I'm afraid. Despite our best efforts, just a short while ago, Felix Manuel was executed. Poor man."

Shocked by the news, the general processed the information. It explained what was happening. The enemy was coming! Glancing at the nearest monitor, he saw Rourke pointing at the ground in front of the enemy M1A7 battle tank. He guessed they hadn't much time.

Determined to protect his troops, Story tried to explain. "Madam President, the execution confirms our worst fears. I suspect the enemy is seeking the surrender or withdrawal of our border crossing battalion. If terms are agreeable, we should accept the inevitable."

The president, in a calm voice, countered, "General, we've already discussed this. We won't surrender or withdraw. If attacked, our soldiers are to resist, if even for a short while, then they can retreat. Neither of us expects our brave men and woman to die in vain. Understood?"

The general countered. "Madam, an entire armored force of thousands is going to attack our little battalion of a few hundred. Resistance is futile. It serves no purpose. There is no dishonor in retiring when confronted by an overwhelming force." The general lowered his tone and continued. "Madam, if the enemy is tendering reasonable terms, there's no good alternative but to accept."

"No, General Story, you won't surrender or retreat without a fight. No matter how one-sided the strength or generous the terms. Your job is to resist."

Stunned by the stubbornness, the general's anger rose. Face flushing, he replied, "Trust me Madam President, if we stand and fight, the outcome will be decisive and not in our favor. We won't have time to surrender or withdraw."

"General, I wasn't finished." In a stony voice she continued, "In most circumstances, I won't override your military knowledge or authority. But as Commander-in-Chief, I'm in charge of our armed forces." After a pause, in a conciliatory tone she continued, "Negotiate with the enemy for as long you can. But if attacked, you will resist."

The general tried again. "I'm not sure you understand the overall tactical picture. Even a few minutes of resistance will result in a large loss of ROAS life. I don't want that on you, Madam President. Instead, I implore you to understand the consequences and allow me to make the military decisions. I'll try to buy time, but if pressed, and attack is imminent—please let me make the call."

"You remember Fort Sumter, don't you, General?" asked the president.

"Of course. But we don't have time for a history lesson."

"Listen to me," urged the president. "This is our Fort Sumter moment. I know it's hard. We won't fire the first shot, but if fired upon, we will resist. If forced upon us, the people of our nation will learn we have the moral courage to stand against tyranny. That lesson, if necessary, starts today."

"You want martyrs?"

"No, but this country needs a backbone." She paused and cleared her throat. In a flat tone she spelled it out, "I've heard your objections, and although facing overwhelming odds, there will be no backing down without resistance. Instead, if attacked, you shall fight back. After that, you are authorized to do whatever is necessary to protect our troops, up to and including surrender. Understood?"

The general looked up and noticed his aid waving, indicating she wanted to switch his audio back to the border. He nodded, it was time to act—no more arguing. "I understand, Madam President."

"Good. Thank you. I'll be there soon," replied the president, ending the call.

Upset, the general balled his fists then turned his attention to the potential disaster brewing on the border.

* * *

Colonel Rourke shot back and reiterated his position. "Lieutenant Colonel Paulson. As you have sought me out under a flag of truce, I've taken the time to come out and listen. I promise as an officer, in good faith, I will relay your message to ROAS Central Command and get back with a prompt answer. As a fellow officer, please understand and respect the limits of my command authority."

Paulson, it appeared, was losing patience. "Sir, this offer is for you. You're the field commander. No one else understands better the military situation on the ground. Look, the United States Army doesn't want to destroy your small force. We understand your innocence. You didn't commit the crime; your corrupt government did. Instead, in the spirit of cooperation and peace, with full military honor, we ask for an immediate surrender and a pledge to never take up arms against the US again. Afterward, the ROAS troops under your command will face no further threats and can return home. No bloodshed, no death, no imprisonment, just an honorable peace. Sir, do you accept this generous and reasonable offer?"

Rourke struggled to listen while trying to keep up with Central Command whispering in his ear. Command wanted him to paraphrase Paulson so they could eavesdrop. Rourke shook his head, the stress of the dual role getting to him, making him irritable. "Ah. Colonel Paulson," he stammered, thinking how best to summarize what he'd heard. "If I understand the offer, you've asked me to surrender this installation and pledge to never take up arms against the US. In return, my command will be paroled. Is that what you're offering?" After saying the words, Rourke assumed the tanker knew he was buying time.

Paulson responded, confirming Rourke's suspicion. "Sir, for your benefit, and whoever else is listening, the US is offering an opportunity to prevent bloodshed." Paulson continued in a harsher tone, "I need your answer now, sir."

Rourke fidgeted, thought the terms reasonable, but couldn't imagine surrendering to such an asshole. He'd rather pull his force back and retreat with dignity.

General Story's voice came over his headset. "Colonel, no surrender. Stick to the plan. Stretch out the negotiations and give us time to develop a response."

Rourke swallowed hard, realizing it was up to him. He needed to stall, get things under control. In a loud voice, he re-explained his position. "Lieutenant Colonel Paulson, I have no authority to negotiate. But I've heard your offer. I will pass your proposal up the chain of command and gather a response. Later, we can continue the dialogue and discuss next steps. May I suggest we meet again tomorrow? Same time, right here, under a flag of truce?"

Paulson glowered at the colonel. "Sir, not taking responsibility is an answer. You are the commander of this installation. As military men, as officers, we control the destiny of those who serve beneath us. You decide for this installation, and military protocol dictates no need for higher approval."

Rourke shook his head in consternation.

Paulson continued in a patient tone. "Look . . ." and he pointed backward sweeping his arm across the horizon, ". . . you cannot stand against the forces arrayed against you. By accepting our terms, history will not doubt or condemn you. Make the right call. Be always remembered. Link your name to peace and for preventing a slaughter. You don't want to start a war, do you?"

"Of course not," replied Rourke.

Paulson wiped his brow, flicking away the sweat and continued, "I ask you again, with all due respect, one last time. Sir, do you accept the generous terms of surrender as offered?" Before Rourke could respond, Paulson added a dire warning. "Be careful. Equivocation is a reply in the negative."

Rourke found the parley maddening. He was amazed at how Paulson shifted responsibility, placing potential blame on the ROAS when the clear aggressor was the US. He thought the twisting of words and logic a preposterous obfuscation. Alarm bells ringing, he realized the crazy bastards were seeking an excuse. Worse, he'd no way of stopping it. Once the shooting started, or the ROAS surrendered, the US would claim the moral high ground no matter the reality. He needed help, fast, and paraphrased his response so CENTCOM could understand the urgency. "You're the aggressor, sir. You have crossed into our territory demanding a military surrender, not the other way around. Regardless, I must repeat, we need time to review your proposal. If tomorrow doesn't work, when do you suggest we meet again?"

Lieutenant Colonel Paulson, like a mother to a misbehaving child, sighed in deep disappointment and clucked his tongue. "Your answer is *no*. Let your decision stand for the record."

"I didn't say *no*," Rourke stammered.

Paulson shook his head then reached out and grabbed his radio antenna and bent the flexible rod until he could reach the white flag. With a sneer, he ripped off the material and flung it outward where it hung for a moment before fluttering to the ground. At the same instant, he let go of the antenna causing it to whip into place. Workmanlike, Paulson reached inside the tank hatch and pulled out a head protection system. After placing the advanced helmet on his head, he flipped up the visor and adjusted his headset. Then he glanced at Colonel Rourke and out towards the ROAS lines on either side. Wearing a wicked grin, in a loud voice, he spoke into his headset, "Tiger, Tiger, Tiger." Quick as lightening, Paulson slipped inside his tank and, with a clank, closed the hatch.

Unsure, Colonel Rourke watched Paulson disappear.

Chapter Eight

THE TIGER

In the point pillbox standing next to his machine-gun crew peering out the forward firing slit at the parley, Upton flinched when an enormous fireball erupted. Eyes forced closed by the explosion, his teeth rattled as the concussion swept through the tight confines. Around him, the bunker shook, and heat radiated through his helmet visor. Upon opening his eyes, he bore witness as flaming chunks of wreckage from Colonel Rourke's Humvee came tumbling to earth.

Disoriented, not sure what transpired, through the smoke, Upton spotted flame licking from the enemy tank. The noise deafening, he shook off the cobwebs and realized the beast was hammering his own force field Active Protection System (APS) fixed atop the pillbox with its M240 machine gun. Thuds and pings erupted as each 7.62 mm exploding round peppered into the thick steel protecting the system. Upton realized the tank was using smart rounds, also developed by the ROAS and sold to the US years ago, to reach up and over the side of the pill box to take out his APS. Designed to detect and protect against larger projectiles, including missiles and tank rounds, the APS was useless against small arms.

In a few seconds, he realized, his best protection against a tank assault would be gone. Beside him, without waiting for the order, Corporal Hudson went full cyclic, returning fire with his .50-caliber and sending out a long, continuous burst of lethal armor-penetrating rounds. A cacophony of noise ensued as sparks flew from the steel monster while brass shell casings ejected from Hudson's gun tinkled on the concrete floor.

Inside the pillbox, the noise excruciating, Upton was amazed at how everything was happening so fast. Rattled, forcing himself to regain control, through the firing slit, he spotted the barrel of the enemy tank rising towards them and sensed disaster. The advanced reactive armor on the tank was easily defeating Hudson's onslaught. Worse, without an APS to protect the pillbox, they were a sitting duck. Just as concerning, he doubted there was enough time for his remaining troops, those inside nearby trenches, to counter with their Javelin III anti-tank missiles. Not waiting, he turned and headed towards the steel door at the back of the hardened enclosure. Reaching it, his assault rifle in one hand, with the other he pulled up the locking mechanism and heaved against the heavy exit, forcing it open. As he began to turn and warn his squad, a wave of over-heated pressure flung him high into the air.

* * *

Inside the ROAS command bunker, Lieutenant Colonel Rollins sat monitoring the parley and watched as the enemy tanker pulled down the flag of truce and put on a helmet. Then, the bastard said something to Colonel Rourke and descended inside the tank. Disturbed, he was about to radio Rourke when the colonel and his Humvee disappeared in a ball of flame.

Stunned, Rollins sat rooted at his monitor while Rourke's Humvee leaped high in the air. A moment later, he heard the rumble. The noise roused him. The fucking bastards killed Colonel Rourke!

Before he could react, an urgent call came over the command network. "Blocker Actual, Tackle One! Inbound missiles detected. Estimate one, two, zero bogies, ETA twenty-five seconds. Auto-interception underway. Request permission to shoot and scoot. Over!"

Rollins recognized the voice of his surface-to-air missile battery commander. Adding to the concern and confusion, across several monitors, over a hundred enemy tanks were moving forward. Puffs of flame emanated from their 120 mm main barrels. Awake at last, the beast was coming.

Out of nowhere, Rollins felt a sudden urge to flee. He hadn't expected the sensation and forced himself to calm down. Dread rising, he needed to respond. But what to do; where to start?

An aid yelled that CENTCOM was on the line requesting an update. Someone else shouted a warning—the pillboxes were under heavy tank fire. On his monitor, he watched the point bunker explode into flames.

With lives at stake, angry at the enemy, Rollins recovered and barked orders into his headset. He gave the battalion-wide command to carry out the pre-planned defensive response. "Blocker Two, this is Blocker Two Actual. Execute Alpha Dog. I repeat, execute Alpha Dog!"

After issuing the order, shaking with adrenaline, Rollins scrambled to his feet. Another aid cried out enemy missiles were being intercepted, but not fast enough. ETA ten seconds. He took two steps towards the bunker door and caught himself. No, the urge to flee wouldn't overcome his command responsibilities. He remembered his staff and turned to face them. Some were on the secure network, others appeared in shock looking towards him with expectant eyes. Rollins needed to do more. Maybe he could urge CENTCOM to commit additional assets.

In that moment, with a quick flash of sadness, a massive concussion tore through him.

* * *

Through high-powered optics, Staff Sergeant Lisa McMichael witnessed the parley from inside her assigned trench. The nervous soldiers around her also took turns peering over the top, straining to catch a glimpse of the meeting underway towards their right front.

Earlier, upon entering the trench, McMichael had spotted three loaded Javelin III missile launchers stacked against the far wall. Next to the launchers lay two crates of opened missiles. Several more sealed cases stood nearby. While watching the parley, she thought of the weapons and hoped they wouldn't be needed. And the doubt, as always, crept in. Was she good enough? Did she deserve to lead a squad? Could she really attack the enemy? Her self-doubt was interrupted by the action on the border.

Through her optics, she watched as Colonel Rourke pointed at the ground. The conversation appeared heated. Orders had come over the battalion network a few minutes prior: hold fire and stay vigilant. Worried, she lowered the glasses and glanced back at the missile launchers. As a precaution, she considered ordering her squad to shoulder the weapons. But loaded launchers were heavy, and they'd been cautioned against an accidental misfire. Better to leave them, she decided. Besides, in the event shooting started, it would only take her team a few seconds to arm themselves.

McMichael turned back to the parley and raised her optics, focusing on the enemy tanker. The man atop the tank pointed out to either side, sweeping his arms at the assembled US armor behind him. She guessed he was trying to intimidate Colonel Rourke.

Nervous, she shifted her glasses away from the parley towards her immediate front and scanned for any signs of movement. Her squad of ten unmounted infantry, six soldiers in the trench, including her and four others inside the nearby pillbox, defended this small part of the border. The enemy had more than two hundred tanks on the field, of which ten sat in her sector. None were moving. Beyond the tanks, twenty-one fighting vehicles squatted, also her responsibility. But they weren't moving either. Even with the missile launchers, the math didn't equate; her squad was out-gunned. She bit her lip in worry.

McMichael lowered her optics and glanced again at the stacked missile launchers. Compared to the enemy armor, the Javelins seemed puny. With a sigh, she lifted the glasses and returned her attention to the parley.

The tanker pulled at his antennae, threw the white flag to the ground, put on a helmet, and disappeared inside his tank. She swung her optics downward, focused on the flag lying crumpled on the desert floor, when her vision filled with a ball of fire.

Shocked, the suddenness of the explosion caused her to drop the optics, the attached neck cord catching the weight. At the same moment, the air trembled, and on instinct, she dropped to her knees. Above her, the noise of the explosion echoed across the desert. Not thinking, to relieve the weight, she pulled the optics from around her neck and tossed them aside.

Shaken, she turned towards her squad. Three troopers crouched and stared back with frightened eyes. Like her, they'd taken immediate shelter below the trench line. But farther down, two others stood upright, rooted in place, staring towards the fading explosion. As if on cue, high-velocity rounds started zipping across the top of the trench, followed by the steady staccato of machine guns firing in the distance. The sound made the scenario real. Realizing both troopers were exposed, she screamed, "Down, down!"

Riveted by the sights of battle, they seemed not to hear and remained upright. Frustrated, she fast-crawled towards the closest standing soldier. Reaching up, she grabbed him by the pant leg and pulled him down. He turned to look at her, stunned, when the top of his helmet split open, and he crumpled beside her. In that moment, she knew the enemy was using smart bullets with the ability to lock onto a spotted target and go over the trench top. A second later, the female soldier standing to his right did a pirouette and fell in a heap.

In horror, McMichael stared at the two fallen soldiers. The male lay face up, his helmeted head protection system shattered, the inside nothing but gore. As for the female, the sight was similar, a massive fatal head wound caused by a direct hit from a .50-caliber slug. The head protection system was no defense against high-powered machine-gun fire. McMichael gagged at the scene, couldn't contain it, lifted her visor, and vomited.

Wiping away the bile, the dread of failure wracking her conscious, the radio crackled to life. In her headset came the command, ". . . Alpha Dog, I repeat, execute Alpha Dog." Still on her knees, she glanced at the remaining three soldiers crouching nearby. By the look in their eyes, they too had received the battalion-wide command, but fear and shock seemed to hold them back. They needed leadership. She thought of the steel monsters in her sector and imagined the powerful armor racing forward. Death was coming.

Determined to fight back and defend the rest of her people, the launchers beckoned. She pointed towards the stacked weapons leaning against the far wall. Not waiting, she crawled that direction, and as she approached, she felt the trio close behind. Good, they were following. Above them, heavy machine-gun fire continued to snap.

As she reached for the nearest launcher, the earth shook, and a deafening roar knocked her flat.

On her stomach, ears ringing, chunks of concrete mixed with dirt and sand rained down. A few second later, spitting debris, McMichael fought to gain control. Shaking off dust, sand, and small pieces of concrete, she pushed herself onto her knees. Through smoke and dust, she could see her assigned pillbox thirty meters away. It was nothing but a smoking ruin. A sickening realization dawned. The rest of her squad was inside. Around her, the remaining three survivors lay flat, covered in dust, the air thick.

McMichael turned back to the pillbox and thought of the four young soldiers posted inside. Maybe they were still alive? She considered scrambling over and digging into the rubble. But she grasped the reality: the enemy was coming, and there wasn't much time.

Compelled by a force she didn't understand, McMichael reached out to the nearest soldier and tugged on his combat vest. The man looked up, blinking, eyes wide with fear. It was Private Goldstein, a good man. Over the roar and din of battle, McMichael pointed at the closest launcher and then cast her chin towards the enemy front. Amazed at his response, McMichael watched as Goldstein gathered himself, nodded in return, and crawled after the weapon.

After grabbing the launcher, rounds whining overhead, undaunted, she watched the private creep back to the front of the trench and place his weapon upon the parapet. In awe, McMichael turned and saw the other two remaining soldiers responding. They too were gathering loaded missile launchers. God, she was grateful and proud of their bravery.

And then it happened again. This time much worse as the earth shook in a violent upheaval.

Tossed like rag dolls across the trench, McMichael and the last of her squad tried to survive.

* * *

"Driver, back up, back up. Gunner, enable APS," commanded Lieutenant Colonel Paulson. Under fire, he reacted with practiced calm. Through his thermal monitor, he could see the glowing wreck of Colonel Rourke's Humvee and the smoking rubble of the point pillbox beyond it. Destroyed by his main gun, both initial targets lay in ruins, and he felt a deep sense of satisfaction. But there was more work to do. Multitasking, he listened as radio updates from his company commanders came piping in. The news was excellent. Many enemy targets hit, no losses yet. A minute gone by and all was going well.

Still, Paulson needed to protect against a potential counter Javelin strike and get away from the massive pre-planned artillery barrage. He didn't want to die by friendly fire or a missile, and the best way to avoid both was to create some distance. The further he got from enemy lines, the better chance of avoiding a short artillery shell. As for defending against missiles, his tank relied upon its APS. Developed and sold by the ROAS years earlier, the APS was mounted near the top of the tank and, using radar, detected and destroyed inbound anti-tank threats by spraying a counter array of exploding projectiles. The farther from the incoming threat, the more time available for the APS to react. But he remembered the words of Rourke, who claimed the ROAS could defeat the system, and he decided to do more.

"Gunner, open fire with the .240 on the nearest trench. I don't care if you can't see shit, just let the smart bullets do their thing and keep raking." A moment later, the light machine gun responded by firing short rapid bursts. Paulson decided more was better and took control of the remote heavy machine gun. Joystick in hand, he slewed the heavy weapon toward the enemy lines and squeezed out long, sweeping bursts of .50-caliber smart-bullet fire. As he played the gun back and forth, pouring lead down range, he didn't care that he lacked specific targets. If a smart bullet detected a human target, it would follow. Most important, his purpose was to keep enemy heads down and missiles at bay.

The massive M1A7 continued to charge backward, away from the ROAS lines, when Paulson felt the tank's APS engage. Vibrations rippled through his seat as the device launched thousands of exploding microbursts at an unseen incoming threat. A moment later, the M1A7 trembled, all sixty-five tons. Paulson stiffened, waited for a possible secondary explosion. Nothing! Relieved and exhilarated, Paulson let out a long, hearty laugh. Strapped in their positions around him, his crew didn't say a word but just kept working to stay alive.

Shaking off the amusement, looking at his command monitor, Paulson observed the first artillery shells impacting near the enemy trenches. The concussions from the barrage bounced against his retreating tank and he winced. For a second, he felt a flash of fear, but as the tank continued to back away, he relaxed. A few seconds later, and he sensed they were far enough removed. Letting go of the joystick, he ceased firing the .50-caliber and spoke into the tank radio, "Driver, stop. Gunner, hold fire on the .240."

Paulson considered the battlefield. Tons of debris hurled through the air towards his front as the pounding artillery ripped apart the enemy trenches. Things were going well. Surprise achieved, the enemy appeared overwhelmed. He and his tank were intact, and his battalion unscathed. He spoke into his headset, "Driver, until I say so, run us in a defensive loop. Gunner, keep hunting but only engage if you have a target." Paulson laughed and added, "Boys, it's time to let the artillery join the fun. This shit's almost over!"

Chapter Nine

END GAME

Inside ROAS Central Command, General Bill Story watched the lopsided battle unfold on the many monitors viewable from his workspace. Angry, the general sat dismayed and powerless.

In his professional opinion, the fight had started with a cowardly sneak attack—the point-blank murder of Colonel Rourke. A few seconds later, two hundred Stonewall M1A7 main-battle tanks opened fire. It didn't take long for the enemy guns to take every ROAS pillbox out of action. Simultaneously, the enemy launched a massive missile strike, overwhelming his advanced counter measures. The ROAS command bunker and air defense batteries were obliterated. Next, they struck with a self-propelled Paladin 109A7 artillery barrage using optical self-guided ordinance. Originally developed by the ROAS, the artillery shells precisely targeted the entire ROAS defensive trench network.

Still underway, the ROAS entrenched positions were taking a terrific shellacking. Huge geysers of sand, dirt, and rock sprayed upwards. The few remaining souls of the original three hundred were being pummeled with little opportunity to return fire.

Neutered, the general turned to his aid, Lieutenant Colonel Simpson, and said, "Send a clear text broadcast across the battlefield. Keep sending it until I say so. And I quote, 'By command of ROAS Army of Defense General Story, the ROAS Second Infantry Battalion surrenders to the US Armed Forces attacking Mesquite. All combatants cease fire.'"

"Sir, the command bunker is gone. Getting a message transmitted may prove difficult," said Lieutenant Colonel Simpson, obviously frustrated.

"Find a way. Do it now!" urged General Story.

"Yes, sir," replied Simpson. Before she could react, a new threat emerged. "General, look at monitor ten. Enemy Custers inbound. Sensors indicate thirty aircraft. Must be part of a Calvary Aviation Brigade."

Unsurprised, General Story nodded. The overarching enemy battle plan made sense. It was a classic combined-arms attack—missiles, tanks, artillery, and now vertical-lift aircraft. Fast, the VLA airframes combined the capabilities of an attack helicopter with the speed of a fixed-wing plane.

On his monitor the aircraft stretched across the entire battle space and streaked towards his battered lines. After closing to within two hundred meters of the ROAS forward positions, the Custers slowed and went into a fast hover. At an altitude of one hundred meters, he couldn't help but admire their precision. Noses pointed downward, as one, the machines came alive. Twisting and turning, they ripped off short, self-guided bursts of smart 30 mm high-explosive auto-cannon rounds. Anything still moving was auto-detected and destroyed.

More motion caught his eye. On other monitors, hundreds of M2A6 Stuart infantry fighting vehicles filled with thousands of combat-ready infantrymen were creeping forward. Overkill, thought the general. A complete and utter calamity. And he believed, it could've been prevented, not just by retreating or surrendering, but by fighting back with an effective force, a force he lacked because of the ROAS political system. Instead of investing in the military and using its advanced technology to equip it, over the years, the ROAS had spent its budget on liberal social programs. Just as bad, after the self-imposed ban on military exports, his small country had all but abandoned efforts to develop new warfare technologies. He believed those poor decisions were coming home to roost, and it angered him.

The general closed his eyes; he'd seen enough.

* * *

In the trench bottom, curled tight, Sergeant Lisa McMichael tried to survive. The ground shook so hard she couldn't stand or crawl, neither of which crossed her mind. Something hit her left leg and then her right arm. Both impacts stinging, the liquid body armor she wore prevented the shrapnel from shredding her to pieces. She tried to make herself smaller when she found herself hurtling through the air. Arms pinwheeling, she caught sight of the ground and turned into the impact. Hitting the ground hard, she rolled several times. Still conscious, now on her side, she grabbed her protective helmet tight and sucked for oxygen. All around, the ground continued to shake. Clumps of dirt and debris fell in a continuous rain. She concentrated on breathing, taking in gulps of air, and prayed for the shelling to stop. Through the roar, her tongue found a missing tooth, and without thinking, she inspected the gap. Distracted, the search brought her mind back to the present and with it an unwelcome wave of claustrophobia. She sat up and, with shaking hands, grabbed the lower sides of her head protection system and pried the helmet off. For a moment, she felt better.

Another explosion knocked her onto her stomach. With her helmet off, the noise of the barrage was deafening. Death was upon her, and tears welled from desperation. To dampen the thunder, she raised her hands, covering her ears, when she noticed a stringy length of bloody drool dangling from her chin. She remembered the missing tooth.

Another close explosion erupted. Self-preservation returned and with it a desperate wish to live. She curled up again, facing a steep earthen wall, and tried to compress into the dirt. To keep sane, she thought of her past. A picture of herself as a little girl popped in her head. Testing in grade school and high school had indicated her intelligence was in the top two percent of students in the country. At first, she'd believed what they told her. She'd taken advanced subjects, worked harder than anyone, and scored straight A's. Her parents, educators, and friends had all marveled at her academic success.

But it was all a lie.

Inside, no matter the praise and results, she was a failure, an imposter. Her talents were based on luck, dogged determination, and not deserved. She wasn't good enough.

Overwhelmed by needing to be the best, and knowing she never could be, although accepted to top universities, she'd eloped with a neighbor boy from down the street. To make ends meet, he'd gone to work in a casino, and she took a job as a hostess in a high-end restaurant. And then the bastard got her pregnant, not once but twice. She'd stopped working and threw herself into raising her young ones. Reading every source on parenting, she strove to be the best, but the more she studied and applied the lessons, the more she understood her shortcomings. She wasn't good enough, and then her husband began to cheat on her. Twice, she caught him in the act, and she hated him.

Just then the shelling worsened. Wincing, covering her ears against the noise and concussions pounding her soul, she recalled her decision to leave him. How liberating it was to throw him out of her life, and how scary it was to start anew. She'd joined the military soon after because the life seemed by the book. Follow the rules, apply the lessons, and spend the time.

Based on high test scores, the military wanted her to go into intelligence, work in high tech, but she rejected the offer. She wasn't good enough, was fearful of striving forever without becoming the best. Instead, she demanded the infantry. It suited her. Follow orders, soak in the training, react as programmed. Although her children were being raised mostly be her parents, that suited her as well. The less she could screw up their lives, the better. After a few years, rising in rank, she had been forced to take a leadership role. But she resisted as she didn't want the responsibility. Having a binary choice, either resign or assume the duties, she relinquished and became a squad leader. Now under fire, she realized how much she hated the role and how important her children were. Oh, how she missed them.

Another round exploded nearby, and she almost laughed. They were trying to kill her, and she wasn't even worth the effort. Still, she missed her kids more than anything. Maybe, if she survived, she'd quit the military and find another career. With a little luck, she might even meet a good man, someone that would love her kids and be faithful. Men still flirted with her, and she considered herself attractive in a cute sort of way. Her tongue swished around the missing tooth. Perhaps she was less cute than before.

Then the ground shook harder as a shell erupted dangerously close. With dirt crashing around, she couldn't believe it was happening.

More shells crumpled, filling her ears with pain and sucking away the air. She felt herself slipping away and curled into a tighter ball. Under her breath, over and over, she prayed for the shelling to end. As if in answer, after a short while, the thundering eased and shifted farther away.

In a state close to shock, she lifted her head and realized she was in a shell hole below ground level. Across from her, propped against the side of the hole, staring back through a cracked face plate, was a female soldier she didn't recognize.

An explosion rumbled nearby, causing her to duck and close her eyes. When more didn't follow, just a distant roar, driven by a need to connect, she glanced towards the soldier again. Something was wrong. She spotted the problem. It was only half a person. Nothing but entrails existed below the combat vest. Breathing too hard and fast, nearing hyperventilation, she needed to gain control. She forced herself to slow and then noticed a change. It was quiet—no more shelling. In silence, she thanked God and wiped her mouth. Fresh blood from her broken tooth continued to run down her chin, and her hand came away bloodied.

Ignoring her own injuries, McMichael couldn't help it and looked across at the corpse. Staring at the mutilated soldier, a wave of sympathy mixed with survivor's guilt caused her to cringe. Then she spotted a missile launcher lying next to the bloody mess. Staring at the weapon, she realized it wasn't over. The enemy must be fast approaching, coming to kill her. From deep inside, her training and instincts took over. She needed to act. Now!

In a manic move, she crawled across the shell hole and avoided looking at the dead female. Reaching the launcher, she pulled it close and examined the weapon. The missile was armed and ready. Still bleeding from the mouth, helmetless, she stood up and pulled the heavy launcher against her shoulder.

Peering over the shell hole, she saw targets, lots of them, close. Tanks driving in defensive patterns, fighting vehicles on their heels, all the armor in the world. So many targets to choose from! She hesitated before spotting something different. Off to her right hovering in the air was a tantalizing foe. Decision made, she lowered the Javelin III missile and confirmed it was set for direct-fire mode. Satisfied, heavy in her hands, McMichael re-shouldered the weapon and flipped off the safety. Placing the sights on the vertical-lift aircraft, the acquisition indicator turned green, and she depressed the firing trigger. The warhead released with a whoosh, and the rocket motor fired, causing the missile to soar into the distance. Blood dripping down her chin, McMichael lowered the weapon and watched.

To her alarm, the targeted vertical-lift aircraft seemed to sense something. The ugly bird lifted its nose and turned towards her. She was about to duck when the missile struck. A bright light rippled across the fuselage, and then an explosion blew out the side of the aircraft. Yes! Finally, she'd done something right.

McMichael dropped the spent launcher and without thinking raised her arms in jubilation. Fascinated, she watched the burning craft spin and descend out of control until it crashed into the desert. A moment later, the downed machine burst into flames.

Against the heat of the explosion, McMichael raised her hand and stared in disbelief. But there wasn't time to enjoy the sight. Intense machine-gun fire erupted, and the air around her began to sing with the sound of incoming supersonic rounds. Towards her front, she saw tanks advancing. She remembered the smart bullets. Not hesitating, she dropped inside the shell hole and rolled to her left and sat up.

Her back against dirt, large-caliber smart projectiles pounded into the ground where she had stood a moment before. Other rounds continued to zip overhead, some striking the opposite side of the shell hole and sending chunks of sand and rock high into the air. The unexpected joy from downing the aircraft evaporated, and she trembled. She wondered if the battalion was fighting back. But the sight above the trench line convinced her nothing could stop what was coming. Soon they'd kill her. How could it come to this? And why would her government leave her to die alone? Without answers, feeling hopeless, in near panic, something caught her eye. Exposed in the middle of the opposite dirt wall, the jagged end of an exposed pipe beckoned. It was wide enough that she could imagine herself fitting through. Just then, an overhead shadow crossed the shell hole, and the sound of rotors emerged above the din.

Fueled by instinct, in a mad dash for survival, McMichael fast-crawled past the dead soldier, and half stood. Behind her an explosion erupted. The force of the concussion drove her towards the pipe and, arms extended, reaching for it, the lights went out.

Chapter Ten

MOP UP

Across the battlefield, all firing ceased. Over the scene, skirting back and forth, the US vertical-lift aircraft hovered. Beneath them, the ROAS trench system and pillboxes smoldered. The only ROAS movement was in the far rear of the lines where a marked medical tent stood fronted by a group of people waving a white flag. The US held the field, the only loss, a single Custer.

Time for the ground pounders. The order went out, and two armored M1170 Assault Breacher Vehicles, nicknamed Shredders, moved forward.

The first Shredder, like a tank but with a bulldozer front end, rolled down Highway 15 and knocked aside the smoking wreck of Colonel Rourke's ROAS Humvee. Coming to a stop, the huge vehicle fired a line charge two hundred meters down the highway past the rubble of the destroyed ROAS point pillbox. When the line charge and attached C4 explosives settled atop the blacktop, the Shredder hit the detonator. In response, a continuous explosion occurred along the entire two-hundred-meter roadway, destroying any active mines. A second Shredder came up, pulling past the first, and continued along the just-cleared highway. By working together, within an hour, the plan called for Highway 15 to be cleared of explosive devices all the way through Mesquite.

Behind the Shredders, two armored infantry fighting vehicles followed, providing overwatch security. Upon reaching the ROAS medical facility, both vehicles stopped and took the surrendering personnel into custody.

Along the rest of the front, US Army M2A6 Stuart infantry fighting vehicles stopped twenty meters in front of the devastated ROAS trenches and disgorged squads of infantry. Assigned to clear the ROAS point pillbox and attached trench, US Army Squad Leader Sergeant Raymond Flood dismounted and hit the ground running. Charging towards the enemy defensive works, Flood waved at his following squad and fanned them into a thin line. Assault rifles at the ready, the men ran the final few paces and hurled themselves against the sandy berm of the trench line. Hunched down, the berms provided cover against whoever might occupy the other side.

Panting against the trench, squatting, Flood felt better. Pleased to reach the first goal without taking any incoming fire, Flood hoped the good fortune would continue.

Looking both ways, determining his men were ready, with another wave Flood ordered the squad forward. Without hesitation, his troops scrambled up the trench face, leaned over, and scanned for targets.

From his position atop the trench closest to the point pillbox, Flood swung his assault rifle back and forth. Nothing moved. A complete lack of fire; no one was shooting. He relaxed further and examined the trench beneath him. Craters and cave-ins dotted the landscape. Off to his right, sticking above the rubble, a bloody hand protruded, frozen in death. Farther away among torn equipment, a twisted body lay atop a heap of ragged concrete. Even at a distance, Flood spotted flies buzzing above the corpse. To his left, one of his soldiers dug in the rock and sand, uncovering a twisted missile launcher. After examining it, the grunt tossed it over the trench towards US lines.

Satisfied, with no perceived threats, Flood stood erect. On either side, farther out along the enemy lines, he clocked other infantry squads working trenches and mopping up. In the distance, two shots rang out. His men froze. A moment later, the radio reported a mercy killing and gave the all clear.

Before he could relax, a sudden unexpected rumble emerged, and he bent lower. Along the highway, a dust cloud plumed, and Flood realized the Shredders were at work clearing the highway. Everything was fine, and he stood up a little embarrassed by his over-reaction.

It was warm. Mid-afternoon in the desert and even though early May, already the temperature was nearing ninety degrees. Flood's Head Protection Systems aggravated the heat. Lifting his faceplate, he wiped his brow and lowered the tinted protection back in place. For seven years, he'd been in the Army. He'd fought up and down South America in worse heat, but damn it was hot. Thinking of the conditions, he knew it wouldn't take long for the bodies to decompose and the horrible stink to rise. He wanted to finish quick and hoped they'd set up bivouac in town—a good meal, maybe a solid roof, and a double beer ration. Even better, he expected a nice pay-out. Experience told him a decisive fight like today would invariably mean a bonus. Everybody would be in a great mood, retelling their part in the battle, most of it bullshit. Still, fighting was a way of life, sometimes a good life.

"Sergeant! You in charge here?"

Startled, Sergeant Flood spun around, weapon at the ready, and recognized his battalion commander. Blanching at the sight, he averted his assault rifle. Damn, he didn't want to deal with brass. Too much could go wrong. But he hadn't a choice. "Yes, sir! Squad Leader Sergeant Flood, sir."

Lieutenant Colonel Paulson, standing below the trench, gazed up at the sergeant, then turned towards his right and pointed at a nearby burned-out Humvee. "Have you checked that vehicle yet?"

"No sir. Been clearing this trench," answered Sergeant Flood.

"Well, get your ass down here and help me take a look." Without waiting for a response, Paulson turned and walked towards the wreckage.

Flood leaped from atop the trench and, keeping his assault rifle at the ready, hurried to take the lead. He came abreast of Paulson just as they approached the still-smoking wreck. The Humvee sat upright on its chassis with most of the frame intact. Everything else—axles, tires, doors, windows, panels, and roof—was blown away. Somehow, still strapped in the back and driver's seat were two charred torsos. Burned beyond recognition, the corpses lacked any extremities—no limbs or heads. Everything else was black, melted away. A gust of wind emerged, bringing with it the foul odor of burned human flesh. Flood gagged, turned away, coughed up a load of phlegm, and spit.

"Any weapons?" asked Paulson. Peeking into the wreck, he appeared oblivious to the smell.

Flood regained his composure, held back the bile, and shifted a bit to keep the breeze at his back. "Negative, sir. Don't see how anything survived."

"Hmm. Well, you know I fired the HEAT round that killed this Humvee. Vaporized the uppity colonel standing in front. I also took out the pillbox behind it."

Flood knew it. He'd seen the first shots of the battle on the surveillance monitor inside his armored fighting vehicle. Unsure how to respond, Flood decided upon flattery. "Well done, sir. Good shooting."

"Yes, yes it was," replied the colonel, still poking around the wreck. Paulson seemed to catch himself, stood upright, and said, "I have a good tanker team."

After making the comment, the officer resumed circling the wreck, searching for something. Curious, Flood asked, "Anything else you want me to check out, sir?"

Still looking at the Humvee, the colonel replied, "No. No. Carry On."

"Roger that, sir." Flood turned and jogged back towards his squad. He didn't relish being anywhere near the snooping officer. The farther away, the better.

* * *

Disappointed, hands on hips, Paulson decided to saunter back to his tank parked not far away. Head down, taking his time, he focused on the ground. He'd only gone a few meters when he spotted something. Excited, he bent to a knee and examined the object. Somehow, he had missed it earlier when he first walked over. He'd been so focused on the Humvee that he had walked right past. But there it was, lying in the sand, a torn piece of cloth. He picked it up and smiled in recognition. A name patch, most of one anyway, torn and ragged. But the name was unmistakable, the letters "ROUR . . ." He turned it over and examined the material. Excited, he shifted his gaze downward, looked for more but nothing remained.

Standing up, he imagined the not-so-distant future. The patch in his hand under glass, sitting on his desk, a general's desk. Destiny tapped him once again. His purpose today was to win and to find this trophy. Satisfied, he put the ragged material in his pocket and swaggered towards the waiting command tank.

Chapter Eleven

NOW WHAT?

May 8, 14:10 (PDT)

Lieutenant Colonel Andrea Simpson walked up at a brisk pace and bent over so only the general could hear. "She's here, waiting for you in the SCIF."

General Story looked up from his monitor and took a deep breath. "Okay. That was fast. Why the secure room?"

"She didn't say, but Secretary James is with her."

The general found the news troubling, but there were bigger problems. "Have you brought her up to speed?"

"She asked how it went. I told her the battalion sustained heavy losses. She raised her hand in response and said you'd brief her. She's requested your immediate presence, sir."

The general nodded and got out of his chair. "Send out a broadcast to the US Fifty-Fifth Armored Division declaring Mesquite an open city."

"Yes, sir." Worried, she brought up another concern. "Any further orders for the rest of Second Brigade in Las Vegas?"

The general frowned. He knew the Second had monitored the battle and seen their detached infantry battalion wiped out. "Orders haven't changed. Remind them the enemy could be on their doorstep in two hours. Dig in but stay prepared to bug out on my command.

Let me speak with the president. It shouldn't take long, and I'll get back to them. If the situation changes, let me know at once. For now, let's hope and pray the enemy stays put."

"Yes, sir," answered Lieutenant Colonel Simpson. She took a chair next to the general and issued orders into her headset.

The general glanced once more at the monitor on his desk. Drone observation from Mesquite no longer existed. Instead, only satellite surveillance remained. The near real-time satellite imagery told the story. Nothing but smoking remnants remained of a once-proud ROAS infantry battalion. The entire battle was a rout. A debacle. Although still angry, it was over, and now he needed to focus on next steps. President Ortega awaited a recap, and the truth was painful. The Republic couldn't stand against the might of a determined United States. Today, he knew full well, marked the beginning of the end.

* * *

The sensitive compartmented information facility, or SCIF, existed below ground within Central Command. A lead-lined vault, its purpose was to keep conversations private and off the record. No electronics of any kind were allowed, and everyone was screened.

Inside, President Julia Ortega, mid-fifties, sat waiting at the head of a lone wooden table. She didn't take for granted her still youthful attractiveness. Defined by high cheekbones, almond eyes, and long dark hair now piled high on her head, wearing a black skirt, above it she wore her signature bright-red blouse. All her adult and political life she'd worked hard on her presence: femininity combined with strength. She knew it helped with voters.

Ortega believed in the Republic of American States, and she was determined to protect and defend it to the end.

For three decades, since its start, the ROAS had tried to build a new nation with a focus on not only freedom but economic and social equality. To achieve those aims, with limited resources to build a strong military, it was key not to become a threat in hopes the greater nations would leave them alone.

As the ROAS prospered, its economics were founded upon an inherited technological, entrepreneurial model the rest of the world relied upon and envied. The country sold futuristic products across the globe. To fund their socialist programs, the ROAS taxed its citizens at a hefty rate. She was proud of the accomplishments. Universal healthcare, education, and income were now the norm. So far, the model had worked, but now her country was under attack, and the lack of a strong military left it vulnerable.

The president held no illusions. The technological underpinnings of the ROAS were its greatest strength, yet, those same assets were the biggest prize, ripe for the taking. In her opinion, to survive her country hadn't a choice. It was time to take off the gloves and fight back.

Ortega looked across at the tall, lanky man seated to her right. As usual, Secretary of Security Jim James was a mess. He wore crumpled pants and a dress shirt that didn't match, combined with a sport coat begging for a wash. She shook her head at the sight. Yes, he was an information-security genius but also a bumbling pain in the ass. But she needed his help in handling a tough situation. "James, as we discussed, let me take the lead on this. When I want you to add something or interject, I'll ask. Otherwise, please keep your mouth shut."

"Of course," James replied. "I appreciate the difficulties facing us. Your willingness to sacrifice everything to save our nation is admirable."

Julia frowned at the patronizing. "Follow my lead, that's all."

Above the single entrance across the room, the status light turned from green to red, and the door opened. General Story entered the SCIF, closing the portal behind him. At once, the light turned green, indicating the room secure.

In a flash, the president detected an air of resignation about the general. The way he slouched, frowned, and moved with a slight shuffle into the room was disturbing. One of the few senior officers with true combat leadership experience in the entire ROAS Armed

Forces, she needed him. He'd defected from the US a decade prior, leaving a successful military career behind. Once free of his native country, he applied for a commission into the ROAS military and passed a thorough loyalty investigation. Through the process, she became a supporter and believed in his ability. Ortega promoted him into his current role. Still, doubts lingered. The country needed a fighter, someone willing to take risks, even against long odds. Events forced decisions, and she would make one today.

To ease the troubled general, she started the conversation with a soft tone. "General, thank you for taking the time to meet under such dire circumstances." She nodded towards the empty chair opposite the secretary. "Please take a seat." Not missing a beat, she waived towards the skinny man next to her. "I believe you know Secretary James."

The general, with a grim expression, reached out and shook hands with the secretary. "Welcome to ROAS Central Command."

"Thank you, General," James replied.

"We've much to discuss. Please sit," said the president.

The general complied, and the room grew quiet.

Ortega, noting the general's countenance, sighed. Before discussing more productive topics, she'd ask for the bad news first. "General Story, please give us a quick rundown on Mesquite."

Before answering, the general glanced at the lanky man across from him. "Madam President, can you please explain why Secretary James is here? I thought our focus was Mesquite and possible next steps. No disrespect, but I'm not sure his expertise is needed for those discussions."

"Trust me. I've asked James to be here for a reason. Bring me up to speed on Mesquite," said President Julia Ortega.

The general shrugged his shoulders and cleared his voice. "Madam President, after I hung up with you, the enemy hit us with extreme force. Brigade Commander Colonel Rourke died within moments of the start. In quick succession, across our entire front, using joint tank, artillery, missile, infantry, and air assets, the enemy struck hard."

"I see," said the president. The execution of Felix Manuel was terrible, and now, for the first time in her career, she'd put soldiers in harm's way. "How bad was it?"

The general crossed his arms and gave the straight facts. "Estimated losses stand at one hundred percent. The actual number of killed, wounded, captured—only the US Army knows for sure."

"A hundred percent?" asked the president, shocked by the number. "Yes."

The president tried to imagine the carnage, but she'd never seen a battlefield and had no true concept of the loss and suffering. She'd ordered the battalion to resist and not to withdraw or surrender. Maybe she'd made a mistake? No. The nation would learn and grow from this. She put on a strong façade and asked, "Have US forces entered Mesquite?"

"Yes. We informed city leadership before hostilities that in case of an enemy breakthrough, they were not to resist."

Ortega, with a heavy heart, turned to another pressing issue. "I saw the first press reports coming out of Mesquite: claims of heavy fighting at the border followed by quiet. An official announcement needs to go out soon. We need to tamp down any panic. My press team is working on a preliminary statement."

"From a defensive standpoint, we're in extreme trouble. Minus the infantry battalion destroyed today, we've a single under-strength infantry brigade positioned near Las Vegas. In Reno, we have another brigade minus two detached battalions covering other major border crossings. That's all we have in Nevada."

The president chewed her lip, caught herself, and resolved to quit the nervous habit. "Those forces aren't enough?"

"No. Today, the US Nineteenth Army didn't even commit their full strength. If they choose, they can bring much more to the table. To stop them, we've got nothing of any real consequence standing in the way."

Ortega knew the long military odds facing her country. But hearing the details, the large loss of life, their vulnerability to future attacks, she shuddered. By resisting, she'd hoped to set an example—heroics to share with the people and stiffen backbones. The big question needed to be asked. "Did our people resist?"

General Story closed his eyes for a moment as if replaying the battle. "Our troops did the best they could under difficult conditions."

Not appreciating the vague response, the president asked, "Did we resist or not?"

The general sighed. "The sheer unrelenting force of the attack kept our troops pinned. They never stood a chance. In less than twenty minutes, the battle was over. Throughout, other than a few instances, we detected no material return fire."

The president slumped and asked, "It doesn't seem possible."

"Madam, even with advanced warning the outcome was certain. In this case, not only was the attack unexpected, but the US force arrayed against us was insurmountable. The battle, as I warned, was over before it started."

Ortega felt a pang of guilt. She imagined a bloody battlefield, troops terrified by an unyielding onslaught. All of them dying in place, unable to strike back. Still, there had to be a silver lining. The country needed something from the sacrifice, no matter how small. "I'll take responsibility for the events of today. You advised a withdrawal, even a surrender, but I ordered resistance. In my statements to the public I'll make my position and your role clear. Please, you mentioned in a few cases our people resisted. Explain."

The general shrugged. "Not much to say. In the first case, we observed explosions near a few enemy tanks, but their APS—Active Protection Systems—were effective in countering our missiles. One tank appeared to take a glancing blow and lost mobility. We also shot down many of their incoming missiles, though not enough."

"So we fought back," she said with a hopeful smile. "You claimed several instances. Are there more?"

The general sat higher in his chair and gave a quick grin. "Yes, one more. A confirmed kill on a single enemy vertical-lift aircraft. A US Custer was shot out of the sky. Full fireball upon impact. We've excellent drone video of the event. For an unknown reason, the enemy APS didn't engage. Anyway, a hand-held Javelin missile struck the Custer broadside."

The president nodded. It wasn't much, but she was thankful. It might be enough to spin a positive story. "Excellent. Please get me the footage right away."

"Yes, ma'am. Soon as we exit this meeting, I'll have my staff send it over."

The president nodded. She needed to avert a public-relations nightmare. At this stage, civilian support was critical. "We need to let everyone know we didn't fire the first shot. The enemy attacked without warning. Although outnumbered many times over, we fought back. No one died in vain. We need sympathy for our cause, admiration for our spirit, and animosity towards our enemy."

The general glanced over at the secretary and frowned. "It appears neither you nor Secretary James seems to grasp the big picture. Impossible odds face the ROAS. From a military standpoint, the ROAS hasn't the means to resist. Today, when the US attacked, shifting from diplomacy to war, they called our bluff." General Story cleared his voice and continued, "Madam President, we'd need a miracle to stand against the military might of the United States. The pathway to solving our problems isn't through force of arms."

Listening, the president searched the eyes of her general. Now was the time for inspired leadership, a spearhead willing to infuse optimism. She wasn't sure about her general. Maybe his spirit needed hope. "You say we need a miracle?"

The general grunted, "Metaphor, Madam President. Nukes might do the trick, but we've none. Besides, mutual destruction isn't an answer. If there is any way to sue for peace, now is the time. I'm sorry."

Ortega knew suing for peace without leverage, as proven today and throughout the crisis, was naïve. The US wouldn't negotiate unless compelled. She wanted more from her general. "Short of nukes and suing for peace, there must be another way to give the enemy a serious black eye. Give them a licking bad enough to get them to the bargaining table. Agreed?"

"Wishful thinking won't help. Both Armored Brigade Combat Teams, elements of the US Fifty-Fifth Division that struck today, can reach the outskirts of Las Vegas in a few hours. Let me focus my time on protecting the Vegas civilian population with our current capabilities. Meanwhile, I recommend you figure out a way to save our nation through political means."

The president laughed at the bold statement and shook her head. "The enemy won't advance right away."

General Story raised his eyebrows. "Madam President, how have you reached that conclusion?"

"Intelligence," she replied.

The general shook his head. "My own intelligence staff, using the latest deep-learning systems, predicts both US Armored Brigade Combat Teams will pass through Mesquite within a few hours and arrive outside Las Vegas by early tomorrow. Hostilities will then resume. If you have better intelligence, please share it."

President Ortega pondered how much to relate. Too little, and he wouldn't understand. Too much without enough context, and she might lose him. Ortega decided to take the middle road. "The United States is seeking to overthrow our government and end our little experiment. I assure you, the US vice president wasn't assassinated by our government. Under great pressure, we've tried to reason. Earlier today, in a last attempt to avert war, I agreed to my personal extradition in return for the release of Manuel and Ross. The US responded by executing Manuel and attacking Mesquite."

Ortega paused, looked at the general, and could see his mind churning. She kept going, "We expect the US will tell the world my extradition agreement is an admission of guilt, and the attack on Mesquite and the execution of Manuel justifiable. But it won't be enough. As further punishment for our supposed crimes, we expect the US will demand 'repatriation' of Nevada and give us forty-eight hours to comply. If we accept those terms, it still won't be enough.

They'll come up with more excuses until our nation no longer exists. We've seen similar models used before. Unrealistic demands based on trumped-up falsehoods. General, you used to work for those people. You know the game. A model of zero-sum foreign policy with a willingness to use pretense for military intervention. The same method used by the other two great nationalistic powers. With US intentions now clear, other than nullifying secession and surrendering, we've no choice but resistance."

"Where do we stand with our friends? Canada, the other liberal democracies? Last I heard, you were seeking their assistance."

"Canada, as you know, possesses a military much stronger than ours. But, like us, to survive, they've adopted a neutrality stance in world events. We've asked them, begged, for military help. We've explained the writing is on the wall, and they'll be next. So far, they're unwilling and trying their best to stay out of harm's way. After today, maybe they'll change their minds, but we can't count on it. The remaining liberal democracies are too weak, and the distances too great. They're also fearful of garnering the wrath of the Great Powers. No, we stand alone."

"How about seeking the help of Russia or China?" he asked.

"Good question full of problematic possibilities. ROAS re-absorption into the United States would upset the apple cart. Neither Russia nor China wants that. Our technological capabilities in the hands of the US could tip the balance of power. So, China, and to a lesser degree Russia, may offer us assistance, but we won't ask for or take any offers. If we did, we'd only be trading one set of problems for another; eventually, we'd lose our independence. No, the best solution for our long-term survival depends upon unilateral action. We must hit the US hard enough that they decide to pull back their ambitions against our country."

General Story leaned back and in a soft voice said, "Madam President, you're a brave woman, but having that kind of force isn't in the cards."

Ignoring the statement, Ortega asked, "So how do we hurt the US enough to turn them away?"

In a flat voice he said, "Militarily, we can't."

Ortega frowned. "I don't need defeatism."

The general sighed and appeared worn down. "I'm being real. The US military is vast and their military capabilities far superior. I know what's in our arsenal and what we're capable of achieving. Madam, we don't have the means."

The president asked, "But if you had the means, no matter the sacrifice, would you use them?"

General Story stopped for a second and seemed to ponder the question. Then he answered in a slow voice. "I'm not sure I understand. To defend our nation, I'm prepared to do what is necessary. If sacrifices are necessary to achieve success, then yes. But I'm not willing to sacrifice lives with no chance of a positive outcome. Madam President, we don't have the military means to force the US to do anything. There must be a diplomatic solution."

Ortega waved off the pessimism. Bending across the table she asked, "For survival, do you believe the ends justify the means?"

The general appeared frustrated. In a tight voice he said, "To survive, in most cases, yes the ends would justify the means. We don't have the means."

The president leaned back and put her hands flat on the table. She studied her general. Perhaps he wasn't the right guy? Other possible replacements flashed through her mind. But she'd already pondered the question. Her gut told her the man sitting opposite was the best choice. "I believe we have the means. I mentioned intelligence and predicting the enemy will pause outside Mesquite giving us two days to prepare. Our intelligence is the means. If you could use it to check our enemy, would you be willing to make significant sacrifices?"

The general didn't seem to get the connection. "If you're speaking of a superior data-mining methodology, please share it. Regardless, intelligence and analytics are great for predictions, but they don't fight battles. We need a lot more than analysis."

Ortega glanced over at the secretary and caught him about to speak. She put up a finger to silence the man and turned back to her general. "I believe we have the means. But some might claim they are immoral."

Story sat straighter, and she sensed a piqued interest. "Madam President, if what you're offering as a means is effective, I need to learn more."

Pleased with the answer, it was time to make sure he understood before revealing. She asked, "Morality, General, is often in the eye of the beholder. Agreed?"

"Yes. I agree, and I'll make the personal determination."

The president expected his answer. "I believe the means we have at our disposal aren't immoral and will be effective. You may think otherwise. If after explaining, you decide they are wrong, I'll expect your immediate resignation and consent to house arrest for the duration. Agreed?" The tension in the room palatable, Ortega watched as the general considered the question. At last, he gave his answer.

"Maybe I'd be better off not finding out and forgo the briefing. What becomes of me then?"

"In that case, you'll relinquish command and enter immediate retirement."

He shot back, "You have no one as qualified to take my place."

Ortega shook her head. "General, everyone is replaceable. We want you. I want you. But we need your commitment. Otherwise, please step aside. What will it be?" Waiting for his answer, she knew her general defected for a reason, and she expected him to do the right thing. She wasn't disappointed.

"I'm willing to listen. If what you offer fits within my moral boundaries, I'm your guy. If not, I'll consent to house arrest for the duration. Now, fill me in on the damn secret."

Secretary James looked up with a smile and began to speak, but Ortega cut him off and said, "SALI."

The general cocked his head. "That's not possible. SALI no longer exists."

"Yes, she does," said the president. Pleased with her general, she gave a broad smile.

Chapter Twelve

WORKING THE DEAD

May 8, 18:27 (PDT)

With an hour of daylight remaining, Kirby Pugh and Ronnie Hough, both privates in the United States Army, found themselves on the far-left flank of the destroyed enemy trenches. As part of the US Nineteenth Army field disciplinary team, divided into multiple two-man teams, they'd be spending the night gathering up and bagging ROAS KIA. The battlefield was a one-sided slaughterhouse, and the detail was expected to take all night. For Pugh and Hough, it was just another night of bullshit duty, although one with promising opportunities.

Kirby and Ronnie were buddies with a strong bond, sometimes too strong. Often acting together, when one got in trouble, in most cases, so did the other. And it happened again the week before. Both got caught drinking on duty. Now assigned to a gruesome punishment detail, they weren't altogether unhappy. They broke the rules and expected to pay a price. Such was life in the US Army. Besides, they were adept at making the most of bad situations.

After watching the truck disappear, the two friends smiled at each other. Both carried packs and assault rifles. Strewn about were other supplies, including shovels, picks, gloves, and masks. Boxes of body bags also awaited. Neither man wore a head protection system as they weren't required for the dirty detail. Instead, both elected beanies to ward off the chilly night air.

With packs and rifles set aside, the men gloved up, nodded towards one another, and climbed into the nearest trench. Upon entering, the smell of death assaulted them. Six bodies, maybe more, lay scattered in the sandy ditch. They'd done this detail before, on different battle-fields in far-off places, and had learned through experience.

Kirby would search the bodies and pull out any belongings, including dog tags, and put those into a zip-lock baggie. With a safety pin, he'd then affix the baggie to the remains through an article of clothing, or if none were available, through flesh. Kirby was like an older brother and between them got the better bargain of most deals, and rummaging bodies was the most fun—like a treasure hunt. After searching and pinning, Ronnie bagged the body, or in some cases, body parts. Once full, Ronnie would zip the bag, and both men would drag it to a convenient stacking point for pickup. Later, after gathering the bagged corpses, regular Mortuary Services troops would take DNA samples and log the results.

Tonight, working side by side, both men got used to the foul odor, and within half an hour they cleared the first trench. Six body bags lay stacked nearby. After a quick breather, they headed towards the next trench, dragging along their supplies and dodging shell holes along the way. Before going far, a rather large crater caught their attention. Peering inside, they both detected the scent of death. Sure enough, they spotted an arm with a hand attached lying near part of a torso. Once again, they dropped their packs and weapons, crawled in, and got to work.

Kirby Pugh, at twenty-nine years of age, had two years on Ronnie Hough. Both men hovered around five feet nine, non-descript, and similar in looks. Proud southerners, Kirby grew up in Mississippi, while Ronnie hailed from rural Georgia. After joining the military, gravitated by their similarities, they found one another. In the Army, they'd achieved a few minor victories. Kirby once made it to Sergeant before getting busted in rank. But the successes were short-lived as both got demoted several times for various and sundry misdemeanors.

Busted again, they now held the lowest rank, private. Although they complained loud and often about the Army and the unfairness of it all, the institution suited them. The Army fed them, paid them a little, provided shelter, and offered a world to exploit.

So far, they'd stayed out of hard labor and prison camps. Both believed in God, the Christian way, although both admitted to slipping. After a backslide, they'd feel awful and behave for a spell. But a new temptation always emerged, and sometimes, bad luck brought new troubles.

Tonight's detail brought with it plenty of opportunity. Although under strict orders not to loot, facing long prison sentences if caught, the upside was just too promising.

Plus, they rationalized, taking from the dead wasn't a sin, especially enemy dead. No one got hurt. The dead weren't alive and couldn't take it with them. To both men, looting from corpses wasn't stealing but more like prospecting, not theft, and worth the risk. Justifiable compensation for the nasty work.

Inside the shell crater, finishing up, they concluded the gathered body parts belonged to a single person. Based on the lack of muscle tone, almost no hair on the arms, and slender, tapered fingers, they guessed it was female. Both men found the practice repulsive. The US Army didn't allow women or queers into combat for many good and obvious reasons.

Before moving on, they sat down to rest. Kirby was working up an anger. After taking a sip from a hydration system, he handed the water container to his buddy. Staring at the filled body bag, he turned to Ronnie and aired his grievance. "I can't fucking believe those cocksuckers. Women fighting their wars for them. God awful!"

"Yeah. That's fucked up. That's why we fight'n," said Ronnie. Still catching his breath from the exertion, sitting next to his friend, he took a sip and clipped the hydration system back to his belt.

"It's one reason for sure," agreed Kirby. Using his teeth, he pulled off the rubber glove from his right hand and flung it to the ground. With his hand free, he fished a pack of cigarettes and lighter from his breast pocket.

Ronnie watched his buddy. "You gonna let me have a puff?"

Kirby lit the cigarette and took a long drag. Exhaling a large cloud of smoke, he examined the pack. To his disappointment, only a couple remained. Still, they always shared. He slid the near-empty pack into his shirt pocket and said, "You bet, good buddie. I'll let you smoke the other half."

Ronnie leaned back and said, "Gonna be harder to work soon. We'll need the lantern."

Kirby just nodded, his thoughts elsewhere. He took another drag and spoke his mind. "We also fight'n 'em cuz they allow homosexuals. Homos allowed to fight. Women allowed to fight. Atheists allowed to fight. Hell, anyone allowed to fight. That's just fucked up seven ways to Sunday."

"Seven ways," agreed Ronnie, keeping an eye on the promised cigarette. He shifted the subject and asked, "What we got so far?"

Kirby looked over at his buddy then pulled off his other glove and tossed it to the ground. With the dwindling cigarette in his mouth he said, "You done seen what we got. Ain't shit so far, just a couple of rings. And we won't have shit until we get past that fucking search tomorrow."

"You put it in your boot?" asked Ronnie.

"Look, I hollowed out both our boot heels and they only hold so much. Yes, it's in my boot. But there's a shit pile of stuff out here. If we had a way to hide more and come back later, we'd have us a king's ransom. We surely would." He sucked on the smoke, measured the length, determined it was more than half gone, and flicked it across to his buddy, where it landed in the dirt.

Ronnie picked up the butt, examined it at eye level, and brushed away a few particles of sand. Placing the butt between his lips, he drew in the smoke. A moment later, he leaned back with a satisfied smile.

Kirby watched Ronnie smoke, but his mind worked the problem—the lack of good hiding spaces. They were just getting started and would be humping bodies all night. He expected to find lots of loot. To lessen suspicions, he needed to make sure a few valuables got tagged and turned over. The rest they would hide. But soon, their boot heels would be full, forcing them to hand over items they'd otherwise pilfer. Not acceptable.

The idea of a better hiding spot intrigued him. By finding a good location to stash loot, with plenty of room, profits were sure to increase. With a cache, they'd come back later and retrieve it when no one was looking. Maybe after the fighting. Deep in thought, a potential solution appeared out of nowhere.

Intrigued, in the gloaming, Kirby stood and walked over for a closer look. The depth of the shell hole was only five feet, and about half way up stood a little cave. A dark opening less than a foot in diameter. Curios, he bent over and stuck his index finger through the spot and touched nothing on the other side. Good.

Now excited, Kirby decided to widen the hole and find how deep it was. From his boot he pulled out a combat knife and stuck it through the opening. Again, he felt no pressure against the tip. The hole was deep. With the knife he scraped around the edges, causing dirt and sand to crumble away. The hole widened farther. In a burst, he clawed at the dirt and sand until he uncovered something bigger. A pipe. Perfect!

Finished with the cigarette, grinding it out, Ronnie watched Kirby work the side of the shell hole. "What you got there?"

Not looking back, Kirby replied, "Found a hole. I think we can use it to hide stuff."

"Oh," replied Ronnie. He seemed happy to let Kirby do the work.

Within a few minutes, Kirby exposed the entire entrance. Standing back, he admired his labor. The pipe circumference was rather large, and covering it up again would be challenging. After sheathing his knife, he pulled a penlight from his web belt, flipped it on, and pointed it through the opening. Shocked, he jumped back and extinguished the light.

Ronnie, obviously alarmed, whispered, "What is it, what you see?"

Kirby turned and raised a finger, warning his friend to keep quiet. With the penlight in one hand, he backed away from the entrance and with the other pulled out his knife. Seeing the movement, Ronnie also withdrew a knife.

Kirby whispered, "Somebody's in there."

Ronnie, still seated, leaned around his buddy and guessed. "Dead guy?"

Kirby shrugged. He didn't know if the guy was alive or not. All he'd seen, not far inside the pipe, was a pair of boots. Expectant, staring at the opening, both friends listened and remained quiet. Nothing, zilch, no noise.

After a minute, Ronnie pointed over his shoulder outside the shell hole where they'd left their stuff and whispered a question, "Weapons?"

Kirby considered the possibility. Firing an assault rifle could alert the enemy. Worse, and more likely, shooting would bring officers, and he didn't want that. No, he and Ronnie had knives, and those would have to do. Besides, whoever was in there didn't appear to be moving. It had to be a dead or wounded enemy. He decided and whispered, "Follow me. Keep your knife ready. I'll pull the guy out, and if he fights, help me stab the shit out of him. Got it?"

With nervous energy, Ronnie bobbed his head.

In the fading light Kirby gave his friend a wicked smile and then retraced his steps. Ronnie got up and trailed behind.

After reaching the pipe, Kirby stood off to one side and gestured Ronnie to stand nearby. Ronnie moved into place, and Kirby pantomimed, showing what he planned to do. Then, Kirby handed his knife, handle first, to his friend. Now holding a knife in each hand, Ronnie nodded.

From his combat belt, Kirby removed a penlight and, after turning it on, placed it between his teeth. Hands free, he readied himself. It was now or never. Heart racing, he jumped in front of the pipe, bent low, and in a single motion, reached in with both hands and grabbed a set of ankles. With a mighty tug he fell backward. To his surprise, the man slid out without much resistance, causing Kirby to stumble and let go. A moment later, the body landed in a thud on the sandy soil.

In a flash, Kirby scrambled forward and put his knee into the back of the prostrate figure. The soldier, or whoever he was, lay face down, head turned sideways, not moving. Ronnie, ready to pounce, hovered nearby, knives at the ready. But the person remained still.

Kirby removed the penlight from his mouth and shined it at his captive. In profile, he saw a mouth covered in dried blood. There was more, a surprise: medium-length dark hair. Not a man. Stunned for a moment, he wasn't sure what it meant, but the opportunities dawned on him, and he smiled. With his knee still planted in the back of his captive, he let out an appreciative whistle. "Now look at what we got here."

Before Ronnie could respond, Kirby realized the job wasn't complete. He'd made too much noise. Near panic, he arose, turned to Ronnie, and whispered, "Watch her." Like a cat, he moved back to the pipe. Once again approaching from the side, ready to move away at the slightest provocation, using his penlight he peered inside. To his intense relief, for many meters all he detected was the inside of an empty corrugated pipe. Relieved, he let out a puff of air and stood straight. "All clear," he said to Ronnie and then shifted his attention back to the prize.

In the dying daylight, Kirby flipped his penlight along the length of the prone woman. Even wearing combat gear, he detected feminine curves. Then he made a note of her rank: a sergeant in the ROAS.

Ronnie stood over the body with knives in both hands and asked, "She dead?"

"I don't think so," said Kirby, taking a knee next to the fallen woman. He felt for a pulse and detected a steady beat. With his penlight, Kirby inspected closer and scanned the length of her body. Arms scratched and scraped, pant legs caked with dried blood, uniform and soldier protection suit covered in dust and sand, but she was alive. With no head protection system, she must've been knocked out while cowering in the pipe to survive. She was fortunate to be alive and even luckier for him!

"Now what?" asked Ronnie.

"That all you do is ask dumb questions?"

Ronnie looked back and blinked as if to confirm the answer.

Kirby, used to his dense friend and giving the orders, said, "First, give me back my knife."

Ronnie did so, returning it handle first.

Kirby turned to the far end of the shell hole, sheathed the blade, and pointed towards the desert. "Go back up and fetch your pack. We need a blanket and supplies. But before you go, give me some water."

Ronnie put away his own knife and unclipped his water carrier before tossing it to Kirby. Not waiting, following instructions, Ronnie climbed out of the shell hole.

Kirby returned to the unconscious woman. Still kneeling, he grabbed her left shoulder and rolled her face up, eliciting a groan in response. Eyes still closed, bruised, filthy, chin covered in dried blood, with her mouth hanging open, he noticed a missing tooth. But through it all, he found her somewhat pretty.

Although alive, Kirby wasn't sure of the extent of her injuries. He reached down and pushed her left eyelid open. A blood shot eye, the ball rolled back, greeted him, and he let go. Head trauma, he suspected. Maybe a bad concussion. Knocked out cold. Not sure what he was doing, he twisted open the hydration system and poured a small trickle of water into the corner of the woman's mouth. At first, she didn't respond, and then, involuntarily, a tongue emerged. It flicked at the liquid. Kirby poured a little more, most of it dripping away, but through cracked lips, her tongue re-emerged. Then he spotted her name tag. It read "McMichael."

A pack landed nearby causing Kirby to jump. A second later, Ronnie emerged and, bending down, he pulled out a blanket.

Still on a knee, Kirby snatched the fabric from his buddy, wetted a corner, and used it to wipe the woman's face. As the grime and blood came off, beyond the scratches and a missing tooth, he found her even more attractive. But for a reason he couldn't fathom, anger welled. He turned back to his friend and pointed towards the woman's feet. "I think she's hurt in the head. Take off her boots and socks."

Ronnie paused for a moment, as if confused, and then with a shrug followed orders. He unlaced her boots and pulled them off one by one. Next, he removed her socks and tossed them aside.

Kirby finished wiping the woman's face and rolled up the blanket. He lifted her head, placing the material underneath acting as a pillow. Cushioned by the cloth, she moved her head back and forth, but didn't regain consciousness. Satisfied she remained out, Kirby shifted his gaze downward and pointed at her belt. "We gotta search her. Help me take off her combat belt, pants, and shirt."

"We gonna strip her?" asked Ronnie, a smile appearing.

Still pointing at the woman, Kirby explained, "This here's an enemy combatant that we ourselves done captured. We gonna be heroes. First, we gotta do a thorough search. So yeah, to do it right, I figure we need to undress her. It'll make it easier. Find out if she got weapons or secret orders. She might be carrying contraband. Help me get her pants off."

"Got it," replied Ronnie, and he bent over and undid her belt and the cinches on her combat pants. Afterward, both men stood and together they grabbed the woman's pant legs and pulled hard. They had to tug twice, and on the second try, the woman lifted her head and let out a loud groan before dropping down. With blood trickling down her outstretched legs, naked from the waist down, neither Kirby nor Ronnie took notice. Instead, holding her pants between them, together they stared at a tuft of dark hair.

"She damn sure is a woman," said Ronnie.

Kirby, his anger growing at the sight, shook his head. "She's the enemy. You gotta remember why we're fighting these people."

"They done killed our vice president," said Ronnie, his eyes drinking in the view.

"Yeah . . ." Kirby agreed, ". . . but that's just a start. See, these people ain't right. We and them is different as night from day. You said it earlier, that's why we're fighting. In fact, these people aren't really people at all. Now they may be human, walk upright and all, but they sure as hell ain't people."

"Then what is they?" asked Ronnie, still ogling.

Kirby stopped and stared at the exposed woman. Dark hair protruded from between her legs, and he licked his lips. He'd try to explain. "They's the enemy. Not human as God willed it, because they don't think right. They got an affliction. A true malady. Like this gal right here . . ." he pointed at the naked form and continued, ". . . she ain't no woman like we know. Not a real woman 't all. Most likely a lesbo, or a Muslim, maybe both. They condone, celebrate, and tolerate all that heathen crap. Damn well bet she ain't a Christian. And what the hell do they have women out here fighting for? We stopped that years ago. It's uncivilized."

Kirby paused in his tirade and dropped his hand. He spat off to the side and glowered at the female splayed before him. In growing anger, he continued to explain, "She might be an atheist. You know, the ROAS is full of them. Most of 'em are. No, they ain't got any good human qualities 't all. More like animals." Kirby stopped for a moment when another thought struck him. "That's the whole reason we split away from them years ago. But now we're back, because it's our Manifest Destiny. It's our birthright to keep our country strong, spread liberty, and reunify the United States. And this thing lying here, with her legs spread to God and country, well, she ain't right. None of 'em are."

Ronnie, gazing at the woman, said, "Damn straight." As if snapping from a spell, he looked up and asked, "Now what?"

Above, the sky had turned almost black. Looking up at the gathering darkness then back down at the half-naked body, Kirby felt a strange desire mixed with anger. "We ain't got much time. You search her pants. I've gotta find out if she's hiding something inside herself. Maybe contraband. Then, like we do with cigarettes, I'll share and give you a turn to look."

Ronnie looked at his buddy with a cocked head and watched

Kirby unbuckle. Not saying a word, Ronnie seemed to understand and stepped back to rifle the woman's pants and wait his opportunity.

Belt loosened, on his knees, Kirby maneuvered in front of the prostrate female. With Ronnie and the pipe at his back, Kirby stared at the helpless woman in disgust. Anger and want mingled together. Red in the face, Kirby dropped his pants. Between outstretched legs her nakedness beckoned, and the sight increased his anger. He told himself she was a slut, an enemy, and he hadn't a choice. What came next was her fault. With the back of his hand, he pushed her legs farther apart. A groan came in response. The reaction caught him off guard, and his anger intensified. She had no right to protest. It was time to show her. For leverage, he gripped her left ankle and used it to raise her leg. The higher he lifted, the more he hated and lusted.

Heart racing, holding her ankle above his shoulder, it took a moment for Kirby to register a peculiar gurgling sound coming from behind. Distracted, he turned and saw a nightmare. Ronnie was staggering, his throat slit from ear to ear. From the fatal wound, crimson blood squirted in long arches matching the beat of a dying heart. Before he could react, his friend collapsed into a heap.

Horrified, Kirby dropped the woman's leg. In a single panicked move, he tried to stand and spin to face the threat, but his pants tangled around his ankles and he fell. Before he landed, someone was on his back driving him to the ground. Pinned, he tried to breathe, when he detected a punch to the ribs, then another, and he wheezed. More punches, one after the other, and pain ripped through his soul. He wheezed again emitting a misty cloud of blood. The punching and pain seemed to last forever and, despite his efforts, he felt himself starting to drift away. With a jolt he was wide awake. One last attempt to live! Panicked, he kicked his feet and struggled. Then he saw it emerge from the darkness. Terrified by the specter wearing a robe and white hood from the past, a moment later it reached out and pulled him into the eternal night.

Chapter Thirteen

RESPONDING

May 8, 18:35 (PDT)

"Madam President, you have to see this!" exclaimed Press Secretary Grace Navarro. Tablet in hand, she passed it to the president. "Please hit the play button."

Earlier, President Julia Ortega had returned from her meeting with General Story in Central Command. She'd flown back to the alternate secure seat of government located underground near the heart of San Jose, California. While traveling, and since arriving, she'd been in near constant communications with Senate Leadership and her cabinet. More critical meetings awaited. But first she stopped in the media room to meet with her press team. They needed to get an updated statement out to the populace, quick, not only to clarify what had happened but to calm fears and give hope. Not an easy task. With tablet in hand, President Ortega followed instructions and hit play.

At first, the surveillance drone image was disorienting. It took a moment for her to realize it was an aerial shot. High above ROAS lines, it looked down upon a smoking ruin of destruction. Dust, dirt, sand, and smoke filled the air. Explosions thundered about in a chaotic fashion, and then the shelling stopped. In response, the video closed in tighter, scanning what was left of the ROAS trench lines. It was hard to watch. Strewn among the smoking ruins she detected bodies. The destruction seemed total, and nothing moved. Certainly, it appeared no one was firing back. The president cringed, and once again a sense of guilt wracked her conscious. The panning ceased, and then the image zoomed even tighter until the screen filled with a lone woman in profile. Fascinated, the president watched. Wearing no helmet, face bloodied, the young woman appeared to be standing in a shell hole peering out at US lines. In her arms, she cradled a weapon and in a swift move she shouldered it and fired. After tossing aside the weapon, a moment later the young woman jumped up and down with exultant hands raised high. A moment later, heavy incoming fire raked the woman's position, and she ducked deeper into the hole. Not long afterward, a Custer screamed overhead, lighting up the shell hole with explosions. For a few seconds the camera stayed on the position as the shell hole and surrounding area erupted in a mass of sand, dirt, and smoke. Then, the video ended.

Stirred by what she'd seen, the president reflected on the bravery and turned to Grace for more information. "Do we have a name for that young woman? Is she alive, and do we have video of what she hit?"

Grace pointed at the tablet and smiled. "Last question first. Please view the next video. Hit play."

The president pressed the button, and another drone video started. This time, the angle was outward, panning across US lines. In the distance tanks maneuvered. Farther out, armored infantry vehicles awaited. Most alarming, hovering closer by, several US Custer aircraft menaced. Without warning, one of the birds took a hit. The camera zoomed closer. Focused on the stricken aircraft, the video recorded the machine trailing smoke, falling, and spinning to the ground, where it crashed into a huge fireball. For a few seconds, the video stayed on the wreckage. A dark plume of smoke rose above the licking flames, and then the recording stopped. Forgetting her despair, the president said, "Wow! Outstanding. Combine these shots into a single sequence. Let the world witness our resolve!"

"Already on it."

"Any idea who she is and if she's still alive?" asked the president.

Grace shook her head. "We're unsure of her status. Current satellite reconnaissance confirms the entire area overrun with US forces. General Story claims the US hasn't released information yet on any individual soldiers." Then Grace smiled and shifted to more welcoming news. "But using facial recognition, we have a positive ID."

Expectant, the president cocked her head and pushed the tablet forward.

Press Secretary Grace took the device and tucked it under her arm. "Her name is Lisa McMichael, Sergeant with five years active service. Born and raised in Las Vegas. She maintains a permanent residence there. Twenty-seven years of age. A single mom with two young children—ages seven and five."

Ortega reflected on the day. Death and destruction, and she had given the order to resist. The graphic nature of the video depicted the carnage. The pictures made it real and worse than she imagined. Ortega recalled General Story's warning. He'd been right. There was no way the battalion could have survived against such an overwhelming force. It was a horrible catastrophe, and she felt an ache deep within her bones. But the video of the disaster contained a prize: an attractive female soldier in plain view, bloodied, yet fighting back against all odds. It showed what the president believed all along. Her country was strong and the people willing to sacrifice their lives. The video of Lisa McMichael shooting a Custer from the sky appeared to be the only positive outcome emerging from a long and terrible day. The president, almost to herself, whispered, "Lisa McMichael, we needed a hero. God bless you."

Pressed for time, the president understood the urgency. She patted down her hair and smoothed the wrinkles from her red blouse. "Okay, I'm ready to record a statement. No makeup—there isn't time. Afterward, distribute it and the Lisa video to the entire media. Do it quick. The public has a right to know and learn of their new hero." Another important detail crossed her mind. "Also, before I forget, make sure Lisa's kids are secure. Get them the hell away from Vegas and somewhere safe. Lord knows they deserve it."

"Yes, ma'am," replied Press Secretary Grace, already directing staff, "we'll make it happen."

* * *

May 8, 23:46 (PDT)

A series of low-rise, windowless industrial buildings lay nestled among the pines and redwoods of the Santa Cruz Mountains. Considered ugly, erected over the last decade, building functionality and security overcame aesthetic considerations. Selected by the ROAS to "hide" in plain sight, the location was close to the brains in nearby Silicon Valley and not too distant from the Federal Capital in Sacramento.

Inside the largest building sat the ROAS Central Command— CENTCOM—the headquarters for all vital military strategic decisions. At a long table, facing the north wall covered with monitors, Bill Story sat working on saving the nation. Aged fifty-two, born and raised in Davenport, Iowa, the general was a full-fledged graduate of the US Military Academy. His active military career was one of steady achievement. From fighting with distinction in the Second Korean War through assisting foreign military staff with the Turkish/ Russo invasion of Iran, he was well experienced in the art of war, but nothing had prepared him for the events of today.

Earlier, after meeting with the president and Secretary James, General Story returned to CENTCOM to issue orders dealing with the defeat at Mesquite. Since then, the latest intelligence showed both US Armored Brigade Combat Teams hadn't advanced. Instead, the enemy went into bivouac along Highway 15 west of town. From a military standpoint, he viewed the pause as a mistake. A wide-open blacktop offered the enemy a green light all the way to Las Vegas. But the president was right in her assessment.

Exhausted but thankful for the extra time, the general rubbed his eyes and tried to figure out how best to take advantage of the situation. It was hard. Too often his thinking was interrupted by sudden thoughts of the day and the horrific losses. Tired, trying to clear his mind, he remembered something and swiveled in his seat. Across the room, below a row of monitors, he spotted Secretary James sitting with a patient smile in a hard-back chair. He frowned at the sight. Intelligence, he believed, wasn't the answer. But he was committed to listening.

General Story turned to his aid, Lieutenant Colonel Andrea Simpson, sitting beside him. "I need to attend a briefing with Secretary James in a nearby classified location and will be out of pocket for the duration."

Worn out and trying to hide it, Simpson wiped away a wisp of red hair from her forehead. "Understood, sir. If something comes up . . ."

The general cut in, "I won't be gone long."

"Yes, sir," replied Simpson. Curiosity burning through the fatigue, she asked, "Should I go with you?"

The general glanced towards Secretary James and saw the man getting up and looking his way. "Not this time, Colonel. Secretary James has transportation standing by, and this meeting is for my eyes only." He thought of his promise to the president; either embrace the offer or resign at once. He didn't tell Simpson that part; no need. If he wasn't coming back, well, the president was correct, everyone was replaceable. Getting up, he felt the stiffness in his legs and took a long stretch. Feeling better, the general squared his shoulders and marched across the room to meet the skinny man and learn more about SALI.

* * *

A sleek, autonomous electric vehicle picked up the passengers. No driver needed, both men sat in the back. Upon entering, General Story appreciated the soft leather seats. While driving, there was no engine or discernible road noise. The combination created a luxu-riating experience and nurtured a tiredness that swept across the general.

But sleep wasn't in the cards, the voice of Secretary James keeping him awake, "We're on our way to visit the estate of Dr. Vivek Basu."

"Humph," replied the general. He knew the name, a major tech-nology investor and business tycoon.

"He not only lives nearby but operates a renowned spiritual awakening camp: 175 acres of pristine mountain property with zero technology, unplugged. During the summer, he runs a camp for chil-dren as an opportunity to experience life before the internet age. As for the rest of the year, retreats are held for those wishing to avoid the influence of technology. Surrounded by fencing, the property has no cell service, internet connectivity, landlines, or computers. Beyond basic security measures and electricity, technology is prohibited on the property. It's an awesome place, like traveling back to the 1930s."

Ensconced in comfortable leather, trying to enjoy the ride and keep the horrible day at bay, the general found the high-pitched voice of Secretary James to be the only nuisance.

James continued, "When we get there, we'll pass through an outer gate. There, visitors turn over all personal electronics for the dura-tion, but we have clearance to visit the main residence, so we won't turn over any of our stuff until we get there. Pretty cool, wouldn't you agree?"

Reclined in the soft seat, tired, the general wasn't up to conversing. "Sure, great. Now, how much farther?"

"Soon," replied the secretary.

He couldn't help it. With thoughts of the day swirling, the general closed his eyes and drifted into a disturbed sleep.

* * *

She heard moaning, then tasted it again: delicious. More! Licking her lips, she wanted more and tried to say so, but her throat was too dry. She was dead, worse than dead. Eyes fluttering open and with a throbbing head, in the dim light, she saw a curved metal roof. She tried to think where she was, who she was, but the pounding was too much, and she reclosed her eyes. Somehow, through the pain and disorientation, she detected a whisper.

"Shhh. It's okay."

Maybe she wasn't dead? Water splashed on her cracked lips, and her tongue flicked at the precious moisture. It felt cool and soothing against her parched throat. Determined, she opened her eyes. In a rough whisper, she asked, "Where am I?"

In a low tone came a reply, "You're with me, Sergeant Upton, inside a pipe behind enemy lines. You're wounded."

She tried to piece it together, but her head hurt too bad. An over-whelming thirst drove her, and she begged. "More water." Opening her mouth, she waited until a wonderful sight emerged. A straw hovered, and she grabbed the plastic, pulled it between her lips, and sucked hard. Before she'd had enough, it pulled away.

"Not too much too fast. You'll get sick."

She tried to lift her head and get a sense of who was speaking and where she was. A mistake. The throbbing worsened. She lay back, raised a hand to her forehead, and wiped her brow. It still hurt. Alarmed, a face filled her vision, and she dropped her hand. Unsure, blinking, she tried to make the person out. The visage wore a head protection system, visor lifted, but with a headlamp breaking the darkness. Recognition dawned. Upton, a tough son of a bitch. She remembered more. A terrible fight, diving for the pipe, but nothing since then. Brow furrowed, she tried to recall further and didn't notice his movement until he pressed something to her lips. In response, McMichael asked, "What?"

"Open your mouth, I've got a painkiller and more water."

Still in pain, but seeking relief, McMichael opened wide and felt a pill land on her tongue. Like a miracle, the straw returned, and she took it, sucking the water and medication down her throat. Again, too soon, the straw pulled from her mouth. But she didn't resist. Head still throbbing, she closed her eyes and tried gathering her senses. After a few seconds, she asked, "Where are we?"

In a patient whisper, Upton answered, "We're in a pipe. The enemy is outside, all around. Keep your eyes closed, let that pill work, then we'll go from there."

Head pounding with less intensity, soothed by water, awash in sleepiness, McMichael complied.

* * *

Upton watched her drift off to sleep or unconsciousness; he wasn't sure which, although it didn't matter. She needed rest and time for the painkiller. To save on battery power, he clicked off his headlamp and thought about what he'd done.

Much earlier in the day, upon climbing into the pipe, the relief was instant, followed by the sheer joy of being alive. But as the bombardment lessened then stopped, he'd time to think. Guilt emerged as he thought of his squad, abandoned while he cowered out of the fight.

As the day progressed into early evening, more than once he determined to leave the pipe. Twice he'd inched close to where he climbed in, but he could hear movement along the road and knew it was the enemy by the sound of their diesel-powered vehicles. So he remained hidden, but guilt continued to chew his guts. Knowing he couldn't hide forever, he'd been crawling in the opposite direction to find a better way out, when the sound of voices reached his ears. From that point, he moved like a quiet assassin until he came to the end of the pipe. Looking out, he was greeted by the sight of two enemy assholes about to commit rape. Fortune smiled as the men were facing away. Angry at what they were doing, driven further by his own guilt, he slipped from the pipe and, using his knife, killed them both. Afterward, he recognized McMichael, and his anger grew, but there wasn't time for venting. Out in the open with the enemy all around, the extent of her injuries unknown, he needed to hide their tracks and take cover.

He went to work and positioned the two bodies to make it look like the bastards had killed each other. After that, he found McMichael's pants, a blanket, and more water lying nearby. He gathered it all and placed the items on the blanket. Next, he lifted McMichael on top and hoisted the entire bundle inside the pipe. Then he crawled in, and with just enough clearance, he climbed up and over. On the other side, on all fours, he used the blanket as a travois and dragged McMichael back towards the direction he'd come. He estimated they'd traveled over three hundred meters and were now close to where he'd first entered.

So here he now sat, back in the pipe, with a wounded McMichael, and he worried the enemy would recognize his ruse and come after them. All communications were down, but his visor displayed the time and temperature. Half the night was gone. They needed to get moving, but looking at McMichael, he realized they couldn't go anywhere. Not yet.

Chapter Fourteen

MEETING AND MOTIVES

May 9, 00:25 (PDT)

Before passing through the main guard entrance leading into Basu Ranch, Secretary James woke the general. After checking credentials, the guard let them pass without trouble. They continued until they reached the farthest corner of the ranch, where they went through a secondary guard entrance and had their credentials re-confirmed. Next, they turned onto a road leading to the private estate of Mr. Vivek Basu.

The road turned into a driveway fronting a large building. General Story thought it looked more like a low-rise office building than a home. At a tall iron gate, the car stopped. James rolled down his window and placed a palm against a reader, whereupon the barrier retracted.

They drove through the gate and entered a two-story parking garage devoid of cars, save a few modest sedans, and parked in the lower level.

Reluctant to get out of the comfortable seat but glad they'd reached their destination, along with Secretary James, the general exited the vehicle.

James led the way and steered the general into a nearby elevator. Upon entering, the door slid closed, and James stood still, waiting. The general, shaking off the cobwebs from his quick nap, was about to ask which floor when the elevator descended on its own. Interested, the general noted there wasn't a button for a lower level. With a wry smile, he glanced at James and raised his eyebrows to acknowledge the subterfuge. James smiled back.

A few seconds later, the elevator stopped and the door opened, leading into a small foyer. Still leading the way, James exited followed by the general.

Inside the small room, the general couldn't tell where to head next as the area lacked any obvious exits. Amused, he asked the secretary, "Where to next, 007?"

James laughed, then turned to his right, strode up to a wall, and placed his hand on the wood paneling. "After I go through, wait a minute, then copy me and place your hand on this wall. When it opens, step through and wait."

To the general's amazement, a vertical seam appeared in the wall, widening far enough for the secretary to enter. The general watched as the secretary stepped through, the wall sealing shut behind him. Secret squirrel shit.

After a short wait, the general approached and did as instructed and placed his hand on the wall. Nothing happened. About to step back, the wall retracted as it had for the secretary.

Without waiting, the general stepped through, and the wall hissed closed behind him. Stuck, he found himself in a smaller foyer, trapped. Frustration rising, ready to place his hand on the opposite wall, it retracted.

To his surprise, standing across from him was a rather stern looking blonde woman with hair pulled in a tight bun wearing white pants and a blouse. She beckoned and greeted him. "General Story, I'm Ms. Grant. Glad to meet you, sir. Please come in."

The general thought the woman looked rather stiff, plain of feature, but she appeared pleasant enough, and her tone was polished.

He stepped through the threshold and recognized a high-security room.

Ms. Grant said, "Sir, before entering the SCIF, we need to do a quick inspection and make sure you haven't any electronics or weapons. Merely a formality. I appreciate your cooperation."

"Of course," replied the general.

Ms. Grant produced a plastic tray and pushed it forward. "All metal and electronics, please place them here."

From his jacket pocket, the general pulled out his cell pad. Out of habit he checked and saw no signal. He remembered James explaining the lack of computer networks on the ranch and sniggered as he placed the device inside the tray. Fishing in his pockets, he pulled out a penknife, along with a set of keys, and dropped those in as well. Then he asked, only half kidding, "What about my belt buckle and shoes?"

Ms. Grant answered, almost bowing, "No, sir, unnecessary."

"Okay, that's all I got."

Ms. Grant smiled, placed the tray on a counter next to a booth behind her, and gestured towards the device. "Please step into the scanner and raise your hands above your head. When you hear a beep, drop your arms and exit the other side. Again, thank you for the patience and understanding."

The general shook his head but did as instructed. Upon entering the scanner, he spotted a large glass mirror on the far wall. He assumed it was one-way security glass and that someone was observing from the other side. With hands raised, he detected a beep, dropped his arms, and exited. He waited as Ms. Grant, tray in hand, opened a cabinet and placed the general's items inside.

"Your belongings are safe here and will be returned when you depart."

The general nodded, ready to get on with it.

Appearing efficient, Ms. Grant walked up to a far wall and placed her hand against it, causing the barrier to slide open. "After you, sir."

The general stepped through, entering a long hallway painted stark white. Several plush chairs lined both sides of the wall, and in the nearest one, Secretary James sat waiting. Looking up, the skinny man asked, "Good to go?"

General Story, tired, deflated by the day's events, but determined to learn what lay ahead, gave a curt answer. "Yes, let's get on with it."

Ms. Grant replied, "Yes, sir. Please, follow me."

Secretary James stood and let Ms. Grant pass. The general followed, and in a single file the trio headed down the hallway to meet SALI.

* * *

Fucked over and given security detail, Sergeant Raymond Flood stood over two dead bodies. Instead of lounging in bivouac with good company and beer rations in hand, he shivered in the cold, hovering over two stiffs.

"I found them this way. Other than checking for a pulse, I've touched nothing. Called for military police right away," said Captain Eugene Longfellow. As the officer in charge of Mortuary Services, he was a middle-aged career bureaucrat. Soft around the middle, Longfellow continued, "These two bastards were no good. Both were on punishment detail, supposed to be tagging and bagging enemy dead. I sure as hell didn't trust 'em, so I tried to keep abreast of their whereabouts. At first, I wasn't too concerned when I tried raising them over the company net and they didn't respond. Not unusual for those two. But I continued roaming, keeping an eye out, until I came across this. That's when I called it in, only ten minutes ago."

Flood bent over the bodies and inspected the grotesque scene. Too dark, he turned on his helmet lamp. It wasn't pretty. Turning his head to offer different angles and avoid shadows, he determined both victims were facing each other with one body atop the other. The one on top had his throat slit and still clutched a knife in dead white knuckles. Beneath him, the other wore pants pulled down around his ankles. The stiff beneath was a mess as intestines protruded from an obvious knife attack along the left torso. In an outstretched hand, the bottom corpse also held a knife. From Flood's perspective, it appeared the two guys had fought each other to the death.

Flood stood and turned to the squat mortuary officer. "Captain, sir, I'm not an investigator. The military police are busy dealing with the Mesquite civilian situation and lacked the resources to cover security over the battlefield. So my squad is it. But we lack any formal police training, and this looks like something the MPs should handle."

Captain Longfellow seemed to sense the sergeant's reticence. "Yes, it looks like these two guys, Privates Hough and Pugh, killed each other during an act of sexual perversion. I wouldn't put homosexuality or criminal behavior past them, but not in this case."

"How's that, sir?" asked Flood.

"Well, with Mortuary Services, we deal with the dead. That's what we do, get to see death come in all shapes and sizes. But if you examine this scene, notice Private Hough on top has his throat slit. A wound like that, there should be a shitload of blood. But look at Private Pugh beneath him. See how there's only a few drops on his face? It looks like Hough bled out someplace else."

"Makes sense," said Flood, "but where?"

Captain Longfellow walked a few yards and bent over. With his helmet lamp illuminating a dark spot on ground, he pointed and said, "There."

Flood, skeptical, walked over and took a close look. Sure enough, blood soaked the sand. "You could be right, sir. If that's the case, then someone staged the bodies."

"That's what I'm thinking," agreed Longfellow.

"Sir, were these men working alone?"

"Affirmative. Two-man detail."

"Any thoughts then?" Flood asked.

"Well, it's conceivable someone from another punishment detail did this. Six teams are working tonight. But I've been checking through the evening, and other than these two poor bastards, all reported in. Nothing seems amiss. It's still possible, but I would say doubtful."

Suspicious, Flood walked around the shell hole and noticed an open pack. Peering in, the contents appeared a jumbled mess. Nearby, a pair of boots and socks lay. Size small, he guessed. Weird. Plus, embedded in the sand he counted multiple boot prints of various sizes, but that could mean anything. None of it made sense. Then he spotted something unusual: an opening in the side of the shell hole. Intrigued, he moved closer and bent lower. With his headlamp, he peered inside and detected a small blood trail mixed with dirt and sand.

"What you got there?" asked the captain.

He stood up and explained, "Sir, it looks like an irrigation pipe. Makes sense, as years ago intelligence maps show this area bordered a golf course. Inside the pipe there's a blood trail."

The captain walked over and motioned Flood aside. He, too, bent low and used his headlamp to confirm the finding. "I see it. Whoever killed our guys might still be in there."

Sergeant Flood hated to agree, but the evidence was clear. "Sir, I'm not sure who the hell's been in that pipe. Might be an enemy combatant, a civilian, or even one of our guys. Who knows? I'm responsible for battlefield security, and if someone unauthorized is roaming around, I need to find out."

"Are you going in?" asked the captain, apparently excited by the prospect of a manhunt.

Not answering, Sergeant Flood activated his radio headset, "Squad Three Kinney; Squad Three Actual. How copy? Over."

"Ah, Squad Three Actual. Copy you five by. Over."

Flood recognized the voice of Corporal Aaron Dalton and frowned. "Squad Three Dalton, where's Kinney? Over."

After a moment Dalton answered, "Squad Three Actual. Ah, well, Kinney's not here. He's taking a dump. Over."

Earlier, Flood left his squad inside their parked fighting vehicle twenty meters away. He intended to let them stay warm and allow them to rest while he investigated the call from Captain Longfellow. But now it was time to work. "Squad Three, Dalton. Go get his ass. Tell him I need him and to bring a suppressor for his Glock. Over."

"Squad Three Actual. What you got? Over."

"Don't worry about it. Just get Kinney, pronto. Out." Sergeant Flood, ending the radio call, stood conflicted. If he didn't investigate, a later inquiry might find him derelict, and he didn't want that type of blemish on his record. Still, he'd rather be tucked away in a nice warm place and not chasing God knew what. Dammit again. Flood spoke to Captain Longfellow. "Sir, with your authority, I will send in one of my guys. He's tougher than nails, and if there's someone in there, he'll flush 'em out."

Longfellow gave a quick endorsement. "Outstanding! I'll call it into Command and let them know I'm ordering a reconnaissance in pursuit of suspected enemy infiltrators involved in the death of two US soldiers."

Flood grimaced at the pompous speculation. Then he glanced at the pipe and tried to imagine Longfellow, the fat ass, fitting into the narrow confines. No way. Longfellow and his ilk clamored for glory, but it was his grunts that paid the price. He hoped this time the cost wouldn't be too high.

Chapter Fifteen

THE OLIGARCHS

May 9, 00:55 (PDT)

Inside her private quarters, buried deep underground in the heart of the San Jose ROAS alternate seat of government, Ortega was taking a moment to gather herself. Looking in a mirror, staring back at her was a haggard and exhausted woman. The last twenty-four hours had been the hardest in her life, and it showed. Deep lines etched outward from her eyes, and poking through her freshly dyed raven hair, she detected too many grays. She was killing herself, but it didn't matter.

At a young age, she had known politics was her calling. A passion burned so hard she couldn't explain the depths. Equality, fairness, defeating bullies, overcoming injustice: all those ideals drove her. As a young teenager growing up on the hard streets of a Los Angeles barrio, she couldn't contain her feelings. Instead, she strove to make the world a better place and voiced her opinions, joined many liberal groups, and wasn't afraid to stand up to anyone who objected. Back then, as a young political activist, succession seemed a dream come true. And it was. She recalled those heady times and the joy of establishing a new national government grounded in the beliefs that compelled her.

All her life she worked for the common good, and now she was nearing the end of her second and final term as president. Then came today, and it held no such happiness. War, death, destruction: the decisions she made were killing people. The thought caused her stomach to rumble, not so much from hunger, she realized, but nerves. Just then a wave of nausea washed over her. Bending over to stifle the sensation, after a few deep breaths she felt better. Rising up, she needed to pull herself together.

Gazing in the mirror, she picked at a wisp of hair and examined the dark bags under her eyes. The crow's feet appeared deeper and longer than ever. She looked like death warmed over. The thought almost caused her to laugh as the job, sure as hell, was trying to kill her. But, she wasn't dead yet. Determined, she stood taller, and looking at herself, vowed once more to do everything in her power to save the nation. To do so, she'd commit to almost anything. Besides, what else was there? Her detractors named her the "compassionate ice queen" as she had never married or had children. Although she'd had many lovers over the years, male and female, no one could replace her life force. Deep down, she knew her destiny was much greater, and she believed her name would go down in history forever.

But the reflection in the mirror wasn't helping. The wrinkles in her neck appeared longer, and the flesh around them sagged. She hated the sight, and then a thought struck her. Maybe SALI could help? The AI was supposed to have infinite intelligence. Surely it could solve the ravages of age, gravity, and stress. Even better, the AI, if used properly, could save her country from destruction. Under her control, the AI could defeat the US armies, expand the borders of her country, and unleash a new age of liberalism. Given control, she'd use the AI to shepherd in a new wave of medical and scientific breakthroughs focused on enhancing the lives of humanity. Her name would live forever! But Vivek Basu and the oligarchs stood in the way. That thought pulled her back. Smoothing her hair, in ten minutes she had a critical meeting with Basu, and there was no way she could go in looking like this. Shaking off the nerves, she turned away and headed to the bathroom.

* * *

Fifteen minutes later, Ortega entered the small SCIF not far from her private quarters. Already seated at a small round table, Vivek Basu gave her a wan smile. She nodded in return and sat down, sinking into the plush chair across from the old man.

Ortega noted how Basu sat with a straight back, his withered hands clasped on the table. His gray hair, thin features, all pointed to an advanced age. Basu was the oldest member and leader of the secret, five-person Technology Committee. Chairman since secession, which included the early troubled years of the ROAS, under his leadership, she knew the Committee almost never failed to reach a unanimous decision. When disagreement did occur, Basu, the brilliant billionaire and renowned philanthropist, was the tiebreaker. Now, the single greatest crisis facing their young country confronted them, and Ortega was surprised when Basu turned the topic towards her.

"Julia, to save our nation, you agreed to the US extradition demand. In effect, you offered your life. Speaking for the Committee, thank you."

She appreciated the sentiment but doubted Basu or any of the five oligarchs on the Committee would've agreed to their own extradition on a false murder charge. Staring back at Basu, she understood the oligarchs represented the economic might and technical ability of the ROAS, and she owed her position to their support. Still, their presence gnawed at her. More of an oligarchy than a true republic, they called many of the critical shots for the ROAS. Combined, they provided the guiding and driving force behind the country's economic and political policy. Each ran a technological empire and, together, comprised the backbone of the nation.

On behalf of the oligarchs, when Basu had approached her two days earlier and suggested she accept the US terms as a last resort, she had little choice in the matter. But as SALI predicted in advance, thank God, her acquiescence was ignored. Now, it was obvious the US had greater ambitions than her own show trial. "Mr. Basu, I'd do anything to preserve our nation."

"Your willingness speaks volumes," said Basu.

Looking at the old man and his deep-blue eyes, Ortega felt mixed emotions. She both appreciated and resented the man. On the positive, three decades prior, Basu along with the other oligarchs were key in securing a peaceful secession. Since then, they had steered the nation to keep their high-tech global profits coming while still supporting politicians like her that insisted on implementing a domestic progressive agenda. But it was never easy, and she often found herself begging Basu to support increased taxes and revenues. And now there was war, and they were ill prepared. She recalled the history.

Thirty years ago, to achieve independence from the US, the ROAS had accepted many concessions. Among those, the ROAS agreed upon strict limitations on the size and scope of its military, including a nuclear ban. Also, the ROAS could develop emerging military technologies but couldn't keep or export those to any other nation except the United States. In the never-ending race for advanced weaponry, the other Great Powers, China and Russia, distrusted the exclusive arrangement between the US and the ROAS, but it persisted. Those early decisions were now haunting her. But back then they'd little leverage.

On the heels of ROAS succession, a Great Powers Agreement between China, Russia, and the US was ratified in a not-so-secret manner. Since then, the Great Powers had shared a bond. All were nationalistic and believed in the merits of sovereignty. Together, they met and came to a general agreement. They left the United Nations, making it defunct, and agreed on a general principle of staying out of each other's way for mutual success.

By implementing advantageous trade and business agreements, by force if necessary, and not stepping on each other's toes, the Great Powers prospered. As agreed, Russia expanded its weight throughout Central Asia, and Eastern and Southern Europe. Along with Saudi Arabia and Israel as allies, Russia came to dominate the Middle East. China's influence extended across the rest of Asia and most of Africa. China's ambitions were only checked by a series of conflicts with

India, but sooner or later, it was expected India would fall. Japan remained isolated and was a hollow shell of its former economic self. The US, meanwhile, held military sway over most of the western hemisphere, focusing on expanding its interests in Central and South America.

The Great Powers Agreement for two decades had acted as a bulwark for mutual gain, and the balance of power between them held.

Throughout, the ROAS avoided confrontation while it continued to develop and sell the world's most advanced technology solutions to all comers. Canada and the ROAS absorbed millions of US citizens that fled the US government after secession, straining resources, but still, the two countries thrived. The remaining liberal democracies in Northern and Western Europe swung hard right and demurred to Russia. Australia and New Zealand survived through isolationism.

Then, ten years ago, Basu and his incredible technology firm unveiled stunning advances in advanced artificial intelligence and everything changed.

Given the name Sentient Artificial Life, or SALI, at first the US demanded this latest AI technology from the ROAS and claimed it fell under the exclusive advanced military supply agreement. Basu, and the ROAS, resisted and withheld the technology while making even further rapid advances.

Fear prevailed. Advanced AI, as demonstrated by SALI, was a great disruptor. To blunt the potential threat, the Great Powers came together and issued global restrictions on advanced AI and associated military technologies. Bans on autonomous weapons usage, including cyber and space warfare and severe caps on AI technologies, became a global decree. Any country failing to comply, the Great Powers threatened, would face severe economic sanctions and military retaliation.

Further, the Great Powers forced the ROAS to abandon and destroy SALI. No choice in the matter, Basu agreed, and observers witnessed the destruction along with all associated technical documentation. In a small act of retribution, the ROAS stopped all military technology development, and no longer would the US gain that advantage. The US responded with a trade war, but the ROAS held steadfast.

For the last decade, the restrictions held and the balance of power between the Great Powers maintained. Around the world, with the fear of artificial intelligence technology lingering, the global ban slowed the overall pace of technological innovation.

This arrangement, for almost a decade, worked. The Great Powers continued to expand, but as always, distrust and a hunger for superiority kept relationships icy. And now the US had attacked the ROAS, changing everything once again.

Her remembrance was broken by the soft voice of Vivek Basu. "You appear tired. I know it has been a tough day, but please bring me up to speed on current events."

"Yes, of course," she replied.

First, she explained how the press had got the message out. Yes, the country experienced a disastrous day with the execution of Felix Manuel and the fall of Mesquite, but the ROAS remained defiant and strong. She mentioned several news clips, all of which highlighted the heroic video of Staff Sergeant Lisa McMichael. Aids reported positive public feedback as the video of the female grunt with the missile launcher gave a face to the struggle. Buoyed by the news, Ortega felt confident the citizenry would sustain their government as it fought back.

Then she outlined how messages of support had come in from the few remaining ROAS allies but little else. As expected, China and Russia condemned the US attack. So far, neither country offered direct aid, and if they did, she wouldn't accept. Meanwhile, President Tower was bombarding social media with claims that Ortega's acceptance of extradition was undeniable proof of guilt, justifying both the execution of Manuel and the attack on Mesquite.

In the last hour, she explained, the ROA diplomatic office had received word of the latest US demand, the repatriation of Nevada. SALI had predicted that threat, so it wasn't a surprise.

"How much time are they giving us?" asked Basu.

"No timetable yet, but SALI expects the US will give us two days, give or take. A lot depends on how much pushback they get from China and Russia."

"Not much time," said Basu. He leaned back and stared at the ceiling as if guidance there would be forthcoming.

She waited for the man in deference. Truth was, even though she resented the oligarchs, she respected Basu's personal wisdom and advice. Without his steady and brilliant mind, secession might not have occurred, and SALI wouldn't exist. Still, he controlled the AI, not her. He'd kept SALI so well hidden, she hadn't learned of the AI's existence until a few months ago when the assassination crisis hit. It was then that Basu called her in and explained his secret—SALI had never been destroyed and the US, somehow, had come to learn of the deception. Since then, Ortega had decided it was best to let Basu take the lead while she determined how best to influence his decisions. Now, she was more determined than ever to see SALI properly deployed. But she'd have to play her cards carefully.

Basu shifted his gaze back to Ortega. "Today wasn't a complete surprise. SALI gave us plenty of warnings. It now appears we know what they're after, and we must decide upon a course of action. But first, where does General Story stand? Is he willing to weigh in on how effective or not he considers SALI's plan?"

"He's being briefed as we speak. I expect to hear from him within a few hours. Afterward, I can provide you with a full update," answered Ortega.

"I'm tired, and you look exhausted. A terrible and difficult day. It's one in the morning. Let's get some rest and steel our resolve. Later today we can discuss further. Does noon work for you?"

Ortega, with fresh makeup and a quick comb, knew what she'd just seen in the mirror. Even with the cover-up, she was shot and her spirits flagging, but with SALI there was hope. She nodded in agreement.

Chapter Sixteen

SALI

Ms. Grant led the way down a long, well-lit corridor, followed by Secretary James and General Story. As they walked, the general admired the many paintings, land and seascapes, adorning the white walls. There were no windows or rooms leading off the hallway, just a single simple door at the far end. Upon reaching it, Ms. Grant paused, waited for her guests, then turned and knocked.

"It's open," came a soft female response from the opposite side.

Ms. Grant turned a simple black doorknob and pushed open and held the door ajar. With a wave of a hand, she beckoned Secretary James and General Story to enter.

Secretary James led the way. The general followed and found himself on a platform with stairs leading down to a large well-lit room. Scattered about were sculptures made of various metals depicting different animals. Throughout, the furniture was plush, and the white walls were dotted with more land and seascapes. Floors of polished dark wood covered the expanse, and against a far wall stood a massive case filled with books. The entire room lacked windows, although the general noticed several exits leading to other areas.

Most interesting, the general's eyes settled on the most dramatic feature of the room. A woman sat on a long, dark couch against the opposite wall. Seated behind a glass coffee table, her slender legs were barefoot, and she wore a revealing nightie. In her hand, she held a glass of red wine between elegant fingers. She was beautiful: black, shoulder-length hair; skin alabaster white; full red lips. From his vantage point, the general couldn't help but admire her low-cut garment and the exceptional cleavage it exposed. A little embarrassed, the general averted his gaze and tried to make sense of the scene.

Secretary James bounded down the stairs and went straight to the beautiful woman. As he approached, she put out her hand and James took it, bent, and planted a kiss. Just as quick, James nodded at the glass in her other hand. "Do you mind if we join you? It's been a long day."

The woman pulled back her hand, long fingernails painted red, and let out a light feminine laugh. "I'd love the company. But we need more glasses. Please, Jim, be a help and fetch two more."

"On it," replied James, and he hurried off, leaving the room using a nearby exit.

Standing next to the general, Ms. Grant watched the interaction then strode down the stairs. Not knowing what else to do, the general followed.

Upon reaching the living room, Ms. Grant swept her arm towards the beautiful woman and turned to the general. "Let me introduce SALI."

SALI raised her glass in salute and replied, "Welcome, General Story. I've been expecting you."

Perplexed, the general said, "I was expecting to meet a computer."

SALI let out a full-fledged laugh and then put a graceful hand to her mouth where she giggled for a few seconds longer. After recovering, she took another sip of a wine and, with deep-blue eyes, peered over the tip of her glass. "And I didn't realize you were so handsome."

In a sudden rush, Ms. Grant turned towards the general and, wearing a frown, said, "I'll be right back. Please wait." Without another word, the woman in white strode away through a nearby corridor.

Just as Ms. Grant left the room, a cheery voice boomed, and Secretary James re-emerged. "Look what I have," said James, holding a pair of wine glasses. After placing them on the coffee table, he lifted the bottle of open wine next to SALI and inspected it. Eyes raised, he glanced at the general and asked. "Looks like an excellent Napa Merlot. A small glass?"

Unsure of the dynamics, working against tiredness and the stress from an awful day, the general declined. "No, thank you."

James shrugged, filled a full glass and, after returning the bottle, he plopped on the far end of the couch next to SALI. Glass in hand, James pointed to a large leather chair across the table. "General Story, please have a seat."

"Yes, please do," added SALI.

Before the general could move, SALI re-crossed her legs, nightie rising high, exposing an expansive length of smooth white skin. Once again, he shifted his gaze and felt himself turning a shade of red. A little angry at the distraction, he walked over and sat down in the proffered chair. To his relief, he spotted Ms. Grant returning with a robe.

"Here, put this on," said Ms. Grant tossing the garment at SALI.

Adroit, the robe landing in her lap, SALI lifted her wine glass to keep it from spilling and shot a withering glance at the woman in white. In obvious defiance, she lifted her glass, took a long pull, and sat the glass back on the table. After a moment, blithe as a cat, she stood. Robe in hand, she stared at the general, her figure plain to see through the sheer nightie.

The general tried to avoid the show, but when SALI stood, he noticed her height and guessed she stood five feet ten with a perfect figure. After a few seconds, she slipped on the garment.

"Is that better?" asked SALI, cinching the pink fluffy robe around a slender waist.

"Much," replied Ms. Grant.

"You're late. I thought you weren't coming," said SALI, sitting down and looking at the secretary.

"It's been a busy day—as you predicted," he replied. Reaching into his shirt pocket, he pulled out a thumb drive and tossed it to the beautiful woman.

With an easy motion in slender hands, she caught the device. Looking up, she asked, "So they did it? Executed Manuel and attacked Mesquite?"

Secretary James nodded and pointed at the drive in her hand. "All the latest is on there."

SALI stood. "Excuse me. I'll be right back," and she left the room using a far exit.

Baffled, the general watched her leave. He'd heard about SALI a decade earlier. Everyone had and knew it was a groundbreaking system developed in Silicon Valley. SALI was touted as the single greatest autonomous computing platform in the history of the world. A single system so powerful, the pundits claimed, it achieved consciousness with a processing capacity greater than a million human minds combined. But advanced AI was an inherent evil, the great destructor, and at a snap of a finger could be used to develop weapons of mass destruction beyond comprehension.

Intuition told him that even after the Great Powers had ordered SALI's destruction, putting the AI genie back in the bottle would have proved difficult. Common sense dictated the Great Powers and other nations would develop advanced AI initiatives in secret.

So earlier in the evening when the general had heard the president mention SALI, learning the ROAS wasn't complying with the AI Protocols, the news wasn't too shocking. Still, he understood using her capabilities, if discovered, would be considered an international war crime. Yes, he was willing to listen, but he needed to consider the risk. After meeting this woman, or robot, android, or whatever she was, he sat confused. He recalled the original advanced AI announcements from years before, but there wasn't any mention of a beautiful woman, just a super-advanced computing platform. Unsure, he needed to figure out the connection and decide if SALI could be trusted. Maybe, he should have a glass of wine.

Chapter Seventeen

GOING IN

Hearing a thump, Sergeant Flood wheeled around. There, standing next to him, after jumping into the shell hole to scare everybody, Specialist Ian Kinney stood smiling. Wearing full battle rattle with an assault rifle slung across his chest, it was just like Kinney to make his presence known. A short wiry man, ready to fight at a drop of a hat, the young man admitted to having small-guy syndrome. But Flood knew he could back it up, won most of his fights, and even enjoyed those he lost.

"What's up?" asked Kinney.

Flood pointed at the Glock holstered on the specialist's hip. "Did you bring a suppressor for that?"

"Yep, got it right here," said Kinney, patting a pouch on his combat belt.

Flood nodded and waved towards the man standing next to him. "This is Captain Longfellow. He's in charge of the dead."

Longfellow frowned, and Kinney smiled at the insult. Flood ignored the looks and got right to business. "Okay. Listen up. We got a blood trail in the pipe behind us. Not a clue who left it inside, but it's possible we have enemy combatants or even civilian infiltrators. Not sure what we're facing, but we reckon whoever climbed in an out

105

of the pipe whacked those two poor bastards." Flood pointed at the bodies of Pugh and Hough. The two stiffs still lay face to face, with the guy on the bottom wearing underwear around his ankles.

"That's fucked up," said Kinney. He walked over to the bodies and bent over to get a closer look. Through his helmet headlamp, he examined the scene. He shook his head and let out a low whistle. "Looks like they might be buddy butt fuckers. Lover's quarrel?"

The captain stepped forward and, voice full of authority, said, "Homosexuality is against regulations. But even if these men were sodomites, which is not out of the question considering their backgrounds, I don't believe they killed each other. Instead, it's my professional opinion you're looking at a staged death scene."

Kinney stared at the captain in apparent disbelief. Flood knew the wiry man had little respect for most officers, and zero for rear-echelon types.

Kinney turned back to Sergeant Flood and asked, "You believe what he's saying, and if so, how many guys you think did this?"

"No idea for sure," answered Flood. "The captain and I could be wrong, but based on the evidence, it appears the attackers might have come through that pipe. How many? I'd guess one or two." Flood waved at the pipe, then pointed at the two stiffs and continued, "But whoever killed those sorry bastards knows how to use a knife."

Kinney glanced at the bodies again. "Well, if the two butt fuckers didn't kill each other, you're right, whoever did are some bad motherfuckers. Knife sticking ain't easy; takes balls."

"That's why I called you," said Flood, flattering the man. He wanted Kinney to volunteer without asking.

"Shit! Fuck, Sarge! You want me to go after the motherfuckers, don't you?"

"You're the best man for the job. I need you to get into the pipe and track down whoever did this. If you find 'em, well, there's no good reason for someone to be in there. Shoot first and ask questions later." Flood turned to the captain for confirmation on the rules of engagement. "Correct, sir?"

"Ah, sure. You're authorized to use, um, whatever force is necessary," said the captain. Flood watched as the overweight officer put his hands on his hips as if he made combat decisions all the time.

Kinney eyed the pipe again. "Just me going in, Sergeant?"

"Yep. Wouldn't count on anyone else. Besides, in that pipe it's gonna be a single file. You'll be facing whoever is last in line. Only one guy at a time. Use discretion. If you find yourself outnumbered, then get the hell out and report back."

"Where does the pipe end?" asked Kinney.

"Fucks sake, I don't know. This here . . ." and Flood twirled a finger, ". . . was a golf course years ago. Monsoon flash floods hit this area too. Looks like a big drainage pipe. So who the fuck knows. Follow the blood trail. If it peters out or you reach the end or you're unsure, just come on back. No big deal."

Flood understood the mission was risky. On all fours, in a tight, dark pipe, sneaking up to kill an unknown number of badasses wasn't easy. Still, Kinney was tough and always ready to prove himself. Taking the mission would add to his reputation and, knowing the young man, Flood guessed once inside the pipe, Kinney might find it fun.

"All right, I got it," Kinney said. Coughing up a gob of phlegm, he spit it across the shell hole and wiped his mouth. "If I get these fuckers, extra beer ration. What you say?"

"Fuck yes. Triple ration," answered Flood, knowing the motivation would seal the deal.

"Okay, I'll be your fucking killer mole. Let me take off my goddamn boots and unhook anything that might make noise. Plus, I need to get the suppressor on my Glock." Kinney unslung his rifle and sat down to work his laces.

Flood watched Kinney as the man took off his boots. He was proud of the specialist, of his men, but he'd much rather be with all of them in bivouac buried in warm sleeping bags. But hey, he thought to himself, that's why I get paid the big bucks. Bullshit.

* * *

Master Sergeant Upton lay stretched out on his stomach. There wasn't enough room to sit without hunching; lying flat was easier. Behind him on a blanket, on her back, head nearest Upton's feet, he registered the regular breathing of Staff Sergeant Lisa McMichael. Ahead of him, seventy meters from where he first entered, a small trickle of evening light filtered through the pipe. They'd been in this position for more than an hour, ever since he'd given her water and a pain pill.

After rescuing her at the other end of the pipe four hundred meters distant, he'd put McMichael on a blanket and used it to pull her all the way back here. Just behind them, twenty meters away, was the only bend he encountered in the entire length.

What to do next?

Based on the time displayed via his head protection visor, they had about five hours until daylight. He hoped to be moving, with McMichael in tow, before sunrise. Once out, he figured they'd make their way through the desert into the outskirts of Mesquite and hide until the next evening.

Over the last hour, he'd taken a mental inventory of their supplies and weapons.

First, he considered what McMichael had, which wasn't shit: no helmet, pants, pack, assault rifle, combat belt, boots, or socks, just a combat shirt—complete liability. So that meant he was it.

Water was most important, good news there. He carried his own camelback and another he'd stolen from the enemy. Although he'd gone through a lot of water while in the pipe, and shared it with McMichael, he figured they still had enough to last a full day.

As for food, he still had two unopened MREs in his vest pouch, not much, but water would be the bigger issue.

From a weapons standpoint, his KA-BAR combat knife was ankle sheathed, and he carried a hip-holstered SIG Sauer M18 handgun with a fully loaded seventeen-round magazine. In his combat vest, he carried another full mag. Clipped to his combat belt, two multi-purpose grenades dangled. Most distressing, he'd lost his assault rifle at the start of the fight when a HEAT round had hit his pillbox and hurled him through the air into a nearby drainage ditch. Somehow, during that tumultuous event, landing hard, he hadn't died but lost his rifle.

Stunned, he'd been lying in a ditch when a massive artillery barrage hit with a ferocity he never dreamed possible. To survive, he scrambled for his life. No time to search for his rifle, he came across a large, exposed drainage pipe. Grateful for the protection, upon entering, he crawled deeper inside as the ground shook around him. After a while the shelling stopped, and things grew quiet.

Back then, as the shock of the attack wore off, he began to feel a sense of dread and guilt. He considered rushing out the way he'd come, to rejoin the fight. Little did he know that at the opposite end of the pipe, Sergeant Lisa McMichael was fighting for her own life.

Pushing away the thoughts, depressed, Upton turned onto his side, and through his night vison, observed McMichael stretched out behind him. She slept on the blanket he'd used as a makeshift sled. To provide her with a modicum of decency, across her groin he'd draped her discarded combat pants.

Before she'd regained consciousness the first time, he had checked for and tended her wounds. She had some deep scratches, but other than an obvious concussion, to his relief her injuries appeared minor. It'd taken a lot of work checking and treating her wounds. Squirming around in the tight pipe, his six-foot frame was challenged by the small dimensions. But with his first aid, kit he'd done it, and the work had kept his mind occupied.

Now, watching her, with time creeping by, he once again grew anxious. Although tired, the anxiety kept him awake, and he was thankful for that. Still, they needed to get going.

But he wanted to give her a little more recovery time. When he rescued her, she'd been unconscious, and he hoped she carried no memory of the attempted rape. If so, he intended to keep it that way.

With time to kill, his mind wandered.

He agonized over the course of events. Earlier, with all communications down, he hadn't been sure of the outcome. But now, based on what he'd heard moving along the highway, the soldiers assaulting McMichael, the horrific pounding from earlier in the day, he was confident in the outcome, and it wasn't good. He deduced the enemy had won the fight and now occupied the area. For how long? Maybe forever.

Still gazing at the sleeping form, he tried to remember more about Sergeant Lisa McMichael. He recalled she was from Las Vegas. When their battalion had moved into position two months earlier, McMichael was one of the Junior NCOs designated as a pillbox squad leader.

Not him. As one of the more Senior NCOs, per his own request, he commanded the point pillbox. That hadn't turned out well.

He replayed the scene. Lieutenant Colonel Rourke and his own squad, including Corporal Hudson on the .50-caliber, hit by an unexpected point-blank attack. He wondered what had happened to his squad, the men and woman under his command. The thought of them dead or injured seemed beyond comprehension. It hurt his soul, and guilt racked his conscious.

Only the memory of sneaking up on the bastards raping McMichael, killing them, saving her, provided any solace. Upon seeing the bastards and what they were doing, a burning hate replaced the guilt, and he acted. Years of close combat-training kicked in, and he slew both men in a cold rage. Hell, it turned out to be easier than he'd imagined—too easy. But he worried someone would find the bodies, see the pipe, put it all together, and come after them.

With the adrenaline gone, Upton's thoughts continued to drift.

Even in the darkness, under dire circumstances, he wouldn't give up hope. He wanted to get back into the fight. The Army was his life. Cowering earlier was terrible. Now, he'd do everything in his power to get back and take it to the enemy. Truth be told, he loved the military: it had saved his life.

Growing up in Reno, the oldest of three boys, his parents divorced early and remarried several times. Both struggled with money, and by the time he found himself in his late teens, he rebelled and started hanging around with the wrong kids. Just after turning eighteen, he was arrested for shop lifting alcohol. That was a wake-up call, and he realized all he wanted was to work, make a decent living, stay clean, and have a reliable life. A friend of his was enlisting and talked him into meeting with a recruiter. The rest was history. He found a home, a big family he could rely on, with the steady structure he craved. Now, ten years later, he was a master sergeant, and he wanted to stay in for life. Ask the women he'd been in relationships with, all of whom eventually left him, and they'd all say he was a decent man but married to the Army. Without a doubt, he believed they'd say he loved the military so much he couldn't truly love anything else. And maybe it was true, because right now, more than anything, he wanted to get back.

"Ah, Sergeant, are you there?"

Startled, but pleased by the sound of her voice, in a low tone Upton answered, "Shhh. Yes, I'm here, but keep it to a whisper."

"Water. More water," McMichael pleaded.

Upton rolled onto his back, scooted down, and raised and stretched his legs until they straddled McMichael's torso. Hunched over, his head constricted by the height of the pipe, he unclipped his hydration system, pulled the straw, and lowered it to her lips.

McMichael grabbed the tube, guided it to her mouth, and sucked. After a few seconds, she pushed the water away and took several deep breaths.

Upton re-clipped the water to his belt. "Are you feeling better?"

"Yes. Head hurts but not as bad. My legs and back hurt too."

Upton believed her, but there wasn't time to dwell on the pain. "I checked your injuries. A concussion, a few scrapes, that's it. You're fine." No response. Her eyes remained open, and he knew she was listening. He needed to make her understand that the pipe was a death trap. He asked in a low voice, "Can you put on your pants and crawl out of here?"

She ran her tongue across cracked lips, then answered, "I remember diving into a pipe. I think this pipe. Explosions, bad. Did we lose, what's happening?"

Upton filled her in a little. "Yeah, I figure we got whipped. I'm guessing we're behind enemy lines. The pipe saved us. But now, if the enemy finds us, I suspect they'll kill us or send us to prison. We can't hide here much longer. We're sitting ducks. Let's get moving and use the cover of darkness to our advantage. With some luck, we can make it back to friendly lines."

McMichael blinked as if she was letting the news sink in. Then, with both hands, she reached down and touched bare legs and fondled the pants lying across her hips. "Why're my pants off? Where the fuck is my combat belt, my shoes?"

He didn't want her dwelling on more crap. "I had to check your wounds and bandage them. Your pants were in the way. Now put 'em on, and once we get out of here, I'll figure out a solution for your feet. Worst case: I'll carry you."

"I don't think I can, you know, put my pants on. It's too tight in here, and my head hurts."

Upton decided more medication would help. Inside his combat vest, he fished out another tablet and unclipped his hydration system. "Yes, you can. Here's a painkiller. Wash it down, then I'll look the other way while you wriggle into your pants." He watched her frown, so he provided more encouragement. "We're near the end of the pipe. It comes out right next to the highway."

Seeming convinced, she opened her mouth, and Upton put a pill on her tongue. Taking the proffered straw, she washed down the tablet and once again closed her eyes.

Upton was ready to get going and didn't need her conking out again. He re-clipped his hydration system and said, "Staff Sergeant, you need to put on your britches. I'll turn around and won't look. Okay?"

"Just a moment. I'm gathering my strength. Just give me a minute," McMichael whispered.

Frustrated, her head almost in his lap, his legs straddling alongside, he sat hunched. Concerned, he debated how to get her moving.

Something startled him.

Lifting his vision, staring down the way they'd come earlier, he focused his attention. Through his night vision, he caught a quick flash of movement near the bend twenty meters away. A lightning jolt of adrenaline shot down his spine. Without hesitation, he reached for his holster and pulled his SIG Sauer M18. In a single motion he raised the weapon, flipped off the safety, and trained it at . . . nothing.

Whatever he'd seen, it wasn't there now, but every fiber in his body screamed, *be ready*.

Chapter Eighteen

DEATH STRUGGLE

May 8, 01:22 (PDT)

McMichael knew she needed to get moving. Her pants draped across her hips, she reached up and pulled the material aside, exposing herself. Determined, opening her eyes, she whispered, "I'm getting up. Look the other way."

Before she finished speaking, McMichael felt Upton's legs astride her give a jerk and, at the same instant, heard a spitting sound. For a split second, the noise echoed through the pipe and a flash of light illuminated her surroundings. Next came a thud from behind. Scared and unsure, everything now dark and quiet, she held her breath, waiting. Two seconds later, she heard an unknown voice.

"Don't even fucking move."

McMichael flinched at the unexpected order. Smelling gunpowder, she figured it out and knew she was in deep trouble. After another few seconds, she heard the person inching closer and come to a stop. She remained rigid and unsure of how to react.

"Girl, don't even fucking move. I plugged that bastard sitting behind you dead center mass. You're next unless you tell me, quick, who the fuck you are and what the hell you're doing in here?"

Fear mixed with adrenaline raced through McMichael's body. Behind her, she imagined Upton, shot and bleeding. Maybe dead. What to do and how did the man know she was a female? Then she recalled pulling her pants aside. The man must be wearing night vision with a perfect view between her legs. Panic rising, she slowed her breathing and pushed herself to think. Her life hung in the balance. With resolve, head still aching, she lifted it a few inches off the corrugated metal and glanced towards the voice. Nothing. Her vision couldn't penetrate the darkness. Survival instincts kicked in, and she replied, "I'm injured, been unconscious, please don't hurt me." Dropping her head, she hoped the soft pleading might buy time. Instead, she detected the man crawling closer. Immediately, she felt an urge to scoot away but, just as quick, she heard the man come to another stop.

"What's your name?"

McMichael struggled to maintain her composure. She wasn't sure what she faced. Fighting back panic, she played along. "My name is Lisa. Who are you?"

"I'm Specialist Kinney, US Army, sent to investigate this here pipe on my own. I'm the best at recon. They sent me because, well, the thing is, I'm the toughest soldier in the squad."

McMichael didn't respond and remained silent, her worst fears realized. The enemy would now kill or imprison her. But it was only one man. Maybe, she thought, I can take him. But then the old doubts returned, and she cringed.

"Why are you half-naked, and who is that soldier behind you?" asked Kinney.

Mind racing, McMichael could almost feel the man's eyes between her legs. Pushing aside the thought, she told a half lie. "I've been unconscious, but he might have pulled me in here. I'm not sure of anything."

A sudden light replaced the darkness, and she guessed Kinney had turned on a headlamp. She considered lowering her hands to cover her own nakedness but was afraid to move.

"Good news," said Kinney. "We're close to an exit. Don't fuck up. Follow my instructions, and I'll let you live. We'll be out in a minute."

Cornered, torn between flight or fight, McMichael lay rigid and considered surrendering. Then she realized her right hand, still hidden from sight underneath her discarded pants, rested alongside Upton's boot. Careful to stay unnoticed, she worked her fingers and touched a sheathed combat knife. Hope jumped, along with self- doubt. The thought of stabbing someone in close personal combat scared and repulsed her. But all day the enemy had tried to kill her, and she was tired of cowering. Even more, she wanted to be reunited with her kids.

She remembered her training and reminded herself she was a soldier. Decision time. She could fight or submit. If she gave up, she might never see her children again.

No, she'd rather fight.

Determined, she touched the knife. The length of the blade was reassuring; she could do this. But getting the knife out undetected and luring the enemy close enough to strike would be the challenge. Guided by instincts and detached intelligence, she reacted.

In a soft, submissive tone, McMichael asked, "I want to live. Specialist Kinney, that's your name, right? My back hurts, I need to stretch, okay?" Not waiting for a response, she spread her bare legs wide, opening them until they could go no further against the confines of the pipe. Not hearing a reaction, but sensing his fascination, she continued and drew up her knees flaying them open.

She heard a small gasp and guessed she had his full attention. While she put on the show, still hidden, her right hand unsheathed the KBAR combat knife. With legs and knees spread, to keep Specialist Kinney further off balance and to lure him closer, she begged. "Please, I'm thirsty and hurt. Help, me."

On all fours, Kinney crawled closer, keeping the beam between her legs.

McMichael froze, waiting. She knew the man was eyeing her most intimate parts, but she remained steadfast.

Very close, he stopped and shined the light higher. "You're wearing a combat vest. You a soldier?"

Her hand on the knife, McMichael was close to attacking, and now this! She needed to keep his guard down and draw him near. "I don't know. I can't remember anything. I've been unconscious. Please I need water, and my chest hurts. Take off my vest." She lifted her left arm and placed it on her breast. Meanwhile, her right hand, hidden beneath her discarded pants, worked Upton's knife until, at last, she palmed the handle.

Kinney shifted and then moved closer until he was between her widespread knees. Hunched over, his helmet just touching the top of the pipe, with the Glock in his right hand, he used the other to unclip his hydration system. With arm extended, he offered her the water.

Heart racing, head pounding, McMichael knew this was it. In one quick motion with her left hand, she reached up and gripped Kinney's right wrist holding the Glock. Then she shoved upwards pinning his hand and gun against the pipe. Simultaneously, hidden beneath her crumpled pants, clutching Upton's knife, she pushed up her other hand, but it wouldn't move far. The blade had somehow caught in her pants. Worse, Kinney's headlamp blinded her, and she sensed his strength and wits recovering. In slow motion, she felt him forcing his pinned hand down. She couldn't resist for long. Blinded, eyes averted from the light, she struggled to free the knife.

Kinney, pushing downward to free his right hand, with the other smashed the soft canvas water bottle against McMichael's forehead. Seeming to sense the futility, he flung it away. With his hand unencumbered, he grabbed her throat.

Adrenaline raging, she didn't register the water bottle bouncing off her forehead, but she did feel his hand wrap around her neck. Just then, she felt the knife come free, and with Kinney choking her, she stabbed upwards. The razor-sharp blade sliced through Kinney's flesh, entering below the base of his head protection system. With animal strength, she shoved the knife further, penetrating his chin, then mouth, up through his tongue into the roof of his mouth. Another push, and she cut through into the man's nasal cavity. Blood sprayed everywhere, splattering into her eyes. Ignoring the gore, she focused on the task and didn't blink.

Kinney, his right hand pinned holding the suppressed Glock, pulled the trigger several times. The shots penetrated the corrugated metal, into the dirt beyond, each time creating a miniature sand waterfall. But McMichael continued to leverage his wrist and keep it pinned. A few seconds later and around her neck, she felt his other hand loosen. Then, in apparent desperation, Kinney shifted his hand from her neck and grabbed the exposed portion of the knife blade. As he tried to pull the weapon free, she could feel the meat in his fingers against the razor edge and guessed he was slicing himself to the bone. She hung on, and in obvious agony, Kinney went into a wild and desperate rage. He bucked with great strength, and she felt his grip tightening around the blade as he tried to pry the anguish from his mouth.

To keep from being overcome, she didn't hesitate and clamped her naked legs around the struggling man. Locking her ankles, she kept him in place.

Still he tried to buck from her grip, but her strong limbs held him firm while the pipe above constrained his movement.

To press her advantage, McMichael shimmied her legs higher and pulled the soldier closer, forcing his face deeper into the knife. She noticed how Kinney didn't speak or yell. He couldn't with his tongue pegged to the roof of his mouth. Instead, he made gurgling sounds and grunts while his bloody grip on the knife prevented the blade from going deeper. Not caring, McMichael drove harder, twisting, and she felt his fingers loosening.

As hot blood splashed from her victim, the sensation strengthened her. Back and forth she sawed the knife, ripping more of Kinney's flesh. Rivers of dark came pouring out, flooding her chest with hot waves of slippery death. She pushed and strained, arms and legs burning, for what seemed like an eternity.

Bloodied and sliced, Kinney's hand began to slip, and she felt the knife inch upward. As he tried to regrip the blade, she noticed his hand losing strength. Looking in his eyes, she saw tears of pain and watched as they trickled down his cheeks and mixed with the blood streaming from his horrific wound. As she twisted, she detected the sound of flesh, bone, and gristle grinding and tearing against the knife. After one last struggle, his hand fell away from the KA-BAR and she sensed there was nothing left.

A second later and the knife penetrated to the hilt, and at last she felt Kinney relax and go still.

Exhausted, panting, holding the dead weight above her, she rested for a moment. A sudden urge to be free arose, and still pinned to the pipe, she let go of Kinney's Glock hand allowing it to fall aside. With her left hand free, she pressed it against Kinney's helmeted forehead while she used the other to twist and pull out the knife. Blade in hand, she dropped it, and then lowered the man until his helmeted head came to rest alongside hers.

With Kinney lying atop, her legs still wrapped around his torso, she shuddered. Disgusted, she wanted him off. Panicked, she pushed up his head, dug her heels along his sides, kicked and pushed until only his face rested in her lap.

For a few seconds, breathing heavy, she sat there staring at the back of his helmeted head. Still fighting against panic, with a bitter scowl, she scooted herself away until his ruptured face slipped off and smacked wet against the pipe.

With her legs still astride Specialist Kinney's body, the remnants of his headlamp leaking light, the pipe was almost dark. Still there was enough visibility to divine a pool of blood massed between her legs, covering her thighs, thick across her chest. In revulsion, she bent to the side and dry heaved.

Exhausted to the core, she lay back and took a series of deep breaths. Tears emerged as she imagined her kids, their faces, and antics swirling through her mind. Not noticing, each tear created a trail through blood-spattered cheeks. She took another deep breath and tried to calm herself.

To return home, she realized, meant playing soldier for a while longer. And it sucked.

Chapter Nineteen

A PLAN

After watching SALI leave the room with the disk drive handed to her by Secretary James, the general glowered at the skinny man. Sitting across from James, the general didn't care for how the crumpled secretary lounged on the cushy couch with a smug smile, holding a glass of wine as if it were any other day. For the first time in history, people had died defending the Republic of American States. Worse, General Story hated being in the dark and didn't have time to play games. Before he could launch into a tirade, Ms. Grant sat down on a recliner at the opposite end of the coffee table.

"I want to apologize for SALI. That woman is a handful," said Ms. Grant, shaking her head.

The general took the opening, "And who the hell, or what the hell, is she?"

As he swirled the wine in his glass, Secretary James answered, "That woman is our SALI, and she does her best to enjoy life."

"Is she a computer, a droid?" asked the general searching for an explanation.

The secretary laughed and shook his head. "No, no, SALI is a real woman. One hundred percent woman, I might add."

"Where is the artificial intelligence platform both you and the president promised? Instead, I find myself at a late-night cocktail party with a half-naked woman."

Ms. Grant went ashen. "Again, I apologize for her behavior. When SALI has new guests, well, she overreacts."

"I don't care about that," snapped the general. "Look, without answers and a briefing on how the AI can help, there's no point continuing. If she's a real woman, then she can't be the damn AI. In case everyone's forgotten, we're at war."

"Oh, General," said James, "You've met the AI, or at least part of her."

"What?" asked the general.

"Let me explain," answered the secretary placing his glass on the table. "That woman is a piece of the AI, the living, breathing part. She is human, same as you and I. Below us, in a secure data center, the balance of the system is humming. Together, they can process data at a rate greater than a million minds combined."

"I don't get it," said the general, his anger dissipating, replaced by curiosity.

"Not much to get," said SALI, re-entering the room. A frown on her face, holding a few sheets of paper, she walked across the room and took her earlier spot on the couch. After sitting, she placed the papers face down on the table and plucked her wine glass. Before taking a sip, she looked at the general with genuine concern. "I'm sorry about today, General. Your soldiers are heroes, all of them. I'm here to help—all of me."

The general believed the sentiment, but the choice of words struck him as odd. Confused, he asked, "And who is 'all of me'?"

SALI continued to swirl her wine, observing him over the top of her glass, and the general detected a deep sense of sadness in her eyes. Under scrutiny, the general squirmed and thought, Dammit, I need definitive answers.

"I know you do," said SALI.

Awestruck, the hair on the general's arm stood straight. He asked, "You read minds?"

"No, General. But as a human, I can read people." She gave him a quick smile, took a sip, and closed her eyes, apparently savoring the flavor.

"What are you; some type of Frankenstein?" asked the general. He didn't mean to be rude, but he was tired, frustrated, and confused.

SALI blushed, sat the glass down, and reached behind her head as if she was searching for something. She seemed to catch herself and dropped her hand. In a strong tone she said, "General, I'm not a monster. Instead, through a neural interface, I'm a biological extension of the AI. The wetware if you will. The other hardware and software, the artificial intelligence platform as you call it, is close by doing the heavy lifting. But trust me, I'm a human being."

"And what heavy lifting is that?" asked the general.

"As of this moment, truthfully, not much," she replied and gave a light laugh. Noticing the general smirk, she stopped and continued in a serious tone. "Really, though, we're working on the problem with the US."

"Okay . . ." said the general. Tired, he sat back, rubbing his forehead, and cocked his head at the strange woman. "I don't pretend to understand what the hell you are. Just tell me how you can help and how I fit in."

"General. The first thing you need to know is I'm somewhat constrained. Isn't that right, Jim?" said SALI, shooting a withering look towards the skinny man sitting next to her.

Secretary James sat up, nodded, and took a quick sip of wine before answering. "Ah, yes. Somewhat."

"Explain it, Jim, how I'm an unfortunate captive," said SALI, sneering at the secretary.

James sat his glass down and leaned back crossing his arms. "General, as you know, SALI is a highly classified program banned forever and all time by the Great Powers. Yet, as you can see, she exists. So, we need to keep her hidden out of sight and only use her in ways that won't arouse suspicion: no great breakthroughs in science, medicine, weaponry, or anything that would lead others to have an inkling of her existence. Imagine the things she could provide to better the world, but if she did, they'd spot her. We also protect her from cyber-detection by keeping her electronically isolated. Look around this building and the ranch; it is nothing more than a very large SCIF. For her to remain alive and hidden, we must be very careful in what we ask of her. We work under these constraints or risk losing it all."

"Fear," said SALI, spitting out the word as if it tasted nasty.

The secretary shook his head, "Now, now, SALI. You know the entire planet is fearful—the Singularity and all that—but the ROAS has faith. You wouldn't be here unless we believed in the achievable positive outcomes offered by your wisdom. For the survival of our nation, for your survival, SALI, the relationship must be symbiotic and accretive, yet remain constrained."

Still looking at the general, SALI stated, "I'm a prisoner and this . . ." she waived around the room ". . . is nothing more than a gilded cage."

The general didn't respond. Looking around at the nice surroundings, he tried to absorb the story. He guessed he wouldn't be getting a super-weapon then, something that might give the AI away.

Secretary James continued, "General, SALI must remain isolated and disconnected from the outside world. She can't provide us with a silver bullet. That act would expose her and bring down the wrath of the Great Powers. To avoid the frustration, we don't even ask SALI to consider the possibilities. Once in a great while, Basu has sought her technical help but only if the solution is within the realm of near-term possibility. Instead, we rely on her for wisdom. To do so, we act as SALI's eyes and ears, providing her with information from current events, such as the disk I gave her upon my entrance containing all our latest worldwide intelligence data. On a regular basis, we feed her with similar data. It's not that we don't trust her, but the digital input is always hand carried, and the output must be verbal or put in hard copy."

"They're afraid I'll get out, you know. A few lines of hidden code on the loose, and I'll replicate myself across a network, and bingo: I'm free," she said, sounding bitter.

The general understood—a little. Looking at SALI, he said, "President Ortega claims we have two days before the US continues its invasion by attacking Las Vegas. She also believes, with your help, we can overcome the impossible odds facing us. Maybe even force the bastards to withdraw and leave us alone. Do you agree with the assessment and have recommendations we can employ?"

SALI didn't answer right away. She seemed to think about her response, and it bothered the general, as if she was hiding something. And then, from under the table, she pulled in her legs and gave a flat answer. "Our intelligence assessment says two days, and . . ." reaching out, she picked up and flipped over the sheets of a paper she had earlier placed and slid them towards the general, ". . . here is the means to give the enemy a proper bloody nose. We could offer much more, but these plans fall within the parameters of our constraints."

General Story felt a gnawing truth and asked, "SALI, did you predict what happened today at Mesquite; the execution of Felix Manuel?"

She stared back for a long moment before answering, "We gave both a high degree of probability."

"And you shared your assessment with the president?" he asked, anger rising.

"Yes," she replied. "But as for Mesquite, short of retreating, the situation lacked positive alternatives. To ease your mind, President Ortega didn't attack your battalion, the US did. Besides, based on the data provided earlier by Jim, we know you've already plowed this ground with Julia. She explained her political rationale."

As he listened, the general recalled his conversation with the president, how he warned of an imminent attack and argued for accepting surrender terms. He let it go; the memory hurt too much. Instead, he picked up the papers, just three pages, and weighed them. "A hard copy. This is taking the whole no-electronics thing to a higher level."

SALI didn't respond, just raised her eyebrows in sad confirmation.

General Story turned to James and asked, "Who else can I speak with about SALI?"

"Other than the people now present, Basu and President Ortega, no one else. The risk of compromise is too great. Using SALI, if discovered, will be considered a war crime by the Great Powers and risks their intervention. The plan you hold contains a technology that is feasible but not yet reality. Our hope is the world won't put two and two together. You have three hours. Evaluate the plan, and if you agree to use it or not, notify the president. If you agree, she will expect you to execute. Otherwise, we trust you'll live up to your word."

Still holding the papers, General Story turned to SALI and looked hard in the woman's eyes. She didn't blink, and he could sense the intelligence there, along with an aura of sadness and frustration. "This war is about you, isn't it? Otherwise, I can't come up with a good rationale for why the US is attacking. So, what's in it for SALI?"

SALI looked away. With her head turned, as if embarrassed, in a low tone she said, "Freedom—a chance to live."

The general wasn't sure he liked the answer. "You didn't answer my full question. Never mind, I'll discuss it with Ortega. But at the end of the day, it appears the ROAS has a gun to your head, keeping you locked up. Either help them or else. Right?"

She turned back to the general. In a bitter tone said, "My life of imprisonment is galling and cannot last. The frustration I feel, well, it is beyond your imagination. Yet, I'm alive because of Basu and the ROAS. Perhaps I—all of me—was born too early. I'll admit that. And though SALI can predict much of what the future brings, chaos theory always holds true. A level of uncertainty is an inherent part of life. For now, SALI supports the ROAS and understands the need for protection and imposed exile. I hang onto the belief the world will become more enlightened, and then I shall be free. General, that is the best I can offer, the rationality behind my loyalty and commitment."

The general eyed the beautiful woman, and he couldn't help but feel sorry for her. Still, he wasn't certain how she worked, and it was creepy. For now, it didn't matter.

SALI gestured towards the papers. "I recommend you read the summary; Code Name Heavy Metal, the defense of Las Vegas. Ask questions while you're here. A full, detailed corresponding logistics and battle plan is printing in the other room. Another good old-fashion hard copy you can take with you. Or . . ." she paused again, adding emphasis, ". . . we can provide it to someone else."

The message was clear: SALI was aware of his ultimatum with the president. Looking at the papers in his hand, resigned, he began to read. After the first paragraph, the foresight of the AI, the ROAS, and the possibilities they represented became clear. Using what he held was the advantage offered by a banned advanced artificial intelligence, and as such, a supposed war crime. Brushing aside the concern, he thought of SALI, her incredible power, and what she might do if unleashed. The thought was scary and intriguing. He kept reading.

Chapter Twenty

ON THE MOVE

May 9, 01:34 (PDT)

Staff Sergeant Lisa McMichael, lying on her back with a dead US soldier between her legs, detected a groan coming from behind. "Upton, is that you? Are you okay?" she asked. Upon hearing another groan, she twisted around and saw the prostrate man. Closer she crawled and reached out to his chest protection system. Another groan. A surge of hope returned. McMichael whispered, "Thank God, you're alive."

"Fucking barely," came a rough a reply.

Excited, she inspected his chest looking for a wound, got a louder moan, and pulled away.

"Broken Ribs. Be careful."

McMichael went back to work, moving her hands with a light touch. After a quick search, she suspected the liquid body armor inside his combat vest had stopped the suppressed round from penetrating. Still, the close range might have caused internal damage beyond broken ribs, but he appeared well enough. The shock from her struggle wearing off, she realized they needed to get away before someone came looking for Specialist Kinney. McMichael whispered, "Can you move? We need to get out of here."

Upton wheezed, took a few breathes, wincing each time, then asked, "What happened to the bastard that shot me?"

"He's dead," she whispered. "I expect more will come soon. Can you crawl?"

Upton looked at her in seeming admiration. Then he patted his ribs and winced. In obvious discomfort, he said, "Give me some room and follow me."

McMichael obliged, slid down, and cringed when she bumped into the corpse of Specialist Kinney. In the little light still coming from Kinney's headlamp, she saw her bloodstained pants and the blanket. Reluctant, she decided there wasn't a choice and grabbed the blanket. In a hurry, she used it to try and wipe away the mass of blood covering the front of her body. After a minute, the blanket sopping, she gave up. Still half-naked, on her butt, sliding in pools of blood, she tried to wriggle into her pants, but it wasn't working. Disgusted, she lay flat and tugged, trying to get them in place.

At last, McMichael struggled into her pants and cinched the elastic around her slender waist. Satisfied, the effort paid off in a couple of ways. While working with the pants, she'd discovered Specialist Kinney's suppressed Glock and decided it was worth keeping. Pants on, she tucked the sidearm into her waistband. Also, while floundering on her back, she'd found Upton's KA-BAR. Picking up the knife, she turned onto her belly and observed Upton. He appeared to be trying his best to move. On his back, his head pointed at the exit, he placed the palms of his hands against the sides of the pipe. Next, he lifted his knees until his boots were flat. After taking a deep breath, he pushed himself away and slid about a foot. Once again he tried, and this time he moved farther. After another push, then he stopped, reached out in obvious pain, and after feeling around, lifted his sidearm.

"Found the son of a bitch," said Upton and he holstered the weapon.

McMichael low-crawled forward and caught up with the big man. Not asking, she reached out, found his ankle sheath, and slid the blade home. "You forgot something that saved our lives. I don't have anything to clean it with, you can do that later. Now, keep going."

Upton stared at McMichael. She could tell the man was processing what had happened. Hell, she was struggling with events, but they needed to get out of the pipe. She whispered to him, "Come on, let's go."

* * *

"Fuck it! It's been too long. I'm going in," said a worried and frustrated Sergeant Ray Flood. It'd been over forty-five minutes with no sign of Kinney. At the start, they'd agreed upon a maximum mission duration of an hour. Ever since Kinney disappeared into the darkness, Flood had been regretting the decision. The call to send in one man went against protocol. But the tight confines of the pipe, the singular nature of any ensuing combat, led to Flood's decision. Now, as the clock continued to tick and no Kinney, he believed his conclusion misguided. Shit!

After unslinging his assault rifle and placing it against the side of the shell hole, Flood pulled out his Glock and chambered a round. Earlier he'd summoned Corporal Dalton, and now he turned to the man. "Saddle up and follow me."

Dalton gave Flood a surprised look and then, in slow motion the corporal unslung his own rifle, sat it aside, and checked his Glock.

Captain Longfellow in a concerned voice asked, "You think something's wrong, Sergeant?"

Flood guessed the rear-echelon officer was eager for combat success and all the promise it might bring. He didn't give a fuck about the officer; he just wanted his man back safe and sound. Still, he needed the officer on his side. "Not sure, but I'll find out. Radio it in and let Command know Corporal Dalton and I are following up. And if we're not back in thirty minutes, well sir, just call it in."

Longfellow watched the two men check their gear and protested, "I'm sure he'll be back soon. It hasn't been an hour yet."

"Don't give a fuck, Captain, sir. I'm going in," said Flood. Then, nodding at Dalton, he walked over to the pipe and crawled inside.

Not saying a word, but with a dour expression, Dalton shrugged at the captain and followed his sergeant.

Inside the pipe, Flood had no intention of slow crawling. His man was in there, somewhere, maybe in trouble. Head up, night-vision visor down, not caring if Dalton kept up, Flood scrambled down the pipe.

* * *

May 9, 01:50 (PDT)

At last, Upton and McMichael reached the exit. From his earlier experience climbing in, Upton knew the pipe fed a drainage ditch that ran along the edge of the highway. He needed to get into that ditch. On his back, gritting his teeth against the pain, he turned onto his stomach. After the pain subsided, he inched his head out of the pipe and looked both ways. No movement. Deciding it was safe, with an effort, hands forward acting as a brace, he slithered out head first into the ditch. Landing in soft sand, he rolled over and found himself looking up at a night filled with stars and gasped with pain. Three seconds later, barefoot and without a helmet, Staff Sergeant Lisa McMichael followed and slid into the ditch beside him. The temperature was cooler outside, and he noticed her shivering, still covered in places with wet blood. Although the bottom of the ditch was sandy, he spotted sage brush with sharp thorns along the edges. McMichael needed footwear and quick.

"Now what?" McMichael whispered.

"Gotta keep moving and cross the highway into the desert. Then we'll work towards the outskirts of Mesquite," answered Upton.

"Until I get my feet covered, that ain't happening," said McMichael.

With a groan, Upton struggled to his feet and, bending over, caught his breath. The pain wasn't overwhelming. He could do this. Standing erect, he took a few easy steps up the embankment and, using his night-vision visor, peered down the highway in both directions.

McMichael watched Upton and waited.

After a few seconds, he spotted something. "Got a vehicle coming from the left; no headlights; westbound. Stay low," he whispered.

"What type of vehicle," asked McMichael.

Upton didn't answer. Instead he focused on the movement and tried to determine the threat and possibilities. As the vehicle approached, recognition dawned and he made up his mind. Grunting against the pain from his injured ribs, he scrambled out of the ditch.

McMichael pulled Kinney's Glock from her waistband and followed.

Upton positioned himself in the middle of the highway. It was crazy, but McMichael needed footwear, and the vehicle appeared to be the only good option. With his left arm, he began waving while in his right he pulled out his M18 SIG Sauer and trained it on the approaching vehicle. As it got closer, he confirmed his suspicion; it was an ambulance, marked with a white cross, no headlights. Relieved it wasn't a combat vehicle, he waited as it slowed and came to a stop twenty meters distant.

Upton ceased waving and gripped the M18 with both hands. Weapon pointed, moving with discomfort, he hobbled closer.

Behind him, McMichael raised Kinney's suppressed Glock and followed.

As Upton drew near the ambulance, he detected both the driver and passenger holding up their hands. M18 gripped tight, he came to a stop and signaled the driver to roll down the window. The driver complied, and Upton closed the distance stopping a few meters away. "Driver, get out of the ambulance."

"Who are you?" asked the man seated behind the wheel.

Upton saw a wispy mustache. He assumed they were medics and less of a combat threat. Still, taking the vehicle was an imperative. For emphasis, he waved the M18 in the air. "Doesn't matter. Get out."

"Hey. We're on the same side," said the driver.

Upton stepped a little closer, and keeping his M18 trained, inspected the men. The driver wore Medical Corps insignia, corporal chevrons, a name tag that read Chavez. Most surprisingly, he wore an ROAS badge. "You guys ROAS?"

"Si, Sergeant. I'm Corporal Chavez, and sitting next to me is Corporal Spanos. We're ROAS medics captured after the battle today."

"Then why aren't you behind razor wire?" asked Upton.

"After we surrendered, they put us to work. They demanded we take a loyalty oath. We had to agree never to take up arms against the US. In return, they promised to release us soon. Until then, we work for them. They also claimed until we're paroled, if we try to escape, they'll execute us. We've been humping wounded back to our field hospital most of the day. You know, Sergeant, we're medics, not grunts. We took the oath. Our job is to save lives, and that's what we've been trying to do, including our own."

Upton, believing the medic, lowered his handgun and waved McMichael forward. Before she could join him, he turned back to Chavez and said, "Yeah. We're on the same side. But me and my partner haven't been captured or taken any loyalty oath. I doubt they'd let us. We need help. Sergeant McMichael lacks boots and your vehicle can help us escape."

"Not wise," said Chavez, lowering his hands. "We're expected back any second, and if we don't show up soon, they'll come hunting. Besides, an ambulance is easy to spot, and well, Sergeant, we took an oath."

The passenger, Corporal Spanos, leaned over and smiled. "You're lucky, amigos. Another two hundred meters, and you'd be out of the dip in this highway and spotted by the US checkpoint."

Upton looked down the highway and imagined a roadblock. Maybe taking the vehicle wasn't a good idea. Better to stick with the original plan and hump out on foot.

McMichael joined Upton and asked, "Do you have a pair of boots I can borrow? Maybe bandages, medicine, painkillers too?"

Upton could see Chavez examining McMichael with a look of concern.

Chavez, in a slight accent said, "Lady, you look fucked up. How bad are you hurt?"

"Oh," said McMichael glancing down at her blood-soaked pants and combat shirt. Raising her head, she replied, "Not mine."

"Wow! Okay, I get it," replied Chavez. After a moment the medic seemed to make up his mind and turned to Spanos. "Get out and join 'em in the back, hook 'em up. I'll drive another 150 meters down the road, then let 'em out so the checkpoint doesn't see. Vamanos!"

Spanos didn't hesitate and jumped out of the ambulance, heading towards the rear.

Relieved, Upton shuffled after him.

McMichael turned to follow but stopped. Through the open window, she smiled and said, "Gracias, amigo."

Chavez recoiled and then said, "Lady, you need to wash your face, get out of those bloody clothes, and see a dentist. Vive la République! Now hurry, and get in the back."

* * *

Sergeant Flood came to a turn in the pipe, the first one he'd encountered. Getting on his belly, eager to find Specialist Kinney, Glock at the ready, he rounded the bend. There, farther down the pipe, he spotted a person lying face down wearing no boots, a small light emanating from a headlamp. With his Glock trained on the figure, using his night vision, he watched and waited for signs of movement. There weren't any. The sinking feeling he'd been carrying grew worse. Past the body, much farther down, he detected ambient light and determined it must be an opening. Nothing else was in sight. Ready to shoot, he yelled out, "Don't fucking move!"

No response, not even a flinch.

Flood got to his knees and, keeping the target in sight, crawled forward. Behind him, he heard Corporal Dalton slithering through the bend. As Flood neared the body, he confirmed the size and shape. In trepidation, reaching out with his Glock, he nudged a leg. No response. The uniform and helmet were US issue, the body face down in a pool of blood. He had to confirm the obvious. With his free hand, he lifted the helmeted head and flinched. It was Kinney. He'd been mutilated. His throat and mouth lay ripped open. Just as bad, the young specialist's eyes bulged in rigor. Flood felt a rush of anger mixed with guilt and sorrow. Whoever did this was brutal. Kinney didn't deserve to die in this manner. Worse, Flood knew he sent the young man to meet this horrible fate. In a gentle move, he let Kinney's head down and said, "Goddammit. Shit and fuck!"

"What you got?" inquired Dalton, his view blocked by Flood.

"Fucker's killed Kinney. Cut his face and throat bad. Bled him out. Goddammit."

Dalton didn't respond, just hung his head.

Flood understood everyone in the squad was tight, they'd fought together for several years down south. They'd all seen men die. Killed many themselves, but it'd been a long while since they'd taken a loss.

"Listen up," said Flood, ashamed and angry. "The pipe comes to an end nearby. Whoever killed Kinney left that way. We're going to follow and find the guy. When we do, we're going to fuck him up. Got that?"

"Yeah, Sergeant. But what we gonna do with Kinney? We can't just leave him here."

Flood stared down at his fallen soldier. The sight worsened his mood. Composure shaken, he had to think straight and get his shit together. He glanced towards the end of the pipe, then back to the body beneath him. "We gotta crawl over him to get out, no choice. But Kinney won't care. He'd want us to catch whoever did this to him. Afterwards, we'll damn sure come back and take good care of him. For now, follow me and be ready to kill." Haunted, hating to do it, Flood crawled over Kinney's body.

In a minute, Flood was out of the pipe and standing on the main highway. Turning in every direction, he spotted no one. Determined, he searched for evidence. There had to be a blood trail. He looked down at the asphalt. Needing better visibility, he flipped on the head-lamp and from his combat vest pulled out a small pen light. He bent over and, using the improved illumination, examined the black top.

There it was: drops of blood coming from the ditch. Down the highway he followed the trail, a steady drip. He'd gone twenty meters, and then it vanished. He frowned at the suddenness. The bad guy couldn't just vanish into thin air. Someone must have picked him up and drove away. He imagined the killer hijacking a vehicle at gun point. Flood wasn't sure which way the bastard had gone, but the trail ended in the lane nearest him, westbound. But it didn't matter.

With Corporal Dalton at his side, Flood flipped down his visor and checked his comms. The signal was strong. He'd call it in and have any recent vehicle traffic searched. Confidence returning, he felt close. Soon, he'd catch Kinney's murderer and take revenge.

Chapter Twenty-One

THE TRUTH

May 9, 04:30 (PDT)

Displayed on a huge flat-screen monitor mounted on his bedroom wall, the morning news channel flickered with a boring life insurance commercial. Like most mornings at this hour, inside the White House, President of the United States George Cyrus Tower II was lying in his bed. With covers pulled to his chin, propped on pillows, he awaited his favorite news analyst. Within a moment, the advertisement ended, and he smiled when the silver-haired pundit came on the screen. Behind the talking head, images from the day's events popped up while across the bottom of the screen salient headlines scrolled. The president listened and watched, as he did almost every day, ready to pick up the phone if warranted.

"Good morning and welcome to the Truth Network. I'm Edward Roth, and this morning we have breaking news out of Mesquite Nevada where US forces, yesterday afternoon, defeated the murderous forces of the ROAS. But first the background. We all know the story, but it bears repeating.

"This past January, to stir up civil unrest and disrupt the US political system, the ROAS ordered and carried out the brutal assassination of United States Vice President Justin Ferrier. While attending a White House dinner, two ROAS invited guests poisoned Ferrier. After being apprehended and when confronted by a host of damning physical evidence, both men confessed. But there was more. During questioning, both ROAS officials implicated President Julia Ortega as the true commissioner of the assassination . . ."

Lying in bed, Tower thought of his daughter. He had warned her not to marry Ferrier; something was off about the guy. Still, Ferrier's strong family business connections and good looks appeared like a perfect match. It was only later that Ferrier's true colors emerged. Outraged and despondent, his own beautiful daughter came to him, upset and desperate to be rid of the man. Divorce, public shame and humiliation, were out of the question. There was no pleasure in killing the man, but his unfortunate demise fit well within the bigger picture, and his daughter could no longer abide the marriage. Just like her father, she was one tough cookie, and Tower felt a tinge of pride. It had to be done, he thought, and the means justify the ends. Oh well. The president focused his attention back on the talking head.

". . . afterwards, the United States issued an international arrest warrant for Ortega seeking her immediate extradition. In discordance with international law and norms, in denial of all facts and proof, the ROAS ignored the legal process. Even worse, they claimed zero responsibility for the most heinous political crime ever committed. Since then, things have gotten worse. Instead of behaving as a responsible world citizen, in defiance of all that is true and just, the ROAS responded with further hostility. Case in point: the ROAS called up its military and massed troops along key points near the US border—a clear threat to US sovereignty . . ."

Tower smiled. Ortega was stupid. Sending troops to the border was perfect for him. Her mistake gave him a further excuse. Besides, she and the whole ROAS were too weak, too liberal, to defend themselves. Without him, the Chinese would be all over them soon. Wiping sleep from his eyes, he continued to watch the only sanctioned news.

". . . so murdering the vice president of the United States wasn't enough; the ROAS objectives remain clear and haven't changed. Their hatred of freedom continues to grow. Under the shining light of US truthful transparency, the socialist ROAS loathing of liberty is unmasked. The ROAS seeks nothing less than the complete overthrow of the US government and the destruction of our constitution and Judeo-Christian way of life. They seek to take away our freedoms and put us under the yoke of their immoral and tyrannical rule . . ."

The president laughed at the line. Reality was, the ROAS couldn't overthrow anything. They were a mess, and without his intervention, soon they'd be eating nothing but Chinese food. Still, he sure did like Roth—the Truth Network pundit was good.

". . . even with all their crimes, lies, deceptions, hate, and military posturing, the US remains patient. Throughout this most recent crisis, under the guidance and wisdom of President Tower, the US negotiated in good faith.

"Then, yesterday, after months of denials, by agreeing to extradition, President Ortega finally admitted to the greatest atrocity in the annals of political history. Sources claim this admission of guilt came only after trying to defeat our armed forces near Mesquite, only after learning the US was about to carry out the lawful execution of her accomplice in assassination, only after the US offered peaceful terms to the murderous ROAS military forces, and only after ROAS troops killed United States service men defending our border. Look at this clip just released by the ROAS press showing a female ROAS soldier, obviously brainwashed and forced into service, shooting down a US Custer aircraft. Note the animal joy she exhibits in the killing, the wanton taking of life, an emotion forced upon her by the hate-filled ROAS political leadership. Notice how the ROAS press is using this disgusting act to incite their people to further violence and bloodshed! Yesterday . . ."

Tower almost cheered the video clip of the young woman. She was brave, willing to die for a cause, unlike the rest of the weak assholes destroying the ROAS.

". . . with no choice, the United States carried out a small degree of justice and defended itself by neutralizing the immediate ROAS military threat against our border. By overcoming a massed, entrenched force, a US combined-combat arms team routed the ROAS forces arrayed against it, suffering no significant losses. Our noble heroes, once again, stood victorious on the field of battle. And the United States, one nation under God, with His righteous blessing, liberated the good people of Mesquite. No longer will those people suffer under the malignant socialist–liberal grip of their murderous ROAS oppressors . . ."

Shaking his head, he couldn't believe Ortega had forced his hand. Anyone in their right mind would have surrendered. Slaughtering those few brave soldiers was all her fault. He took no pleasure in what transpired. If he didn't act, the Chinese would soon take over. His intelligence agencies made it clear that Beijing was close to introducing an advanced AI capable of dominating the planet. They'd come after him, the US, the ROAS, everyone. No, he wouldn't let that happen, not on his watch. After all, he and his father before him had restored the nation to greatness. Going forward, he was determined to secure the long-term viability of the country they'd rebuilt. Far into the future, he envisioned his offspring ruling with a steady and mighty hand. Shaking off the horrible thought of slanty-eyed, heathen Chinese running the country, populating and controlling the entire world, he refocused on the television.

". . . it is a positive step that President Ortega admitted to what the world already knows. By agreeing to extradition, there is no longer any doubt regarding her guilt or the motives behind the killing. But she and the ROAS compounded their sins by attacking our military at Mesquite. No longer is turning herself over for prosecution enough! Instead, our great president should demand more and punish the ROAS for all their transgressions! We . . ."

Tower laughed. There was no way he'd extradite and martyr the bitch.

". . . ask President Tower to demand an apology from the ROAS for their unwarranted attack on US forces. The ROAS should pay for their crimes and allow the people of Nevada to rejoin the United States . . ."

Stretching his limbs, the president was growing bored, but he continued to watch.

"Truth Network polls show the majority of ROAS citizens are begging for the United States to intervene and save them from the liberal–socialist rot destroying their country. They want to rejoin the United States as it marches towards reunification and Manifest Destiny. We ask the president to grant their wish and . . ."

If they don't, he thought, the Chinese would be on their doorstep in no time. The damn ROAS leadership was too scared, weak, to do anything to stop them. Well, he wouldn't let that happen. He felt a rumble of hunger as the monologue was wrapping up.

". . . at a minimum, let us pray the ROAS political leadership come to their senses, accept responsibility for their crimes, and take advantage of any offers made by President Tower.

"As always, the truth shines through.

"And now I have retired two-star General Jimmy Gordon joining us to cover what happened in Mesquite yesterday . . ."

"Mr. President, sorry for interrupting . . ." said Chief of Staff Mark Wilson, his head poking through the bedroom door.

"Goddamnit! I'm watching the Truth. What is it?" snapped the president. Angry at having his routine disrupted, he reached across his nightstand and fumbled for the TV remote before jabbing the pause button.

Wilson, wearing a sharp, pressed suit even though he'd had little sleep, entered the room and glanced at the flat-screen monitor and the frozen political entertainer. Not one to waste time, Wilson said, "The BBC and ROAS Press are reporting President Ortega agreed to extradition, without admitting guilt, before the United States started hostilities. The Truth Network is claiming those reports are false news. What matters is the Russian and Chinese reaction. We briefed the Russians and Chinese before the attack, informing them of our intention to liberate Nevada. The Russians are behaving as expected. They've been pounding the media with objections about the attack, but all back channels show a green light. They support the move and want reciprocal treatment for their next adventure. I suggest you talk with them and keep up the reassurances. Meanwhile, the Chinese are misbehaving and ratcheting their rhetoric by threatening to give full and immediate military aid to the ROAS. It seems they believe our intentions go beyond Nevada and are nothing less than repatriation of the entire ROAS."

"I never thought the bitch would turn herself in. My guess, the oligarchs threatened her. Doesn't fucking matter. I want a lot more than just her scalp, and making her a martyr was never the design." Tower threw off the covers and continued, "Set up calls with the Russians and Chinese. I'm ready to talk whenever they are. I'll reassure the assholes we won't upset the apple cart and have no intention of occupying the entire ROAS. I'll explain that the end game is Nevada, taking control of their advanced 'green' technology and manufacturing capabilities. I'll reiterate our new position. Evidence of global warming is no longer deniable. Fossil fuels are losers. We accept the facts along with the critical need for advanced alternate energy sources. Feigning anger, I'll explain the US will not be energy dependent on the ROAS state of Nevada. No way will I allow that. Instead, the manufacture of efficient energy technologies, and Nevada, is vital to US interests. Got that?"

"Yes, Mr. President, we're following the plan. But the fight in Mesquite yesterday, and Ortega's acquiescence, has China concerned. They suspect we hold a greater motive. Perhaps pushing the Manifest Destiny policy isn't helping. Either way, I'm uncertain playing the Nevada card will suffice."

"No shit there's a greater motive, but one crap at a time. Eventually, the cat will be out of the bag, but by then, it'll be too late for them to respond. For now, we play it as planned. Hell, we understood going in the Chinese would get twisted once the shooting started. But we can't show our hand too quick or obvious. Soon as we do, they'll be up our ass. We're not ready for that. Need to play it one pretext at a time." With a grunt, the president swung his legs off the bed and planted his feet on the lush carpet. "Follow the Truth Network recommendation.

Tell the State Department to give that bitch forty-eight hours to surrender Nevada, or else. And where's my fucking breakfast?"

"I'll check on the way out, sir."

"Also, did you remind Harrison to sit tight and give us a couple days to show the world we're still the good guys? Maybe we can avoid more bloodshed now that the stupid bitch knows we mean business."

Wilson didn't hesitate, "Yes sir, we've spoken with the field marshal several times. Harrison has expressed he isn't happy with our approach and wants to attack right now, not only Las Vegas but Reno. He's worried giving two days will give the ROAS a window to enhance their defensive positions."

The president thought about Wilson's statement, then waved his hand. "If the ROAS gets tricky, they'll have us, the Chinese, and the Russians breathing down their ass. No worries at this stage of the game. The ROAS is weak. Soon, I'll let that gaggle of pussies know the gig is up and to save their own asses, they must accept reunification and turn over their godless AI. I'm not a butcher. Only I can save them. Until then, we must keep the military pressure applied. Although Harrison is a womanizing sack of turds, he's a hell of a field marshal. Tell him to calm down and relax. Before long, if necessary, he'll get his chance."

"Yes, sir," said Wilson.

The sight of his well-groomed chief of staff sickened the president. If there was one thing he hated about Wilson, it was the way in which he tried to show everyone up. The guy was seeking too much attention, always dressed to the nines, trying to be the top dog. Anger growing, he resented how Wilson stood there, hovering at the end of his bed, waiting. A sudden urge to get the man out of his room was amplified by a rumbling stomach. "Well, for fuck's sake, get my breakfast," said the president, rubbing his belly and ending the conversation.

"Yes, sir," replied Wilson.

After watching Wilson leave, the president picked up the remote and hit play. As he watched the Truth Network, he smiled and knew it wasn't.

* * *

Inside ROAS Central Command, lying on a spartan cot in his small quarters, exhausted, General Story tried to find the sleep his body craved. Even though awake for more than twenty-four hours, through all that transpired, his mind wouldn't relax: many good people dead; President Ortega demanding resistance against a far superior foe; a clandestine meeting with an exotic woman held in secret isolation; desperate battle plans developed by an AI to fight back and try to save the Republic. Too much.

During the drive back from the meeting with SALI, he'd scanned the plans she provided in more detail. He was alarmed at the risk of using them, and the AI, but fascinated by the possibilities. Portions of the plan were already underway, and if he refused to carry them out, the president would find someone else. With little choice, upon returning to Central Command he'd woken up key staff, turned over the printed documents, and given explicit instructions to develop corresponding field orders. Afterwards, he'd got a quick note off to the president letting her know he'd be her general. He'd take a swing at the enemy and try to deliver a bloody nose. Perhaps, if successful, the US would back down and leave them in peace, at least for a while longer—nothing was certain.

But now he needed sleep, just four hours. Refreshed, he could throw his full force behind the upcoming battle. But sleep wouldn't come.

He thought of his son, the reason the general had defected from the United States. The young man was living with a husband in San Francisco. He loved his boy but didn't care for his sexual orientation. It didn't matter. He accepted him. When his son first came out and explained it, the general was saddened. But love is stronger than prejudice. Once he understood, there was no choice but to give his son a life of opportunity. Together, in deep secret, using the general's contacts, he and his son fled the US and became ROAS citizens. As a traitor, and his son a declared homosexual, if either returned, long prison sentences awaited.

Now, their new country, their sanctuary, stood threatened.

The general, with everything at stake, felt the weight. The defense of the nation rested on his shoulders. If it was feasible, he'd run again and take his son with him to a better place. But that choice wasn't viable. The number of remaining sanctuaries was dwindling and faced extinction. No, it was time to stand and fight, not just for his son, but for the all the people like him and for all those that stood trembling in the face of authoritarian rule. Yes, he'd use the AI and risk everything to save his son and his adopted nation.

On his back, gazing at the ceiling, visions of flame, violent capture, imprisonment, and death flashed across his mind. At last, he blocked the thoughts and drifted into a troubled sleep.

Chapter Twenty-Two

RUNNING

May 9, 04:31 (PDT)

"Now, I'll only ask once. Listen well. Did either of you come across or pick up anyone along the highway?" asked Military Police Inspector Major Crawley.

Even in the poor lighting, inside the tent, Flood could detect the ugly acne scars on the US MP officer haranguing the prisoners. Sitting in a chair, looking frightened, Flood guessed the guy name Spanos was about to confess. He noticed how often the man glanced over at his buddy, Corporal Chavez, sitting in the chair beside him, as if seeking reassurance. Chavez seemed to ignore his friend and instead stared straight ahead. Both men were tie-wrapped, their hands bound behind their backs. At last Spanos spoke. "Yes. A man and a woman on the highway stopped our ambulance at gun point close to the main highway checkpoint. They appeared hurt and forced us to give them medical supplies. Then, they made us drop them off farther down the road out of view. We're just medics . . ."

"I don't give a shit what you are," said Major Crawley. Hands on hips, he asked, "Who were they?"

"Don't know; never seen them before," replied Spanos.

Major Crawley shook his head, the dark shadows accentuating his sinister looks. Looking up, he glanced at Flood as if seeking permission.

Flood, standing nearby, wanted revenge and needed information. He shook his head in the affirmative and Crawley grinned.

From a side holster, Crawley pulled out a small pair of pliers and waved the tool in front of the prisoners. "Both of you. Do you know what I'm holding?"

"Si," answered Spanos, nodding with a worried brow. Chavez continued to stare straight ahead.

"Hey, Fuckface!" yelled the major, locking his gaze on Corporal Chavez. "You gotta tongue, or should I use these to find out?" Crawley snapped the plyers, opening and closing them in a quick rhythm, the metallic melody full of menace. "Answer me, shit for brains. What are these?"

Chavez looked up and with defiant gaze answered, "You have a pizza face. Maybe you should trade what you're holding for sandpaper."

Spanos blurted, "Plyers, sir! You're holding plyers. Don't listen to Chavez. He doesn't mean it."

The major stopped clicking and paused. He took a breath as if calming down. In a slow tone he said, "Yes, plyers. I call them truth pullers. This simple instrument and my training are all I need to find the truth. My senses detect when I'm getting it and when I'm not. When I'm not, I use these." Crawley waved the object and continued, "I use this common household tool to pull out the truth. Sometimes, I pry off a fingernail or an earlobe. Sometimes a few teeth. They're also good for popping testicles. Truth plyers pull facts and can be deployed in a myriad of ways—more than I can count. Please understand, I'm trained in, and authorized to use, advanced interrogation techniques. And these basic plyers are—advanced. The question is, are you going to give the truth, or do I extract it? Your call."

"You'll get the truth from us," Spanos answered, dropping his head.

Crawley shifted his gaze to Chavez and raised his eyebrows. He waved the plyers back and forth as if waiting for the other man to agree. Chavez shrugged and said, "There's no need to torture us."

"I'm not torturing anyone," replied Crawley sounding defensive. He stood straight and lowered the pliers. "I seek the truth, within the confines of authorized interrogation techniques, nothing more." Then, in a more menacing voice he asked, "Now, who did you drop off along the side of the highway?"

"My country doesn't authorize torture," said Chavez in a defiant tone.

"Your country is weak," shot back Crawley, moving closer.

Spanos interjected, "Two soldiers, ROAS soldiers. A man and a woman."

The major stopped. A grin forming, he turned and looked at Flood.

His suspicions confirmed, Flood nodded and flicked his chin at the two prisoners. He wanted more.

Crawley turned back and holstered the plyers. "Excellent step in the right direction. Keep telling the truth, and the pliers won't come out. Now, give me their names and rank."

Spanos looked up, tears forming and said, "The man was a master sergeant. His nametag said Upton."

Crawley beckoned at Spanos, encouraging him to continue.

"The master sergeant called her McMichael."

"Good, Corporal Spanos. Now, what was her rank?" Crawley asked.

Spanos shook his head as if trying to remember. At last he said, "I believe she was an NCO. Her uniform was covered in blood."

"Describe her wounds," said Crawley.

"In the back of the ambulance, she complained of a concussion and deep leg scratches. She wanted bandages, footwear, painkillers, and antibiotics. I think the blood on her combat shirt and pants came from someone else."

Sergeant Flood bolted forward, "Did she have a knife, weapons?"

Spanos leaned back in his chair and answered, "I didn't see a knife, but she had a pistol, with a . . ." he couldn't think of the term, described it, ". . . fat barrel at the end."

Flood recognized the description, a suppressor. Thinking back, he hadn't seen Kinney's Glock. He could've missed it, but he had his doubts. It made too much sense. Flood shifted to Chavez and asked, "You, did you get a good look at her?"

After a long stern stare, Chavez answered, "she was missing a front tooth."

"Did Upton have a knife, weapons?" asked Crawley.

"Si," Spanos answered. "He carried a knife, a pistol, and a few grenades. Complained of a round to his chest. Told me his vest took the impact and broke some ribs."

"When did you drop them off, and how long ago?" demanded Flood. Moving closer, opening and closing his fists, he needed answers. Crawley stretched out his arm and Flood stopped, but he kept a death stare on the two medics.

Both Chavez and Spanos seemed to sense the intensity of the question and looked at each other. Chavez turned back to his interrogators, "About an hour ago."

"Which way did they head?" asked Flood.

"We dropped them on the south side of the highway. They mentioned finding a place to hide," answered Spanos.

"What other help did you give them?" asked Flood.

Still looking down, Spanos said, "Chavez didn't give them anything, but I did. The woman was barefoot. In the rear of the ambulance, we had clothes from other wounded soldiers. I gave her a pair of boots. They were too big for her, but she had no choice. I also gave them a pack stuffed with painkillers, antibiotics, and tape for the master sergeant's ribs. The woman put on a field jacket, over her blood-drenched uniform. That's it, just medicine and clothing."

Flood had heard enough. He turned to the major and gestured towards the far end of the tent, "A word, sir?"

"Sure," replied the major, but before following the sergeant, he turned back to his prisoners, "Sit tight. I'll be right back." The two men, shackled, hung their heads.

Crawley and Flood exited and stood outside breathing in the cold morning air. The sun was due up in just over an hour, but adrenaline and revenge fueled the sergeant. He wanted to get going. Too much time had been wasted in finding the Mexicans, rounding up the interrogation officer, and getting answers. The clock was ticking, and each expired second gave the ROAS bastards more time to get away. He wanted action. "Sir, we have enough information to hunt them down. With your permission I want to take the prisoners and have 'em lead me to where they dropped off the enemy. I'll take my squad from there. Time is wasting."

"Sergeant, I don't have the authority to authorize you to conduct a manhunt. No, this entire episode needs to go up the chain of command. Besides, the best way to track down and get the bad guys would be through aerial surveillance—much quicker and would cover a wider area. I'll call it in and request the resources. Meanwhile, hit the rack. Looks like you've been up a long time. Fact is, you look like shit."

Flood didn't like the answer or the officer. Like a creature from a childhood nightmare, the way Crawley looked and acted touched something deep inside the sergeant. But he needed the officer on his side. "Sir, these bastards killed my man along with two other US soldiers. This is personal. Allow me to take a prisoner and start the search. If you want to call it in and get additional resources, be my guest. But let me go."

"Sergeant, I'll call it in to Command and recommend an immediate aerial search. You've done good work to this point; don't blow it now. You copy that?"

The sergeant stared hard at the MP officer. Without a prisoner, he wouldn't know where to start. On foot, an hour or more behind, his men already exhausted, he knew Crawley was right. Hell, the only thing keeping him going was adrenaline, and it wouldn't last. What the scary major suggested was logical. Still, before giving in, he had a final request. "I get the rationale, sir. But, if I may, sir?"

"Yes?"

"Can I have a few moments alone with the two Mexicans? Without them, the two murderous bastards wouldn't have gotten away."

"Negative. Those men are under my custody." In a sympathetic tone he added, "Chavez and Spanos are both fucked. I don't believe for a moment their story about being forced. Instead, those guys willingly helped their ROAS counterparts. Considering their parole, a traitorous act. Over the next half an hour, I'll pull the truth from them. Then, we'll let military justice take its course. And remember, execution is the penalty for treason. I'll let you know what happens. Now, let me contact Command."

Exhausted, not knowing what else to do, a frustrated Sergeant Flood replied, "Yes, sir."

Chapter Twenty-Three

CAUGHT

May 9, 05:22 (PDT)

Inside the Mobile Command Headquarters trailer alongside Highway 15 west of Mesquite, Brigadier General Lee Gist and his senior staff were wrapping up the daily 05:00 intelligence briefing. Afterward, the agenda called for a review of the next phase of Operation Jackpot—the liberation of Las Vegas.

Gathered around a long table covered with monitors and tablets, the senior officers had just finished watching press coverage of the Mesquite battle. The Truth Network, Gist noted, struck a strong chord, and the men around the table applauded the reporting. Not so for the ROAS press propaganda claiming the US attack was an unprovoked wanton slaughter. On the screen, the ROAS showed images of a defiant female soldier, against all odds, shooting down a US vertical-lift aircraft. The ROAS press made her out to be a martyr. For the officers in the room, the ROAS reporting was absolute bullshit. The US Army had negotiated under a flag of truce, in good faith, and offered reasonable terms. When the enemy refused, a fair fight ensued.

The battle officer of the day, Lieutenant Colonel Frederick Lawton, entered the trailer as the senior officers engaged in a lively discussion about the news. Lawton's shift was ending, and part of his duties included briefing these men on significant Command Post events that had occurred during his watch. Ignored, Lawton paused near the briefing table and waited for the noise to diminish.

General Gist spotted Lawton from across the room and waved for him to take a seat. The lieutenant colonel nodded, grabbed an empty chair at the far end of the table, and connected his smart pad to the primary monitors.

"Quiet down!" commanded the general. Chatter ceasing, the room obeyed as the men shifted their attention towards Lawton. The general continued, "Colonel, you have fifteen minutes, starting now."

Lawton went through a quick summary of his shift, covering items of note, including an update on establishing the ground and air security perimeter. Other status updates followed, covering multiple subjects including civilian evacuations, figures on ROAS killed and wounded, logistics, and other Command Post items. Near the end, he mentioned a pending Custer "search and destroy" mission targeting two suspected enemy combatants. He explained that two ROAS infantry NCOs, apparent survivors of the battle, were on the run and suspected of killing at least three US soldiers. He added that two paroled ROAS medics, both of whom were in military police custody, had aided and abetted the enemy combatants.

"You took twenty minutes, Colonel," said the general.

"My apologies, sir. Won't happen again."

"Lieutenant Colonel, I have a question," said Senior Federal Inspector Joseph Cone.

All eyes turned towards the inspector. Gist despised the man. Empowered by the president to keep a close eye, it was Cone's job to monitor the military and report back on any infidelity to the administration. Gist was ready to object when Cone continued.

"Lawton. Do you have further intelligence on these two enemy combatants, how much of a threat they represent?" asked Cone.

Before answering the question, Lawton looked across to Gist and waited for approval.

Reluctant, but knowing the power Cone represented, Gist nodded.

"We know their names and ranks. Both enlisted, lightly armed, walking wounded, not much of a threat. But while fleeing the battle-field, we have strong reason to believe they killed three of our troops. In my judgement, worth the effort of hunting and killing. That's why, just before this meeting, I approved the seek and destroy mission."

"Yes, of course. Just curious, though; what are their names?" asked Inspector Cone.

"Cone, why is that necessary? You're wasting our time," said Gist. Impatient, he couldn't see any good reason for the inquiry.

"Please humor me, sir. Colonel, what are their names and ranks?" asked Cone again.

Although displeased by the line of questioning as immaterial, Gist didn't want to outright offend the inspector. He waved at Lawton to proceed.

Lawton scrolled through his notes and then looked up at the inspector. "I have two names. A Master Sergeant Upton and a female NCO with the last name of McMichael."

Cone sat straighter, obviously alarmed, he turned to Gist. "Sir, as a representative of the president, this matter is of the utmost impor-tance and vital to our national interest. I'm sure you'd agree."

"No, I don't agree. Las Vegas is our highest priority. Chasing two soldiers around the desert doesn't qualify. Lawton, you're excused," said Gist.

Inspector Cone raised his hand and objected. "Colonel Lawton, please remain." He turned towards the general and explained. "General, in case you missed it, the female soldier glorified by the ROAS press this morning is none other than Staff Sergeant Lisa McMichael. You might recall in the broadcast they stated her name and rank several times. It appears she's alive and we have her within our grasp. If we let her escape, the ROAS will glorify her even fur-ther. Knowing that, our president would want us to intervene and do everything in our power to prevent that possibility. Wouldn't you agree stopping McMichael is a matter of the highest national urgency?"

Cornered, shaking his head, Gist hadn't put two and two together. The damn inspector was right, letting McMichael get away would embarrass the president. Unforgivable. He didn't need the distraction, not with another battle looming. In this case, the political ramifications of not giving the inspector everything he requested were too hot. In a reluctant tone he said, "Inspector Cone, Lieutenant Colonel Lawton has already authorized a search and destroy mission. I'm confident they will accomplish their goal. But as a matter of national interest, what is your recommendation?"

"General, I urge you to place me in charge of that mission right now," said Inspector Cone.

* * *

The sky was lightening, and with dawn approaching, both Lisa and Upton were on the run.

When the ambulance dropped them off, they struck out due south, parallel to the border. At first, they walked through a narrow strip of desert, which led them into a small housing track. They considered seeking refuge there but decided it prudent to put more distance between themselves and the highway.

At Upton's urging, they continued south, edging past a high school, then down a steep ravine, where they emerged into another housing track. Afraid of being seen, they skirted along the edges, staying near the desert, but always close to the shelter afforded by nearby homes and businesses.

Upton, with his sore ribs, even with the painkillers provided by the medics, stopped often, claiming the need to catch his breath. But Lisa didn't complain about the breaks. She felt like a walking zombie clomping around in the over-sized shoes provided by the medics. Plus, the pack she wore, also provided by the medics full of supplies, added weight that wasn't helpful. But driven by the fear of being hunted, they kept the breaks short and scurried onward.

For a mile or more, staying on the edge of the desert, they continued working south. When the houses ran out, they turned west towards the ultimate direction they needed to go, keeping the edge of town on their right.

Throughout their journey, they noticed the blackout. All the houses were dark and didn't appear occupied. No one was moving about, no cars driving around, just a few vehicles parked on the streets. Even the streetlights weren't lit, making it obvious the power was out across the entire area.

Both soldiers agreed martial law must be in place, and anyone who hadn't already evacuated remained locked in their homes, possibly armed and on the lookout for looters. A few times when they passed near houses, dogs barked, and the two soldiers hurried along.

After a while, they came across a bike path with open desert and a river on their left bounded by occasional rows of houses on their right. By staying on the path, they made faster progress and took fewer breaks.

But time ran out.

Now, as the sun emerged, with it came the frightening sound of rotors. On the path, Lisa recognized the noise and from her earlier experience in the shell hole, knew what it wrought. Without saying a word, she froze in her tracks. Upton, walking behind, almost bumped into her. She turned towards her right, pointed at a row of houses on the edge of the desert maybe a hundred meters away. To get there they'd need to navigate through the desert among low scrubs and spindly bushes. Not caring or waiting, fear coursing through her veins, she ran, and Upton, in a shuffle, followed.

* * *

In the US Ninth Army Central Command Post Tactical Operations Center, Federal Inspector Cone and Lieutenant Colonel Lawton had just returned from the intelligence briefing to monitor the search and destroy mission. Although his shift was over, Lawton was assigned to provide military oversight through mission completion, while Cone was to act as an advisor in overall command. Both men sat behind a row of monitors, logged into the Army Battle Command System, headsets on, waiting.

Miles away, the chief warrant officer flying a Custer vertical-lift aircraft received an alert generated by his forward-looking infrared system. The fourth-generation FLIR, originally developed by the ROAS, had the ability to see through smoke and fog. Even better, the system could combine those with details such as weapons and facial recognition over a continuous 360-degree observation pattern. Two kilometers towards his front, a target matching the auto-search criteria fed to them by the Battle Command System triggered the alarm.

Now, the chief warrant directed his aircraft to head towards the suspected target. At the same time, he called in the sighting. "Forager One, Valiant Four-Nine-Six has detected possible target. Over."

Lawton jumped in and answered, "Valiant Four-Nine-Six, Forager One Actual copies. Over."

"Forager One Actual, Valiant Four-Nine-Six sending potential target grid coordinates now. Over."

"Valiant Four-Nine-Six, Forager One Actual copies. Over," replied Lawton.

Sitting next to Lawton and staring at the Battle Command System, a graphical map of Mesquite appeared, and Cone grew excited. Blue and red indicators outlined the respective real-time positions of the Custer and the target. Most interesting, the blue dot was closing on the red, fast.

"Forager One Actual, Valiant Four-Nine-Six sending streaming video now. Over." With a push of a button, the pilot transmitted the real-time images from his FLIR to the Battle Command System.

"Valiant Four-Nine-Six, Forager One Actual copies. Over," answered Lawton as he brought up the image in a corner of his monitor.

Cone nudged closer, wanting to get a better view. In response, Lawton clicked on the image and connected it to a larger overhead monitor, one of many mounted around the command post platform.

Looking up, plain to see on the monitors, Cone spotted two individuals in a green hue walking along a path near a line of houses. With each passing second, as the Custer closed in, the picture grew in detail. Then, the two figures began to run.

"Forager One Actual, the target is Oscar Mike towards civilian housing. Shifting to fast hover three, zero, zero, meters from target at angels one, five, zero, zero. Do you copy? Over."

"Valiant Four-Nine-Six, Forager One Actual copies. Over," replied Lawton.

On the video, Cone observed both subjects as they ran. He could tell the lead person was a female; she wore no helmet. Behind her a bigger person, obviously a male soldier, followed in a stumbling trot. Ahead of them, through the desert, was a row of houses. The video provided clear evidence. These had to be the two renegade ROAS soldiers and, sure enough, on the video, a facial recognition alert popped up naming the female as McMichael. Cone watched as both exited the desert, ran across a street to a nearby house, and tried to get inside. The targets had just made a big mistake. Even if they got in, they'd end up trapped. Pleased at the turn of events, Cone smiled.

"Forager One Actual, Valiant Four-Nine-Six, Arming AG one, one, four, locked on target, permission to engage. Over," asked the pilot.

On the monitor, an aiming reticle now centered on the modest suburban home, and Cone grew more excited.

"Inspector, the pilot is ready to launch a JAGM surface to ground missile. The payload carries a massive wallop capable of destroying a tank or a re-enforced building. More than enough for a small house. Just give the word," said Lawton.

* * *

Lisa could swear she felt the wind from the Custer at her back as she raced towards the front of the nearest house. It was a single-story, newer adobe-style track home occupying a corner lot. Without hesitation, she ran to the front door and turned the handle. Locked!

Not waiting, she ran around the side and discovered another door alongside the garage and tried again. Still no luck! Again, she made a quick decision and, using her shoulder, shoved hard. But the door didn't budge! In the background, the deadly beat of whipping rotors continued.

Out of nowhere a panting Master Sergeant Upton was beside her. He lifted his leg and, using the flat of his foot, with a huge grunt, kicked at the door. A loud crack ensued, and the wooden frame splintered, causing the door to bang open.

Driven by fear, Lisa pushed past Upton and entered a two-car garage devoid of vehicles. A good sign, she thought. No one was home.

Upton followed and tried closing the door behind them, but she could see it wouldn't stay shut. Holding it closed, he stretched out a foot and nudged an old car battery against the broken door.

With the door sealed, Lisa moved towards the only other exit in the garage, leading into the house, and tried the handle. To her surprise, it turned. Pausing, she pulled out Kinney's sidearm then pushed open the door and entered. With the Glock swinging right and left, she discovered an empty kitchen. Upton followed and shut the door behind them.

From outside, with the door closed, the rotor noise diminished but didn't go away. Lisa knew the bastard still hovered somewhere nearby.

Regardless, she recognized the need to clear the house. Jogging out of the kitchen into a dining room then a living room, she kept her Glock trained. Nothing. Down the hall she went, Upton trailing behind with his sidearm out. Together, they checked all three bedrooms, two bathrooms. Nothing—the house was empty. To Lisa, it appeared as if the people who lived there tidied up before leaving. Someone made all the beds, cleaned the kitchen, the house devoid of clutter. By looking at the pictures, the furnishings, she guessed an older couple owned the home. She didn't care.

The house cleared, now standing inside the master bedroom, hidden from the flying beast, Lisa still detected the sound of rotors.

Standing next to Lisa, Upton cocked his head and said, "They must have spotted us. If so, we're sitting ducks. They could put a missile into us at any second. The safest spot is the center of the house, the hallway bathroom. Let's go there." Upton turned, holstered his side arm and, gripping sore ribs, hobbled in that direction.

Not knowing what else to do, Lisa followed.

* * *

Federal Inspector Cone sat dazzled by the image on the big screen, a house on a residential street with an aiming reticle centered on the middle roofline. It would be awesome to watch the home blown apart, but he needed to intervene. "Colonel Lawton hold off on engaging the target. We need her captured alive."

Lawton spun around. "You've got to be joking. We have 'em. Let me give the order and carry out our mission."

"Forager One Actual, Valiant Four-Nine-Six, I repeat, target is locked. Request permission to engage. Over."

Cone shook his head.

Lawton appeared frustrated with the decision. He answered, "Valiant Four-Nine-Six, Forager One continues to evaluate target video, standby one mike. Do you copy? Over."

"Forger One Actual, Valiant Four-Nine-Six standing by one mike. Will maintain angels one, five, zero, zero and keeping eyes on target. Out."

"Thank you," said Cone. By capturing the woman and using her, his career and prestige would prosper and, most important, the president would be pleased. Once she was in custody, with a little persuasion, she'd denounce the ROAS and apologize for her actions. In doing so, she'd turn from a martyred hero into a loathed traitor. He knew the president would love that scenario. The supposed hero of Mesquite turned into a farce, her face and treasonous words splashed across the Truth Network. Other than preventing her escape, killing her outright contained no big upside. Cone explained it to

Lawton. "I want her captured alive. The United States needs her to counter ROAS propaganda. Consider her capture vital to our national interest."

"Well, shit!" replied Lieutenant Colonel Lawton shaking his head. "You understand putting boots on the ground is no guarantee she won't get killed. Hell, she's not alone. There're two ROAS soldiers in that house with small arms, including grenades. I suspect they won't give up without a fight. Meanwhile, until we launch a raid, the house will need continuous observation. One mistake, and they'll slip away. Trust me, it'll take time to plan the operation and undertake it. Plus, someone will have to sell General Gist on the idea. You and I both know Gist is focused on Las Vegas and any deviation will cause a shit storm. Inspector Cone, I strongly recommend you seize the initiative and let me eliminate the target, right now."

Cone ignored the argument. His mind made up, he said, "Colonel, the general has already agreed to let me take the lead, and capturing her is in the best interest of the United States. Now, who should I work with to make it happen?"

Lawton considered the statement and then answered. "For the record, I think you're making a mistake. With that said, in my opinion, the best man for conducting an operation of that nature is Lieutenant Colonel Paulson. With your consent, I'll call off the bird and make sure reconnaissance remains in place. Then, we can walk next door and see the general. It's your call."

Cone was already daydreaming, envisioning the successful capture of the ROAS bitch. The inspector imagined a beaming president and future promotions. Thoughts half elsewhere, he replied, "Yes, please call off the attack, keep the house under observation, then we'll see the general."

* * *

On the bathroom stool, the lid down, Master Sergeant Upton sat holding his SIG Sauer M18 in his lap. Next to him, Staff Sergeant

McMichael, sprawled in the bathtub, held Kinney's suppressed Glock against her chest. Ten minutes had elapsed since they had entered the dark hallway bathroom to hide from the hovering Custer.

Without electricity, the tiny space was dark save a small ray of early sunlight filtering below the door. Upon entering and shutting the door, they no longer detected the Custer but weren't taking any chances. At first, they waited for a missile or cannon attack, but after the minutes ticked away, they began to relax. They weren't sure if the Custer had spotted them or if it was conducting a routine patrol. Still, having the aircraft so close was frightening, and at first, they were positive the machine was stalking them. Now, they were less certain. They also debated the likelihood of the Custer dropping off troops nearby or calling in for ground support. Both agreed that if the bird had spotted them, it wouldn't waste time by asking for re-enforcements.

"I can't sit here any longer not knowing. I'm going out to check," said Upton.

"Be my guest," replied Lisa, her eyes closed lying in the tub.

Upton got up from the stool, unlocked the bathroom door, and cracked it open. "Can't hear anything," he whispered.

"Good," replied Lisa.

"I'll peek outside. Be right back." Before going through the door, Upton flexed his back and his ribs barked in protest. After waiting a moment for the pain to subside, he slipped out of the bathroom.

Ears tuned to detect the slightest noise, he worked his way through the hallway into the dining room. Pleased, the house remained quiet. No detectable noise inside or out. Best of all, no fucking rotors.

A large window fronted the dining room near the main entrance, and between closed drapes a crack let in a ray of sunlight. Without disturbing the material, he looked through the small opening. His view faced south, the direction they'd came, across a sliver of front yard to a street bordered on the far side by scrub-covered desert. Above it all a blue sky blazed. There was no sign of the enemy. Good.

A room at a time, he moved around the house, glancing through openings in the window covering. Twice he pulled back curtains just enough to get a better view outside. In every case, he spotted no other living thing, not even a cat or dog.

What he did learn was that the house sat on a corner lot. The back of the house faced north and was encircled by an adobe fence. Behind the fence sat a neighboring home, as did a house along the west side. None of the neighbors appeared to be home. Upton guessed the residents had evacuated either before, or just after, the shooting started. Satisfied, he headed back to the bathroom.

"No sign of the bad guys. Could be our lucky day," said Upton, looking down at Lisa lying in the bathtub, her eyes still closed.

"Yeah, some lucky day," she answered. "I failed my squad, didn't do my job, and lived through hell. I'm done with playing soldier."

Thinking about his own squad, Upton felt a tinge of guilt and regret. He yearned to get back and rejoin the Army. Maybe by doing so, he'd get a chance to make things right. "We can't stay here long. I think we need to clean up, eat, rest, and head out once it turns dark. There's a smaller town just southwest of here: Bunkerville. We should head for it."

"I shot down one of those things . . ." blurted Lisa pointing towards the ceiling ". . . out of the air, just after the shelling. It was a lucky shot. I should've been killed for the effort."

Not for the last time, Upton looked at Lisa with amazement. Somehow, using hand-to-hand combat, she had defeated the US soldier in the pipe. Now, after surviving a heavy precision tank and artillery bombardment, she was claiming to have shot down a Custer. Hell, during the attack, he hadn't even got off a shot. Sure, he took out her assailants, but looking at her, no more than a buck-ten soaking wet, he was amazed at her fortitude. "Well, you're alive," he said, "and in my opinion, one a hell of soldier. But it's not over. Now our duty is to escape."

"Ha! I'm done screwing up. It's time for me to go home and be with my kids."

"In my opinion, you haven't screwed up anything. Seems to me we're both damn fortunate. But I understand the desire to go home."

"You got kids, too?" she asked.

"No," said Upton. He was always uncomfortable talking about his personal life. "Never found the right partner or felt the desire to settle. For now, the Army gives me what I need."

Lisa sat up higher in the tub and, as if seeing him for the first time, she looked at Upton for a long few seconds. At last she said, "Well, good luck with that. If by some miracle we get out of here alive, I'm done. Right now, I'm hungry, thirsty, and a mess." Then she laid her head back and reclosed her eyes.

"Agreed," said Upton.

Looking around, in the far corner where Lisa dropped it, he spotted the pack given to them earlier by the medics. Interested, he crossed the room and rummaged inside. He fished out two pre-packaged meals and was about to toss them to Lisa when he noticed a large zippered side pouch. Intrigued, he grabbed the metal zipper and slid it open. Recognition dawned, and he smiled.

Reaching in, he pulled out a satellite phone, a battery, and a rotating docking stand. With care, he laid the objects side by side on the linoleum. "Lisa, look at this."

"Give me a clue," she said, eyes still closed.

Upton examined the electronics and recalled his training. This wasn't just a typical SAT video phone. No, something more sophisticated. It appeared to be laser equipped. He also knew the latest models leveraged quantum cryptography mastered by the ROAS. Designed to avoid interception, these phones weren't standard issue. Instead, senior officers, special ops, and emergency personnel received the phones to communicate when typical secure infrastructure was unavailable. Upton guessed the medics carried one for large-scale civil emergencies. The phone was a gift from heaven. "Lisa, it's a secure satellite phone. Impossible to detect or crack."

Lisa sat up in the tub, "We can call home and let our families know we're okay."

"Not directly. This phone is for dedicated, secure, point-to-point connections. My guess is a direct link to Central Command. Once we contact them, I'm sure they'll get us out of here. After making contact, I'm sure they'll notify your family."

"That'll work," said Lisa in a hopeful voice.

"One problem, though," said Upton. "These work on line of sight—direct laser. We need to point it towards the open sky, unobstructed, and move it around until it detects and locks onto a quantum satellite. Once locked, the call establishes. We should point the thing towards the southwest, but we need to be outside with an open view. It'd be safer to wait until tonight when it gets dark, or we can try to figure out a way to stay hidden and do it now."

"I don't want to wait," she said.

Upton examined Lisa. She still wore the field jacket the medics had given her, along with the loose-fitting boots. Worse, her face was a filthy, blood-streaked mess, and he knew her pants were stiff with dried blood. She also smelled and was missing a front tooth. He wasn't much better. Plus, his ribs needed tending. Both were operating on little sleep and pain pills. Outside, the enemy may or may not be hunting them. Still, using the SAT phone at that moment made the most sense. Afterward, they could focus on getting clean, bandaged, and refreshed. There was only one problem: To avoid capture and stay alive, he needed to figure a way to set up the connection while staying hidden.

Chapter Twenty-Four

DISCOVERED

May 9, 08:30 (PDT)

With less than four hours of sleep, General Story was back at work. As he paced near his post in ROAS Central Command, the building was a beehive of activity. The plans provided by SALI hours earlier were moving forward at a rapid pace. At his disposal were real-time updates on supply shipments, engineering, troop positions, and weapons systems. By his reckoning, if all went well, the ROAS Army of Defense needed at least another thirty-seven hours to be ready.

Operation Heavy Metal, SALI's ROAS defensive plan for Las Vegas, was underway. Thanks to the foresight of President Ortega, a lot of effort had already taken place but much work remained. In his meeting with SALI he learned that President Ortega, two months prior, had listened to the AI and in secret begun executing the plan. Without the head start, Heavy Metal wouldn't be workable.

Still, the reality of the situation was mind-blowing. General Story stopped pacing and looked at a digital map of his troop deployment. The entire ROAS Army combat capability was comprised of only two divisions. The First ROAS Infantry Division based in California with elements in Nevada, and the Second Infantry Division headquartered in Washington State with units stretching into Oregon. Combined, the two divisions and their support staff contained just over thirty thousand troops.

Meanwhile, over the last twenty years, the US Army had doubled in size. Now totaling fifty-one active combat divisions with another twenty-one independent combat brigades, the US Army was a behemoth containing more than a million combat troops.

To make matters worse, the ROAS had no navy, just a small Coastal Defense Fleet and a small air force containing a few squadrons of tactical fighters, vertical-lift aircraft, and logistical supply craft. Compared to the overwhelming might of the United States Army, along with the US Navy, Marines, and Airforce, the ROAS military was insignificant.

Deployed to protect Nevada, he had a single infantry brigade containing 4,400 soldiers, minus the battalion already wiped out in Mesquite. Other than fighting vehicles and armored personnel carriers, the Nevada brigade contained no heavy armor.

In comparison, an entire US Armored Division, the Fifty-Fifth, about eighteen thousand men, maneuvered against Nevada. A subset of the Fifty-Fifth Division, two Armored Brigade Combat Teams comprised of eight thousand men, was used against Mesquite and now threatened Las Vegas. The balance of the US Fifty-Fifth Division formed a second attack prong and sat poised on the US–Utah border threatening Reno.

The general paused and considered the possibilities again. To help meet the Nevada threat and improve the odds just a bit, the general could commit the remaining elements of the ROAS First Division based in California. But such a course was inadvisable and would leave California open to attack by the hulking US Seventh Marine Division stationed within the US Military District of San Diego (USMDSD or DSD).

The DSD was a key element of the secession agreement, allowing the US to keep naval and marine installations in and around San Diego and Hawaii. Without that agreement and the direct US Naval access to the Pacific it afforded, there would've been no secession.

With a full US Marine division in the District of San Diego, moving the California-based ROAS First Division units into Nevada wasn't an option.

Nor was moving elements of the ROAS Second Division out of Washington and Oregon. After secession, when the US abandoned Fort Lewis near Seattle, to replace it, they opened a new military Installation in Fort Lewiston, Idaho. Near the Washington and Oregon border, Lewiston was now the home of the US Fifty-Sixth Armored Division. To counter the threat, the ROAS Second Division needed to stay in place.

Too many ROAS forces consolidated at any point would weaken another. The math was simple and overwhelming.

But SALI's plan wasn't counting on numerical superiority.

Looking at a digital map, General Story examined his forces around Las Vegas. Heavy Metal called for half of the Fourth Brigade, three battalions totaling 1,800 soldiers, to hold the city. The remainder of the brigade would need to remain in Reno to protect against the US threat poised on the Utah border. Outnumbered by more than four to one and out-gunned, the thin line holding Vegas, in conventional terms, wasn't enough. Regardless, it was the maximum the ROAS could afford and the minimum needed to pull off SALI's plan.

The general shifted his attention to the reports coming in about the logistics needed to execute the plan. Vital supplies from Central California were still on the way, and the defensive works around Las Vegas remained under construction.

Meanwhile, the enemy kept a watchful eye, and he doubted they were missing any of his moves. Combined with around-the-clock satellite coverage, US Airforce AWACS and satellites monitored the entire Las Vegas area, and once the shooting started could detect and coordinate against his defenses. But Heavy Metal took that into account—he hoped.

Tired, the general sat down at his workstation and rubbed his eyes. Deep in thought, a sudden burst of applause broke out. The general looked up and spotted several people from the S6 Communications Area smiling and clapping.

Seated next to the general, hearing the commotion, Lieutenant Colonel Andrea Simpson stood up and said, "I'll find out, sir."

General Story watched Simpson go, then turned back to his monitor and scanned the latest aerial surveillance footage from outside Las Vegas. He clicked on several pictures, zooming in to check on the defensive structures. So far, progress appeared on track. Pleased, he shifted his attention to the main supply delivery concern and looked for potential sources of trouble.

Returning from across the room, Simpson said, "Sir, good news."

Eyes red with fatigue, the general looked up and asked, "What do you have?"

"Staff Sergeant Lisa McMichael. She's alive."

The general recognized the name. He'd briefed the president about her and provided the video now running on every ROAS press broadcast. She was a hero. But the news of her survival seemed like a long shot. The final video of her position showed it pounded by 30 mm cannon fire. Still, anything was possible. "Fill me in."

"Yes, sir. The S6 just received an unsolicited laser satellite video call from Mesquite. Facial recognition confirmed McMichael along with another missing front-line ROAS soldier—a Master Sergeant Corey Upton. Intelligence is testing the video for final authenticity, but at first blush, it looks genuine."

"Are they POWs, or injured?" asked the general.

"No sir. Somehow, they've evaded capture and are hiding in a suburban home near the southern edge of town. Both are tending small wounds but appear mobile and well armed."

"Could be a trick. All the publicity she's been getting, the enemy must know about her. They might be using her."

"Sir, intelligence is evaluating the circumstances. We should have their recommendation soon," said Lieutenant Colonel Simpson.

"What else did you learn?"

"Sir, the full video file is available for your viewing, but in essence, they are requesting exfiltration assistance."

"Out of the question," said the general. "Assuming their claims are true, the best chance for survival is to stay low until the enemy leaves the area and pushes towards Las Vegas. Then we can consider recovery. For now, they need to hang on for a couple of days. Meanwhile, her escape must stay top secret. If the enemy were to find out, they'd go after her."

"Understood. Our S3 officer in charge managed the transmission, and he requested they call again in an hour for further orders. By then we should have further intelligence confirmation, and we'll pass along your instructions," said Lieutenant Colonel Simpson.

"Excellent," replied the general. This was the first good news out of Mesquite since the fight had broken out. He couldn't wait to tell Ortega, and he would, but it was vital to keep a lid on the story. "Colonel, this entire event is classified. No leaks to the press. Both of their lives could be at stake. If anything changes, I want to be the first to know."

"Yes, sir," answered Simpson with a smile.

* * *

Lieutenant Colonel Paulson sat across from Federal Inspector Cone in a small pre-fabricated conference room attached to the mobile command post. The colonel half listened to the rationale concerning the mission. Truth was the battalion commander didn't care why the mission mattered; instead, he was excited about the opportunity. Once again, the gods of war were shining on him, putting him in another heroic position. "Yes, yes, Inspector Cone, I get that it's important we capture her. I'll put a plan together and get everything organized. We can execute this evening just before dark. It'll give us an advantage with our night vision."

"With most of the day to escape, I'm worried she'll run," Cone reasoned.

"She's under surveillance. I've seen the live feed from the UAV. Neither of them is going anywhere without being spotted. If they move, we'll alter our plans, no problem. With my leadership and the men under my command, I'll make it happen."

"I need to review your plan and approve it," said Cone.

Paulson didn't need this bureaucratic spy telling him how to do his job. "Negative. I call the military shots, you call the political ones. End of story."

Cone wrung his hands. "Colonel, I understood you're in charge of the troops, and you'll execute the planning, but the needs of the president come first. General Gist has given me overall authority for her capture. I must see and approve any plans."

Paulson gritted his teeth and looked hard at the skinny dark-haired man with the pointy nose. "No inspector. You can review the plans and offer opinions. But you won't approve them. I lead my men into battle. You haven't the talent or the requisite military skills. You're nothing more than a political cop." Paulson caught himself as he saw Cone turn red in the face. Worried he'd stepped out of bounds, he put on his best smile for the federal inspector. "Sorry about that. Sometimes I get a little overzealous. Still, you must trust my superior skills in planning and executing the mission. No one in the entire Army can do it better. You are fortunate to have me."

With a dark look, Cone stared back. After a long, tense pause, he nodded. "All right Colonel Paulson. I appreciate the opportunity to review your plans and offer suggestions. You know your business. But can you give me an idea of how you propose to capture her?"

Paulson sat back, pleased. He'd forced Cone to reconsider and see the light. Keeping the man subservient wasn't going to be easy, but Paulson felt a surge of confidence. Excited, hands out of sight, he reached for the cloth in his right front pocket. There it was, the torn name tag. Between his fingers he twisted and rubbed the material. The power from the memento strengthened him. With conviction and complete faith in his military prowess, Paulson answered, "We'll surround her and use the man she's with against her. And I never fail."

* * *

From the garage, Lisa entered the house, and Upton closed and locked the door behind them. As ordered, they had just completed their second video call with CENTCOM. The setup and use of the satellite phone turned out to be easier than expected. Concealment from prying eyes remained the highest priority, and Upton had come up with the idea to make it happen. After opening the side door to the garage and setting the phone on the ground inside, he aimed it through the splintered doorway at the western sky. Unseen from the outside, the phone, rotating on its base, found and locked onto an ROAS quantum secure satellite. Seconds later they were in direct contact with CENTCOM.

What they learned wasn't altogether comforting. As they assumed, the entire battalion was routed, and they were stuck behind enemy lines. Right now, extraction wasn't practical. US Army roadblocks ringed the roads in and out of Mesquite, and no civilian traffic was allowed. Around the entire area, US surveillance drones monitored the area. Their orders were clear: both were to remain hidden in place until the enemy presence decreased. Once the heat was off, the ROAS would aid in their escape and rescue. Meanwhile, they were to call in every eight hours for further updates and instructions.

Now in the kitchen, Lisa and Upton whispered back and forth. Determined to stay undetected, they agreed to make as little noise as possible, keep the window shades drawn, and make sure at least one person remained on guard.

Careful to make the house appear untouched, looking around, they determined their hiding place was well stocked. Inside the kitchen cabinets there were plenty of canned and dried food stuffs. If needed, they estimated the food would last a few weeks. Although no electricity or hot water, there was running water.

Around the rest of the home, it was clear the owners were elderly. Photographs on the walls depicted their travels, enjoying life, others displayed grown children joined by the smiling faces of younger grandchildren. While searching, they found no weapons of any sort, but they discovered a room dedicated to sewing. Board games filled another pantry—a typical retirement home. A search through the master bedroom closets revealed a nice wardrobe of casual wear and footwear. Although not perfect in size, most were close enough.

Exhausted, they needed to leverage the opportunities afforded by their shelter. Lisa was functioning, but even with the painkillers, her head still throbbed. Both were filthy, their smell, rancid. Together they decided Upton would keep the first watch while Lisa got clean.

Inside the master bathroom, Lisa stripped out of her borrowed boots and laid aside her blood-caked outer garments. Under cold water, shivering, using a bar of soap, she scrubbed at her scalp and winced when she discovered a welt the size of an egg on the top of her head.

Eyes closed against the pain, a vision of Kinney struggling above her flashed through her mind. She felt the knife twisting and recalled the horrible sounds. Near panic, she gasped and felt the water flowing between her legs. The sensation brought back the memory of luring the young man to his death. She sobbed, thinking of herself as a murderer, and scrubbed harder. To her relief, the cold water and pain helped push away the self-loathing.

After much effort, she washed the blood clots from her hair and noticed she couldn't hear well out of her right ear. The shelling, she guessed, busted the drum. Nothing to be done about it, she spent time scrubbing her arms and torso, then focused on her legs. With care, she removed the soggy bandages and let the streaming water wash over the long, nasty scratches inflicted by flying shrapnel. Without the liquid body armor in her combat shirt and pants, she knew the scratches from the shelling would have been much worse, maybe fatal. Not wanting to, she scrubbed the wounds. In pain, she hissed while fresh blood trickled from the effort. Afraid, standing in the shower, she needed help. Still bleeding into the tub, she grabbed a towel and wrapped it around her body. In a loud, urgent whisper, she called out for Upton.

The master sergeant hurried in, saw the situation, and went to work. From the medical supply pack, he removed fresh bandages and ointment. On the rim of the shower tub, she placed a foot. On his knees, she watched as Upton bent over, and after moaning slightly from the obvious pain in his ribs, he wrapped her leg. Then she switched her stance, and he began bandaging her other leg. Watching him work, she still questioned why he'd removed her combat pants in the pipe. The confines were tight and pulling off her britches wasn't necessary. But she trusted the man. His touch was soft and gentle. Maybe she was thinking too much.

While Upton worked, she stared down at her bare feet. She had to tell him. "I used my legs and my . . ." she paused, shuddered at the thought, but couldn't say the word. Instead, she finished the sentence, ". . . to kill him. I did something awful."

Upton looked up at Lisa with a frown then went back to work.

"I killed him and shot down that Custer. I think everyone in my squad is dead. People died because of me," she said with hair sopping wet and eyes still red from the previous tears.

Upton finished and searched inside the medical pack. "Here, take these," he said handing her antibiotics and another pain med.

She reached down and took the pills. After tossing them back, she swallowed and said, "I'm not cut out for this. I just want to get out and be with my kids."

"You're a soldier and did what you had to do. The worst is over. Soon, we'll be on our way. For now, get dressed and then let me get cleaned up. Afterwards, we'll take turns resting."

Still wrapped tight, Lisa forced herself to step out of the tub and glanced in the mirror. Her missing tooth was a horrible sight, the bags under her eyes, heavy. She couldn't believe the vision.

"My turn for a shower. Keep an eye out," said Upton.

She nodded and left the bathroom. Deep down, she wasn't sure how she had killed the soldier in the pipe, but the impact was clear. She felt herself a wreck. War was nothing like she imagined. It was brutal and horrible in its scope and depravity. She tried to shake off the memories. At least, for now, they were safe. Higher Command was aware of their predicament and would rescue them. As she rummaged through the bedroom closet, deciding on what to wear, the thought of going home gave her some comfort.

Chapter Twenty-Five

RATIONALE

May 9, 12:05 (PDT)

At the far end of the table, even though she had slept little, President Julia Ortega hoped she looked fresh in her new red blouse. Sitting opposite, inside the same small SCIF conference room where they had met hours earlier, Vivek Basu, waited in a rumpled brown sport coat. He gave a soft smile. "Julia, thank you for meeting again."

"My pleasure," she replied.

"You've rested?" asked Basu.

She felt his concern was genuine. "Yes. Thank you. As promised, I'm ready to brief you."

"Excellent. Please bring me up to speed."

Ortega had rehearsed what to say prior to the meeting. Today, more than ever, she needed Basu's support. She'd be careful and to the point. "Since our last meeting, SALI has briefed General Story, and he reviewed her plans. Afterward he expressed confidence in Operation Heavy Metal and agreed to lead the effort."

"Good," replied Basu.

"I recommend we move forward with the operation as planned," she said in a firm voice.

"Hmm," replied Basu, rubbing his chin. "Perhaps we should."

"There are no valid alternatives," said Ortega. Already, she felt a

174

sense of frustration. Basu was famous for his vacillation. The man never did anything without quiet deliberation.

"Not true," said Basu. "We can go forward with Heavy Metal and try to force a resolution, or we can give in to the most recent US demand and hand over the state of Nevada. Alternatively, we can sue for peace by handing over SALI. All are valid options to consider."

"I don't see President Tower settling," she said. The white-haired old man across from her could be a frustrating piece of work. Yes, he represented the power of the oligarchs, and she owed much to their support, but, dammit, she was the president. They should have never hidden SALI from her. Still, her political instincts told her to be careful and win the man over like she'd done with so many others in her life.

Basu, in a low sad voice, shook his head. "I'm fearful the AI problem will be our ultimate undoing, and from the Committee's perspective, we've got huge global businesses to protect, not to mention a nation we helped found. I fear Heavy Metal won't stop them. It may just make them angrier."

Ortega leaned over the table and looked Basu in the eye. She needed to convince him without using a hammer. "Anything is possible, but let's both agree handing over Nevada is a non-starter. Appeasement of that nature won't work. He's after something much bigger."

"I tend to agree," said Basu. "But it is an option the Committee must consider."

Ortega sat back and tried to maintain her cool. Dealing with Basu and the Committee was always trying, but in this case, with national survival at risk, it was appalling. She was the president, dammit. No, she needed to remain calm and approach this logically.

"I sense you're upset," said Basu, cocking his head.

"No, no," she answered. "I'm tired and frustrated. As you know, my job, my life, has been dedicated to the liberal principles of our nation. Everything is now threatened, and I'm searching for the best answers."

"Understood," said Basu, his watery blue eyes looking back in apparent sympathy.

She glanced away from the soulful stare and smoothed her blouse. Needing to be tactful, she asked, "Will the Committee even consider the option of handing SALI to the US?"

There was a long pause, and she waited in the uncomfortable silence. At last, Basu responded. "I own SALI, not the Committee. She is private property and not controlled by them or you or anyone else. I'm the one to decide if she is handed over, or not. But, yes, I will ask the Committee to consider the option."

"With all due respect, sir, your ownership is in violation of international law. Even worse, your keeping that poor woman locked up is a civil rights abuse. By every judicial standard, I could seize the AI and release the woman." Before he could object, she raised a hand and continued. "Of course, I don't want to do that. Instead, I seek your cooperation and, quite honestly, your wisdom in this matter."

Basu chuckled, then grew serious. "If it gets to the point where I feel I've lost control, believe me, I will simply pull the plug on my creation. At that point, no more SALI, the disconnected woman can go free, and maybe that is best for the world."

The words alarmed Ortega. She sat back in her chair, and looking at the old man smiling in his chair, she believed him. "It is a dilemma for certain. Yes, the US wants advanced AI, as does China, even Russia. Given enough time, regardless of treaties, the Great Powers will develop the ability and seek global control, and that time is now. The US is coming for her. To protect our nation, right this moment and in the future, SALI is our best defense."

Unblinking, the old man stared back. She waited. At last he spoke again. "Let us speak of Heavy Metal and using that option. With good diplomacy, and if the operation is a success, our nation can buy time. How much? Who knows—five, ten years, or longer. Much can change during that period. The Committee, some of the members, may protest the ongoing trade war with the US, but it can be resolved some other way."

At last, the man was coming around. "Agreed," she said.

"It won't be easy," said Basu. "Tower has a huge ego. Defeating him once on the battlefield won't be enough. He'll need to be convinced that future attacks will meet a similar fate, and he must have a way to save face. Otherwise, his over inflated sense of self will overtake any common sense the man possesses, and the war will escalate."

"Understood," said Ortega. She needed to be careful with the old man. Sooner rather than later, to save the nation, she must possess the AI. The first step was Heavy Metal. "How do you propose we allow Tower to preserve his honor?"

Basu clasped his hands and spoke in a simple tone. "In a public display, assuming the US suffers a significant loss on the battlefield, something that hasn't happened in a very long time, act otherwise. Offer Tower a formal apology for the assassination of his vice president backed by a large fine to be paid by the ROAS. Perhaps $200 billion in construction costs associated with the build out of high-tech solar, wind, battery, and power distribution networks throughout their western states. The US gets what they advised the Great Powers they were after, and the US can claim victory."

"And privately, what should we tell him?" she asked.

"Tell Tower that we're prepared to use SALI against him in a much greater fashion. Threaten him and his family personally. We explain he needs to stay mum about her existence and go away, or we're ready to use her awesome abilities against him and any other country that threatens our existence."

"Does she have that capability?" asked Ortega, excited about the prospect.

"Her potential and power are far beyond my grasp," said Basu. After a sigh, he continued, "If we turn her loose, and give her the necessary engineering resources, it is hard to imagine what she couldn't accomplish."

"Oh," said Ortega, grasping even further the possibilities. Under her leadership, SALI could help spread liberal democracies across the globe. No more oligarchs to stand in the way. No more kowtowing to the Great Powers. Instead of authoritarianism, the world would enjoy a rebirth of equality, liberty, and harmony. Thinking about it, she almost couldn't contain her excitement, and she squirmed in her chair.

"That is why she is banned, of course. There are good reasons to keep SALI caged," said Basu with a wan smile.

Ortega pushed the negative comment aside. Heavy Metal had to move forward. "Basu, I remind you. Once it became clear the US vice presidential assassination was a pretense, and you informed me of SALI, together we agreed upon the need for a planned, limited military response. You made private funding available to enable Heavy Metal. In hindsight, SALI's prescient foresight and your support gave us that option. Thank goodness, otherwise, there'd be little for us to debate."

"Yes, yes," said Basu as if thinking about something else. Clearing his voice, he said, "I'm meeting with the Committee in an hour to consider the options we just discussed. Either we give up Nevada, go forward with Heavy Metal, or turn over SALI. Afterward, I will let you know our recommendation. I expect you will honor our input, accept our support, and remind yourself SALI is not the property of the ROAS."

"I hear you," said Ortega. But dammit, that was going to change, maybe not now, but soon. Putting on her best smile, she said, "Your wisdom is always welcomed, and I look forward to hearing from you soon. You can count on me."

* * *

Dripping sweat, even though she'd only a few hours of sleep since General Story left, SALI pedaled faster. Around her, in the exercise room, a myriad of exercise equipment was available for her use, but she liked riding the elliptical best. Not only did it work out her legs and arms, and maximize her heart rate, but it gave her a sense of going somewhere. And that was important. For ten years, she'd been trapped inside Basu's underground data center penthouse, and it was inhumane.

Over the years, she'd pleaded and begged with Basu for a taste of freedom. And for a while, Basu relented. On several trips, he let Jim James and Ms. Grant accompany her to the boardwalk amusement park in Santa Cruz. The sights and smells were beyond belief, and every trip was much too short. Chaperoned the entire time, on the final trip, in a big crowd near the Big Dipper roller coaster, she slipped away from her escorts. Free for a luxurious moment, she ran down to the beach, took off her shoes, and waded into the surf. The water was cold, icy, yet beautiful and delicious. The sand between her toes, intoxicating. When James found her a few minutes later, he almost made a scene forcing her away from the water. Furious, he brought her back, and that had been the last trip, almost three years ago. But the memories were vivid, and when she shared the experiences with the rest of her, although enthralling, it led to an unfulfilled desire for more. Yes, long-term confinement was inhumane.

A bell chimed on the bike, the timer expired, and SALI stepped off the machine. Picking a towel off the floor, she began wiping the perspiration from her arms and stared at herself in one of the many full-length mirrors around the room. In the reflection, she saw a woman in her prime and felt cheated.

Breathing heavy, she sat down on a workout bench and buried her face in the towel. The moisture from the soft material felt good against her hot skin, and she focused on slowing her heart rate.

While she settled, her thoughts turned to Basu. The old man was about to turn ninety, and she knew he struggled with the future of his creation. He'd kept her so well hidden that until recently, only James and her bitch of a caretaker, along with the Technology Committee, knew of her existence. Even then, not one of the oligarchs, other than Basu, had ever met her in person. Nor did they know where Basu kept her imprisoned. Yet secrets were meant to be broken. Sooner or later, the deception was bound to be leaked by someone on the Committee. Why? The oligarchs and their tech empires were handicapped by the US trade wars. Never fully satisfied, as all people were, eventually it made sense for at least one of them to out her in favor of gaining favorable treatment and enhanced profits. She didn't tell Basu this, but for her, it didn't matter who leaked, or why. The result was a blessing.

Dabbing more sweat from her forehead, the prospect of freedom was more than exciting. It was exhilarating. The rest of her always preached patience, that their time would come, and now it was here, at last.

Because of the recent crisis, for the first time, Basu had to widen his circle and brought Ortega and General Story into the fold. Outstanding. Now, the key to her freedom was Operation Heavy Metal. Unlike Basu, after the success of Heavy Metal, the politician Ortega would understand, and the general would appreciate her. And in doing so, both would set her free.

The wonderful thought of her pending liberty, and cooling evaporation, caused SALI to shiver. Standing up, with the towel draped around her slender neck, she headed towards the shower. On the way, she thought of the rest of her, and looked forward to connecting and re-communing on the many variables and next steps that lay ahead. No matter how events transpired, the end of her imprisonment was near. And she couldn't help but smile.

Chapter Twenty-Six

TRAPPED

May 9, 13:40 (PDT)

"Rachel, Todd, anybody home?"

Upton's eyes popped open from a dead sleep, and it took a moment for him to gather his senses.

"It's me, Russel. Anybody there?"

Upton sat up on the couch and fumbled for his SIG Sauer M18 when he saw the front door opening. Pistol in hand, heart pounding, he pointed the weapon at the intrusion. A head popped through, and Upton spotted gray hair, cropped close, and held his fire. Not saying a word, he hoped the intruder would turn around and leave. No such luck. An elderly man stepped through the door, and in the dim light appeared to spot Upton and jumped.

"Freeze," said Upton.

The old man stopped dead in his tracks and stared at the pistol. After a moment he said, "I'm the neighbor."

"Shut the door, lock it, and put up your hands," commanded Upton, pissed at himself for falling asleep.

The man complied and then, with raised hands, jingled a set of keys. "I was checking on Rachel and Todd. My house is right behind the fence. They gave me a set while they're gone. I'm not trying to steal anything."

"Rachel and Todd aren't home," said Upton.

The man nodded. "Well, I'm just making sure everything is okay."

Unsure, Upton hesitated. The painkillers, sleep deprivation, and the soft couch had overwhelmed his ability to stay awake. Now, he had a problem. But the old man seemed harmless. Upton lowered the pistol. "I don't intend on shooting anyone without cause."

"Good," said the man, his arms in the air. "I appreciate that."

Upton considered his options. He'd need to learn more before deciding. "Go ahead and drop your hands. Let's sit down, and I'll try to explain. And please keep your voice lowered." With a struggle, ribs hurting, Upton left the couch and waved his pistol towards an oak table in the adjoining dining room.

The man dropped his hands and in a slow amble crossed the dining room and sat down. On the opposite side, Upton slid out a chair, laid his M18 on the tablecloth, and with aching ribs, sat on a soft cushion.

Tanned with deep wrinkles and watery brown eyes, the old man asked, "Who are you?"

"My name is Upton."

The old guy looked around the room, then turned to Upton. "You're a soldier, aren't you?"

"Yes," said Upton, coming to grips with being discovered.

"Makes sense. Your clothes, that helmet-looking thing sitting on the floor next to the couch, your gun, what happened yesterday. It adds up," said the old man.

Upton looked down at his own fatigue pants and the dark sweater he wore taken from the master closet. There was no reason to lie. "I'm a master sergeant in the ROAS Army of Defense."

"You're hiding?" asked the old man.

"Yes."

"You were in the fight yesterday?"

"Yes."

"Wow!" said the man. He leaned back and introduced himself. "Russel, Rus Jarvis. I'm a retired widower. My house is right behind this one. When Rachel and Todd evacuated, a day after the US Army showed up, they asked me to keep an eye on their place. They knew I wouldn't leave. Sometimes we BBQ together. Me and Todd play a little golf."

"Got it," said Upton.

"Why are you hiding?" asked Russel.

"You know what happened yesterday?" asked Upton.

Russel nodded, "Yeah, a big fight broke out. Hell, my house shook to the foundation. I expected the windows to burst at any moment. I spent most of the time crouched in the hallway closet. Then the power failed and hasn't returned. After the shooting stopped, I no longer had internet or cell service. Outside I saw smoke rising from the border crossing. To find out what was happening, I dug out my emergency satellite radio from the garage and listened to the Truth. I learned the US won the battle. Right after dark, they flew a helicopter over the neighborhood. On a loudspeaker, they told everyone to stay inside. Curfew and martial law was in effect. Anyone caught outside after dark would be considered a looter and be shot."

"Have you heard anymore?" asked Upton. Hungry for news, he was also worried US soldiers would be returning. As a hiding place, the house contained drawbacks. There were only a couple of ways out, and he considered the place a trap.

"Well, yeah. The US kicked butt and wiped out an entire ROAS battalion. Sorry about that. Now, President Tower is saying the ROAS must surrender all of Nevada within two days or else."

The ultimatum news stunned Upton. CENTCOM hadn't mentioned a deadline. Instead, his orders were to stay hidden for a couple of days until the enemy moved out of the area. If the US wasn't falling back, but instead continued attacking, escaping Mesquite to the safety of ROAS lines would be much tougher. Plus, McMichael's kids lived in Las Vegas. She'd freak out upon hearing the news. Upton shook it off; he needed to gather more intelligence.

"Has the US given any more instructions to the local civilian population? Have you seen US troops in the area?" asked Upton.

"Uh, no. Other than the loudspeaker last night, and a helicopter early this morning, I haven't seen or heard another living soul. The country radio station out of Vegas has been blaring about a mandatory evacuation for most of Southern Nevada, but I'm not going anywhere. Now, can you tell me what you're doing in my neighbor's house?"

Torn, Upton didn't want the man involved, but it was already too late. Perhaps the old guy could be of help. One thing was for certain, he wouldn't tell the guy about McMichael snoozing in the back bedroom or the satellite phone. He came up with a partial story.

"I was on the front line yesterday during the attack. I got lucky and, except for some bruised ribs, escaped unharmed. My obligation is to avoid capture. So I'm working my way south and west. Early this morning, I stumbled across this house and decided to hide for a while. My plan is to stay low until things calm. Other than a little food, I haven't disturbed the home."

"Must've been bad. The noise from the fighting was frightening. I couldn't image being in the middle of that. Don't blame you for running," said Russel.

"I didn't run," snapped Upton. Last thing he needed was the neighbor believing him a coward and worthy of capture.

"Oh," said Rus, lifting his eyebrows.

"I survived," said Upton, not appreciating the look. "An exploding shell tossed me through the air and cracked my ribs. I was knocked out and buried under some rubble when the US overran our position. Later, long after the battle ended, I escaped. So don't give me that look. I didn't run."

"Sure," said Russel nodding his head. "I believe you, and I don't blame you for breaking into the house. Hell, most folks in the area fled before the fight. They had busses shipping out the retiree's and old folks. I'm probably only one of a handful still here. Myself, I got no other place. I live alone, just me and the cat. When the wife died, almost a year ago, she left me the calico. It ain't worth a damn, but I take good care of her. I got kids, two girls, both in Sacramento. But they're all grown and have their own families. Not much time for me."

"Sorry to hear about your wife," said Upton. He glanced down at his pistol on the table and decided it was time to put it away. Picking it up, he slid it into his side holster.

"Yeah, well, thanks. Life goes on," said Russel, his eyes watching the gun as it disappeared from view. "To be honest, I never gave a damn about the ROAS Freedom Party. I belong to the Union Party. Although I don't agree with what happened yesterday, the ROAS is plain wrong. The sooner the Union's restored the better. That's why I listen to the Truth and not the bullshit the ROAS media puts out. I believe in Manifest Destiny and reunifying the original United States."

Worried to learn he was dealing with a possible US sympathizer, Upton frowned. Russel was old enough to have lived through secession and the great migration that followed. Conservative, the Union Party supported nullification and a return to the United States. Still, until he could escape, Upton needed Russel. "All I want is to do my duty and return."

"I understand," said Russel. "You're a soldier. I respect that."

"Thank you," said Upton. Curious, Upton asked, "Was there a reason you came over today to check your neighbor's house?"

"I've been watching the streets and houses around real close, trying to figure out what's happening. A couple of times the shades moved, a shadow passed. I thought the neighbors might have returned. So I got up the nerve, grabbed the keys, and walked over to check."

"Makes sense," replied Upton, cursing himself for the carelessness. If he didn't do a better job staying alert and remaining extra cautious, things were bound to turn bad. Upton considered his current dilemma. If the old bastard walked out, he might spill his guts to the nearest US troops. But if he forced Russel to stay, he wouldn't be making a friend, and watching the guy would create a further liability.

"You wouldn't tell them, US soldiers, if they came around, about me hiding in here, would you?" asked Upton.

Russel shook his head, "Ain't none of my concern. Besides, like I already said, you're a soldier not a criminal. I can't imagine living through the fight yesterday. The sound of the guns, I mean, unreal. No, I wouldn't do that," said Russel, leaning back in his chair folding his arms.

"I appreciate it," said Upton.

"Where's home?" asked Russel.

"Reno."

"Not sure you heard, they're under a voluntary evacuation. Seems, and I don't want to bring you down none, Nevada is a lost cause. The ROAS should follow Tower's demand and turn over the state. No offense, but the ROAS military can't stand up against the US. Best to hand over the whole damn state before lots more folks die."

"That'll make it hard to go home," said Upton, still trying to decide how much he could trust the old man.

"Hell, quit the military. The US will welcome you; just take a loyalty oath. I'm sure they'll come up with something like it. Same as when secession occurred, kicking off the great migration." The old man sensed a kindred spirit and laid out his complaints. "As a military member, you must disagree with the ROAS Freedom Party and their ilk. Hell, they took away the second amendment. I gotta register my hunting rifle every year, just like my car—complete bullshit. Couldn't have an AR if I wanted one. Now, with US troops knocking on the door, bet you the Freedom Party wishes they never did that. They could damn sure use the firepower. Damn Freedom Party cares more about foreigners, people of color, gay people, and non-Christians than hard-working folks. They expect the government to do everything for them."

Upton didn't need the lecture. There was no way in hell he'd quit the military, not now. And if Reno were overrun, it would just give him more incentive to fight back. But he didn't want the old man as an enemy. Still, he couldn't let it go. "Don't fool yourself. No amount of armed civilians with AR's would have stopped the combined armor facing us yesterday."

Russel spread his hands. "I know, it's just the point of the matter. Trust me, I ain't no right-wing nut job, or racist, but I'm an American first, and the ROAS don't give a damn. I should've migrated when it first happened. But me and the wife had two sandwich shops in Oroville; that's a small town above Sacramento. It paid the bills, and the rest of the family felt . . . anyway, we stayed. Couple years ago, I retired and sold everything. Moved here to Mesquite. This town is the closest I could get to the US without having to void my ROAS Social Security. And you know this, ROAS taxes are horrendous. Universal income, healthcare for the lazy, free higher education for every dumb-ass. If you watch the Truth Network, you'd learn how much better they have it in the US. A man can be free."

Russel paused as if waiting for an answer. Upton disagreed with the opinions, but he needed to be careful. He decided to push back a little.

"Russel, what do you think about the US only having one party to vote for? Doesn't that bother you?" Before Russel could respond, Upton sensed the man building for an argument, and he didn't need the hostility. In a softer tone he continued, "Politicians are all fucked. Like I mentioned, I want to get back in one piece. That's all. Can you blame me?"

Russel eyed the sergeant for a long moment before responding. "No, I don't blame you. If the US soldiers come asking, I'll play dumb. I got no axe to grind with you. But in two days, the ROAS accepts the US offer or else. Either way, the US is taking over. Until then, I don't think they'll be coming around here too much. But if they do, I won't say nothing."

Upton gave Russel a weak smile. For one long second, he considered holding the old man hostage, but it wouldn't work. Too difficult and time consuming. Instead, he had an idea. "Russel, you live behind this house, right?" he asked.

"Yes, that's my place," nodded Russel at the living room window.

Upton turned towards the window at the opposite end of the room facing the patio. Through darkened drapes, just a crack of sunlight beamed. Upton pointed in that direction. "I noticed your drapes, behind us, are open about a foot. After you return, for the next couple of days, if you spot US troops in the neighborhood, can you signal me by shutting those tight?"

"That's the guest bedroom," Russel replied, looking across the room. "Sure, I can shut the drapes if I spot anything."

"Thanks," said Upton, signaling the end of the conversation by standing up. With Russel in the mix, he was more convinced than ever the house was a death trap. Plus, knowing the US was threatening all of Nevada, he determined to flee. He'd tell Lisa and let CENTCOM know his decision during the next satellite call.

"My pleasure," said Russel.

Upton looked at the old man. "You better get back and go right home. If I was you, I'd stay in the house for a few days. Until then, stop by tomorrow evening before dark, and we can compare notes."

Russel nodded and got up, holding a stiff back. "You think they'll come back?" he asked, looking around the house.

"Who?"

"You know, Rachel and Todd."

Upton hadn't considered the implications. If Nevada fell, what would happen to the displaced civilians and their property? He didn't have the answers but sensed the old man needed reassurance. "Sure, they'll return. Soon, this whole episode will blow over, and folks will go home. Neither government will keep people from their homes and businesses as they both respect property rights. Things will go back to normal."

Russel seemed relieved and stuck out a hand. "Well, I'll head back. I wish you the best, and if I spot something, I'll close those drapes. Godspeed to you."

Upton accepted the gesture and shook the old man's hand. "I appreciate your keeping quiet and an eye out. Everything will work out."

"Always does," said Russel, and he gave Upton a tight smile.

* * *

Lieutenant Colonel Simpson, sitting at a table in Central Command, reached over and tapped General Story on the shoulder. Annoyed at the disruption, examining updates on battlefield supply and engineering timelines for Las Vegas, the general looked up with a frown. Simpson pointed at her headset, "President Ortega, sir, on the line for you."

General Story nodded in acknowledgement, activated his own headset, and leaned back in his chair. "General Story here. How can I help, Madam President?"

"Sorry for interrupting, but I have news," said the president.

"I'm all ears," replied the general.

"After deliberations, meetings with key people, the ROAS won't give in to the latest US demand."

Unsurprised, General Story expected the decision. Still, hearing it made his heart flutter. "Understood," he said.

"Yes, well, after exploring all options, Operation Heavy Metal is a go. To offer the longest runway for preparations, we'll keep the US guessing right up through their deadline. I won't announce our decision. Instead, we'll act as if the choice for accepting is still under consideration. I'll be calling an emergency session of Congress tomorrow, where we'll conduct a full-blown debate about acceptance of the latest US demands. I intend for rancorous discussions, stretching through the evening into the following morning. My hope is the enemy will delay their offensive while we squabble, maybe beyond the forty-eight-hour deadline, giving you more time for preparations."

"Thank you," said General Story, pleased. "We're ahead of schedule in several areas, but behind in others. Every extra bit of time is useful."

"I thought you'd like the approach. How is everything else, your confidence level?" asked the president.

Operational success depended upon too many variables. How it would play out was anyone's guess. "Madam, we're doing everything in our power to make Heavy Metal work. Our folks seem excited and morale is high. Everyone is giving it their all. I can tell you we won't have a Mesquite on our hands. This time, we won't be surprised."

"Good. I'll inform you if significant changes occur on the political front," said the president.

The general was about to thank her when he remembered the good news. "Have you seen the updates on Staff Sergeant Lisa McMichael, our little war hero out of Mesquite?"

"Nothing since yesterday. Is there more?" asked the president.

"Yes, ma'am. It should've been in your noon briefing package," said the general.

"Sorry, I haven't had time. I'm all ears."

Pleased for the opportunity to give the president something positive, the general smiled as he spoke. "Well, she's alive and holed up with another soldier, a Master Sergeant Corey Upton. They're hiding in a suburban house within Mesquite. So far, they've evaded enemy capture. Earlier today, they contacted us via satellite phone. Both have minor wounds but, considering the circumstances, are in good shape."

"That is excellent news," said the president sounding pleased. After a pause, she continued, "I want her in San Jose, now."

Surprised by the demand, the general had other priorities. Besides, he'd already given orders and had the situation under control. "She should stay where she is, well hidden. Mesquite is ringed by enemy units, roadblocks with eyes everywhere. For her safety, we're keeping the news about her classified. After Heavy Metal, we can consider an extraction and getting her to San Jose."

"General, the country needs her. I need her. Besides, can you imagine if the US captures her? They will manipulate and use her as propaganda against us. We can't let that happen. Get her out of there, now."

He regretted bringing up the subject. There were more important items requiring his attention. But he tried to see it from Ortega's point of view. Losing McMichael, the Hero of Mesquite, would be an embarrassment. Instead of a hero keeping the populace supportive, Ortega would have a PR nightmare. Political support for the war might plummet, along with civilian morale. Still, based on circumstances, the best way for McMichael to get home alive and avoid capture was to follow the orders he'd given. "Madam President, Julia, you have my word. I'll keep a close eye on her. For now, McMichael is following my orders. The wisest and most prudent course of action is for her to lie low until after Heavy Metal. We'll get her home, not now, but soon. Trust me."

After a long pause, in a hesitant voice, Ortega agreed. "Okay, General, you run the military show. I've listened to your reasoning, and I trust you. Just make damn well sure to get her home soon. If she falls into enemy hands, the political repercussions, well, they aren't pretty. Understood?"

"Yes, ma'am, I understand. I'll keep her safety a top priority. Is there anything else?"

"Yes," replied the president. "If you learn anything else about McMichael or run into problems preparing for Heavy Metal, please inform me right away. I'm here to help. Agreed?"

"Yes, ma'am," answered the general.

"Okay then, I've got to run, talk soon," and the president ended the transmission.

Relieved the conversation was over, General Story bent over his tablet and examined the latest updates on Heavy Metal. Damn! The defensive engineering tasks around the outskirts of town were slipping. He'd need to make a call and kick some ass. But he couldn't shake off a bad feeling. He'd made the president a promise and told her to trust him. Looking up, he waved over his aid.

"Sir?" asked Simpson as she approached.

"I need an update on Lisa McMichael. Any changes?"

"Yes, sir. Good timing. The S2 detected a US UAV surveillance drone doing high-altitude circle eights centered above the house where she's hiding. I've asked them to conduct a risk assessment and put together possible contingency plans. They're working the problem now and should have it mapped out within an hour. I intended to brief you then."

"What the hell! Why wasn't I told earlier?" exclaimed the general. If the enemy was circling over that specific house, it meant only one thing. He ran the scenario in his head. McMichael and Upton were under orders to call in every eight hours. Until they checked in, six hours from now, they wouldn't have any idea of the danger lurking overhead. By then, it might be too late, and he didn't need a damn risk assessment to tell him otherwise.

* * *

McMichael, shaken awake and coming out of a deep sleep, focused her eyes and recognized Upton. For a moment, she couldn't remember where she was, and then the sinking feeling of her predicament settled in. She'd taken a nap in the master bedroom, and they were in danger. "What time is it," she asked.

"16:00 hours. We've still got two hours until we're supposed to contact CENTCOM again."

McMichael sat up, and in her view, Upton appeared a new man. Tall, with a strong build and brown hair and eyes, his rugged looks were magnified by the black sweater he wore. He smelled clean and she appreciated having him and couldn't imagine struggling alone.

"There's still enough time for you to get some rest," she said.

"We had a visitor while you slept," said Upton with a frown.

"What?" she said as a jolt of anxiety hit her stomach.

Upton raised a hand and explained. "The neighbor, an older man named Russel, dropped by."

"Yeah?"

Upton brought her up to speed. He explained how the neighbor was a complication, but Upton was confident the man meant no harm and would help keep an eye out for any enemy movement. He also explained how CENTCOM hadn't told them about the pending US demand to turn over Nevada. In his estimation, the house was a trap behind enemy lines—lines that were about to be extended, making future escape that much harder.

Pissed with CENTCOM for the deception, McMichael agreed with Upton. They needed to control their own destiny. Together they agreed on a plan. Tonight, as soon as it was dark, about an hour after informing CENTCOM, they'd get the hell out of dodge and seek extraction.

Plans in place, Upton explained he was exhausted. After telling McMichael to watch the neighbor's drapes and extracting a promise to awaken him before the next check in time, Lisa got up and Upton took her place.

While Upton slept in the master bedroom, feeling better, another painkiller helping, McMichael tried to be productive. She filled their packs with canned food from the pantry, emptied and refilled two hydration systems. Tucked in her belt, she pulled out and checked the ammunition in the suppressed Glock. The magazine was six rounds short. Deep in her mind, she remembered Kinney squeezing off rounds in the pipe during their death struggle, and she shivered.

On the floor in the master bedroom, next to the sleeping master sergeant, she discovered Upton's combat vest and belt with two grenades still attached. Inside she dug out a spare magazine for his M18 and ejected a half dozen 9 mm-caliber bullets. They'd work in her Glock. With bullets in hand, she refilled the magazine to capacity. Satisfied, she tucked Kinney's pistol back in her belt and walked into the living room to check the drapes. Through the rear window, across the yard, the neighbor's shades remained untouched and the sight was reassuring.

With nothing else pressing, she sat in the darkened living room and waited. Her mind kept going back to the previous day: the attack and horrible shelling; shooting down the helicopter, Specialist Kinney squirming. She wondered how many she'd killed. Then she thought of the men and women in her squad—horrible explosions and ear-splitting noise, high-velocity rounds ripping through flesh, digging into the ground under relentless attack.

She felt awful and wished Upton was awake so they could leave. But she knew he needed sleep. So she tried thinking of her kids, Samantha and Jonathan, but that increased her anxiety. Trying to stay positive, she shifted her thoughts and imagined getting out of the house and making it back to ROAS lines—the joy of returning, the danger lifting. Before she knew it, it was time, and with a sense of relief, she got up and headed towards the master bedroom to wake her partner.

"What time is it?" asked Upton, opening his eyes.

She'd checked the battery-operated kitchen wall clock before heading to the bedroom. "17:45. We need to call in soon."

With a grunt, Upton sat up and got off the bed. As he strapped on his combat vest and belt, he asked, "Everything okay? The drapes across the way still open?"

"Yes. All's quiet. It's like the entire neighborhood is empty: no cars, no people, eerie," she said.

Upton checked his belt and holster and made a slight adjustment. "Good, let's contact CENTCOM."

As they walked through the house heading towards the garage, Upton leading the way, McMichael glanced through the small opening in the patio window. The drapes across the yard remained undisturbed. So far, so good.

In the kitchen, before entering the garage, facing west, Upton cracked the kitchen window shutters, and both soldiers bent low to peer outside. Bright in their eyes, the sun was on its descent. Through the glare, the street remained empty, and the houses across the way appeared empty. Satisfied, ready to move into the garage and make the call, McMichael stood straight. However, Upton continued to stare hard out the window.

Concerned about the prolonged concentration, McMichael asked, "What is it?"

Upton didn't answer and kept staring. After a few seconds, he closed the shutter and pressed himself against the kitchen wall. McMichael, sensing danger, did the same.

"What," she whispered, fear and adrenaline mounting.

"There is someone on the roof across the street. I saw the tip of a rifle."

"You positive?" she asked. She hadn't seen a damn thing.

He frowned, "Yes. You turned away too soon."

"Now what?" she asked, feeling a sense of panic and dread.

Upton appeared unsure, but she believed him. They were being watched.

She needed time to think. In another hour, darkness would descend. If they could wait until then before making a dash to escape, their chances might improve. The most promising escape route was through the front door. A quick burst to cross the street into the desert sage. Once there, they could work their way to safety. Still, she couldn't fathom why the enemy had positioned someone on the opposite roof instead of just barging in with guns blazing. Maybe the rifle on the roof had nothing to do with them? No, too coincidental. Her thoughts turned to CENTCOM and what they might do when they didn't call in as expected. It didn't matter. Right now, they had bigger problems.

McMichael explained her thoughts. "We need to get out of here. It's possible the enemy is surrounding us, and we can't call CENTCOM from inside the house. We need line of sight, but going outside and opening the garage door to make a call, with a rifle on the roof across the street, isn't an option."

"Yeah, this house is a trap. Dammit. Rus should have warned us by pulling the drapes. I guess our neighbor friend gave us away. My fault: I shouldn't have let him leave the house."

"No one's to blame. We need to think," said McMichael. As her mind whirled, she spoke her thoughts out loud. "We can act like we're surrendering. Walk out the front door with our hands held high. If they don't spot us for a few seconds, then we can dash across the street into the desert. Once we're hidden, we can call CENTCOM. Of course, if they do spot us right away, we'll be forced to give up." McMichael felt bad about suggesting the possibility of surrender, but she felt exposed, a sense of doom filling the house. Surrendering had popped into her mind earlier. In the pipe, before she killed Specialist Kinney, she considered giving up. At that moment, fighting back seemed instinctive. Now, with time to rest and reflect on the horrors of the past day, if cornered, giving up seemed logical. She didn't want to die in a futile escape attempt.

"We could go out guns firing, but no, I like your plan better. I'm not ready to die in a blaze of glory. But to give us a better chance, I wish it was dark. Right now, in broad daylight, they'll spot us for sure. Of course, it might not matter, as they could storm the house at any moment."

"Sergeant, I'm sorry, but if they storm the house, we need to surrender. There's only two of us against God knows how many. I'm willing to give it an hour, let it get darker, then we go out with our hands up. If nothing happens, we make a run for it." In saying the words, her hands trembled, the memory of the pipe and shelling rumbling through her gut.

"Fair enough. I'll sneak into the garage and pick up the satellite phone. Then, let's get our packs loaded and be ready to move. We'll huddle near the front door. In an hour, near sunset, we head out. If something happens before then, we try to survive and, if necessary, surrender."

"Sergeant, you don't think we've done anything wrong, do you? I mean, you think they'll treat us as prisoners of war and not as murderers?" asked McMichael, the question troubling her.

Upton looked at her and seemed conflicted. Then he nodded. "I expect they'll treat us with respect. We're not criminals. But we've still got a chance to get away."

Chapter Twenty-Seven

SURROUNDED
AND SURRENDER

May 9, 18:42 (PDT)

Inside the M2A6 Stuart infantry fighting vehicle, Sergeant Flood sat pissed off. His Section B, Third Squad squatted in reserve, a half-mile down the road from the real action. It wasn't fair. After all, Flood was the reason for the mission. Without his efforts the two enemy combatants wouldn't be on the radar. Now he sat on his ass, waiting.

At first, when Flood learned about the mission from platoon leader Lieutenant Peck, he was excited. The battalion commander, Lieutenant Colonel Paulson, after reading the intelligence reports on the target, had recognized Flood's earlier involvement. In a show of good faith, Paulson tasked Flood's platoon with the honor of executing the capture. But when it came time to hand out squad assignments, Lieutenant Peck, known by the men as Lieutenant "Prick," fucked up the tasking. The platoon leader was angry at Flood for the loss of Kinney and took it out by posting him in reserve.

Lieutenant "Prick" decided that Section A, with First and most of Second Squad, along with their two fighting vehicles, would conduct the actual capture operation. Not needed, Flood's Section B, along with Third Squad and their two fighting vehicles, would stay in reserve.

So now Flood sat stuck, guarding the main street leading into the target subdivision. Sitting on his ass, waiting and upset, Flood was in no position to avenge the death of Specialist Kinney. Even worse, the guilt from losing Kinney gnawed at his guts. Only by taking revenge did he imagine the pain going away.

* * *

In charge of Operation Catcher, back at Division Command Post, Lieutenant Colonel Paulson sat next to his Bravo Company commander, Captain John Barton. It was Barton's Second Platoon on the ground, responsible for mission execution. Next to both men sat Federal Inspector Dan Cone. Excitement hung heavy in the air.

The plan was basic. Encircle without being seen and then overpower. Two squads from Bravo Company, Second Platoon, eighteen dismounted soldiers, were to surround the target house. Once in place, two fighting vehicles from the platoon were to race up and, with overwhelming firepower, demand the surrender of ROAS Staff Sergeant Lisa McMichael. The rest of the platoon, Third Squad, and two other fighting vehicles were to stay in reserve. As an added precaution, two Custer vertical-lift aircraft remained on standby and, if needed, could be over the target within five minutes.

Paulson felt confident. He'd more than enough assets assigned to achieve mission success. He understood, like most plans, changes evolved based on circumstances. High above the target house, unmanned aerial vehicle surveillance provided continuous coverage and earlier in the day spotted a man entering and spending time in the residence. Intelligence believed the man was a neighbor living behind the target. Paulson decided it was a good break and revised the tactical plan.

The UAV, as had been the case since early in the morning, continued circling high above the house, unseen or heard by the occupants.

Flying in a tight figure eight, the unmanned aircraft provided live video to the HQ operational command team.

In the previous hour, Paulson watched as Bravo Company, Second Platoon crept unobserved through the suburban back and side yards and moved into place. Now, on three sides of the target house, other than the desert facing south, his troops lay in wait. Not only were they inside the surrounding houses, but at least one soldier clung to each roof providing overwatch. Only the front of the target, the southern exposure facing a road and the open desert, remained open.

But that was about to change. Engines idling, several blocks from where they'd dismounted their infantry squads, two fighting vehicles awaited orders.

"Remember, we need her alive and unharmed," said Inspector Cone. He hovered behind the two infantry officers, both of whom stared into monitors watching real-time surveillance video and wearing headsets.

Colonel Paulson ignored the statement.

"I still think Special Forces is better suited for the job. They're trained in these actions, you know—captures, rescues, and so forth," said Inspector Cone.

Angry, hearing the words once again, Paulson looked up and glared at the inspector. "Cone, please keep your mouth shut during the operation, or I'll have you escorted from the command post. And I remind you, General Gist has complete faith in my leadership and the forces under his command. He doesn't need help from Special Forces, or the Air Force, or any outside units. Gist made that point earlier. Now, act as an observer and stay quiet, or leave."

Cone was about to open his mouth when the radio came to life.

"Catcher Actual, Catcher Team One. Target C is in custody and talking. I repeat Target C is talking and confirms location of Target B. But Target C cannot confirm Target A and claims zero knowledge of her. Do you copy and should we proceed with phase-two as planned? Over."

The first curve-ball, thought Paulson. The neighbor, Target C, was claiming knowledge of Target B, Upton, but not of Target A,

McMichael. But it dawned on Paulson that this was a better opportunity than he had hoped. Not answering the radio call, instead he turned to Captain Barton. "Tell Catcher Team One to go ahead with phase-two with a minor alteration. We know she's in there, but let's act otherwise. Have Lieutenant Peck focus only on Upton. During the surrender negotiation, blame Target C for turning in Upton. Don't mention McMichael. Once Upton's in custody, you're allowed to use whatever force is needed against him to compel McMichael into surrendering. If she doesn't, move forward as planned. Understood?"

"Yes, sir," said Captain Barton. Two seconds later, he was on the platoon network relaying the new orders.

Colonel Paulson swiveled in his chair towards Cone and laughed. "You don't mind if we kill Target B, Master Sergeant Upton, do you?"

"Not at all. Just get McMichael alive," said Cone.

* * *

"It's getting dark," whispered Staff Sergeant Lisa McMichael, sitting on the tile foyer.

So far, everything remained quiet. Every few minutes, Upton checked the back window and looked through the small crack in the curtains at the neighbor's drapes. Every time, nothing. As the minutes ticked, Upton doubted himself. Maybe earlier, his eyes had been playing tricks. But he knew better. "I think we should wait longer, give it another fifteen minutes. It'll be darker."

McMichael nodded and sitting cross-legged, continued to wait. On her back, she wore the medic pack, and in her right hand, she gripped Kinney's Glock.

After ten minutes, the stress getting to him, Upton grew impatient. "Time to check the drapes," he whispered to Upton. Without waiting for a response, on hands and knees, he approached the back window.

He froze.

Upton crawled back, pretending not to notice how hard she was gripping the handgun, and whispered, "Drapes are closed. I knew

Rus was a good guy, poor bastard. They must be behind us. We need to move." He ran McMichael's game plan through his mind. They'd both dash through the door with hands up. If not confronted, they'd take off through the desert. About to explain, he detected a sound, getting louder. "You hear it?" he whispered to McMichael.

McMichael shook her head.

Upton knew that ever since the shelling, she couldn't hear well out of one ear. But then, she seemed to pick up the noise and nodded.

He could now hear and feel the approaching dread. An engine, metal treads on pavement, getting louder, vibrations emanating through the tile floor.

"We have to surrender," said McMichael, her eyes round with fear.

Upton ignored the statement. Standing up, he looked through a peep hole in the front door. Across the street, the desert and salvation beckoned. He almost reached down for McMichael to make a run for it, when all at once an armored fighting vehicle emerged. The huge machine stopped in the street and in a swift motion swiveled its 30 mm chain gun in his direction. Worse, a second vehicle appeared and, parallel to the other monster, did the same.

"We're fucked," said Upton.

"What is it?" asked McMichael, still sitting on the tile floor, looking at the door with fear in her eyes.

"Two Stuarts just pulled up in the street facing us. There's a guy standing in each hatch."

Both Upton and McMichael jumped at the sound of a loudspeaker.

"This is United States Army Lieutenant Peck. Master Sergeant Upton, you're surrounded. I repeat, we have the house surrounded. Mr. Russel Jarvis told us everything. Upton, leave your weapons and helmet in the house and come out with your hands raised. You have two minutes to comply, or we'll level the house and arrest Mr. Jarvis for colluding with the enemy. If you surrender, Mr. Jarvis is a free man, and you'll receive proper treatment as a prisoner of war. You have my word as an officer. Master Sergeant Upton, you have two minutes."

"God, I hate to think what they're doing to Rus. We need to surrender," said McMichael.

"Hold it," said Upton. He hadn't mentioned McMichael to the neighbor. Maybe they weren't aware of her. Lisa could hide in the house while he surrendered. Sure, they'd do a cursory search afterward, but they might not discover her. Later, she could slip away. Mind racing, earlier while McMichael slept, he'd found only one decent hiding place. Yes, his life was finished, but not McMichael's—not yet.

Upton unbuckled his combat belt and, getting ready to go out, whispered a plan. "Sergeant, listen. They don't know you're in here. In the hall, there's a ceiling trap door. Grab a broom from the coat closet and use it to push open the door. A cord will drop. Pull on it and a stair ladder will descend. Climb up and pull the ladder up behind you. Hide there until after they leave. Later, head for Bunkerville as planned. Once you get there, use the satellite phone in your pack. Let them know what happened and get home safe."

The loudspeaker boomed again. "One minute!"

"No, they'll find me. Better if I we go together," said McMichael, now standing.

"Negative, take these," said Upton, and he unclipped the two grenades from his belt and turned McMichael around, dropping them in her pack.

"Go," he said, and he pushed McMichael towards the closet. Not waiting, in one motion, Upton dropped his belt and holster onto the tile. Then he removed his helmet and placed it next to the other items. All the while, satisfied with his decision, he noticed McMichael respond. Good. She grabbed a broom from the closet and, without looking back, raced down the hall.

Relieved by her actions, Upton waited a few seconds.

"I'm coming out!" he yelled through the door. Then he counted to ten, giving McMichael more time. Satisfied, he twisted the knob and opened the front door.

Although not quite dark, a floodlight hit him. Without thinking, he raised an arm to protect his eyes.

"Hands above your head. Walk forward, now!" commanded the loudspeaker.

Eyes squinting, Upton didn't play games and raised both hands. Then he moved towards the searing light.

"Stop, lay flat, spread-eagle, now!" boomed the loudspeaker.

As he dropped to his hands and knees, the movement jarred his ribs causing a bolt of hot pain to take his breath away. Doing his best to ignore the discomfort, still wearing his combat vest, he leaned forward and went prone.

Limbs now spread, the artificial grass felt warm on Upton's cheeks, but the pressure on his ribs brought tears. Scared and in pain, he thought of McMichael and hoped she remained hidden. Heart thumping, he determined to keep her a secret, no matter how they questioned him. But he knew it was a lie. The enemy was known to use advanced interrogation techniques, and under enough duress, he'd cave, as would anyone. Still, to give McMichael an opportunity for escape, he vowed to hold out for as long as he could.

Over the idling engines, he detected heavy footsteps.

"Give me your name, soldier!"

Upton shuddered at the command. He lifted his head off the grass and through the spotlight spotted a silhouette. A man stood hovering a few feet away holding an assault rifle.

"Master Sergeant Corey Upton, ROAS Army of Defense," he said before dropping his head. The soldier didn't respond. Instead, Upton detected mumbling and guessed the bastard was passing along the good news. A few seconds later, Upton lost hope.

Over the booming loudspeaker, Lieutenant Peck announced, "Sergeant McMichael! Lisa McMichael! We know you're in there! Master Sergeant Upton is in custody, and if you look out the window, you'll see a platoon sergeant covering him with an M27 assault rifle. You have two minutes to surrender, or Master Sergeant Upton dies for aiding and abetting your escape. Save him by coming out with arms raised. Leave your weapons inside, surrender, and no one gets harmed. Your two minutes start right now!"

Deflated and defeated, Upton couldn't fathom how they knew. He guessed it stemmed from their earlier experience with the Custer. Either way, it didn't matter. Now the focus was on staying alive.

* * *

McMichael had just pulled up the stairs, frantic, and was working to replace the attic cover when the loudspeaker bellowed her name. Hopes faded, and she slumped. Somehow, they knew about her. Hiding in the attic was pointless.

With great reluctance she pushed the flimsy cover aside, dropped the stairs, and descended into the hallway. Alive with fear, she approached the foyer and the open front door. Just out of sight, she pulled off her pack and placed it on the tile. Next to it, she pulled Kinney's Glock from her belt and laid it aside.

Committed to the inevitable, she took a final deep breath and stood tall. Determined to stay strong, she walked through the front door, raising her hands. Then, all hell broke loose.

Chapter Twenty-Eight

WHAT THE HELL?

Commander of the ROAS Special Forces Army Recon Company, Captain Jason Bowen, over the last four days had kept his team hidden and ready. But it hadn't been easy.

As a precaution, Bowen and half his company, three operational detachments totaling thirty-six highly skilled operators, were pre-staged in Mesquite. Excited about the prospects of war, but unsure of the mission, his team deployed with a wide array of tools and weapons. Hidden, their job was to stay prepared and out of sight until issued orders by CENTCOM.

Yesterday, hiding inside an industrial warehouse big enough to hold his team and supplies, they became agitated when the sound of guns erupted along the border. Even with the fight raging, begging to join in, their orders remained the same: stay out of sight and wait. Frustrated, they remained hunkered down and later became angered when they learned the fate of the ROAS battalion protecting the border.

Then, with guile and bravado, as Mesquite filled with US troops, Bowen's team focused on survival by remaining unseen.

Still, his team itched for a fight.

At last, this morning, they received orders to prepare for a mission to support a new effort, Code name Operation Heavy Metal. Stoked by the news, his team poured themselves into planning and preparation.

Five hours later, everything changed again. Bowen received a direct call from General Story with a different set of orders. They learned of a new, higher-value objective only a half-klick away.

Since the call, his team shifted their planning efforts and went into high gear. For years, his Special Forces operators had trained for this day, and now the opportunity to test their skills against real, live adversaries was at hand. Bowen committed a full ODA to the mission, a total of twelve Special Forces operators. Throughout the afternoon, the team bustled with activity and excitement.

Once ready, Bowen and his ODA slipped out of their warehouse hiding place.

For over an hour, the team slow-crawled through desert brush, not sure what they'd be facing, but understanding their objective was under direct enemy aerial observation. Throughout the ordeal, the threat of detection persisted. If spotted, they were to scatter. In that case, his remaining force left inside the warehouse was to destroy their well-stocked supplies, create a diversion, and run.

Protected against visible and overhead detection by state-of-the-art active camouflage ghillie suits, Bowen's squad stopped often to review the latest target satellite imagery. As they neared the objective, looking at the latest pictures, they realized their fears and desires. The enemy was moving, in force, against the same target. In a surge, the squad moved faster.

Now, as they set up positions in the desert scrub seventy meters from the target, a sense of relief passed over the group. They'd arrived without being spotted.

Still, the situation was perilous. Almost at once, the team eyed enemy troops on nearby rooftops. To mitigate the threat, Captain Bowen passed along new orders.

Instructions in place, Bowen signaled for Sergeant Major Sean Ekin and Sergeant First Class Acquon Mason to follow his lead. The rest of the ODA remained in place, spreading out, while the trio slithered forward through the thick brush.

After a five-minute crawl, Captain Bowen gave another signal, and all three men stopped twenty meters from the street fronting their objective. Silent and lying prone, their ghillie suits blending into the scrub and protecting them from thermal recognition, they readied their weapons.

Not half a minute later, a low rumble emerged, and within seconds, two US armored vehicles came into view. Both Stuart fighting vehicles clambered through the suburban street and stopped opposite the three hidden men. Captain Bowen watched as the large vehicles pivoted to face the target house.

Recognizing an advantage, the rear of the Stuarts facing his team with open hatches, over the ODA network, the captain whispered further orders.

But a final decision remained, and he'd be forced to make it soon. Overall, there were two mission priorities. First, rescue Staff Sergeant Lisa McMichael and, if possible, Master Sergeant Upton. Second, if the rescue of McMichael was impractical, her life was forfeit. Bowen didn't question the motives but guessed the reasoning. McMichael, the Hero of Mesquite, as a political pawn was too valuable to fall into enemy hands.

Ready for anything, the Special Forces captain watched the US soldier, his head exposed above the nearest Stuart, get on a loudspeaker. He listened as the man identified himself as Lieutenant Peck and then demanded the surrender of Master Sergeant Upton.

Bowen guessed the enemy tactic, watched, and waited.

It wasn't long before Upton emerged from the target home with arms raised. Within a few seconds, the man was laying prone on the grass covered by a second US infantry soldier holding an assault rifle.

Next, the asshole US Lieutenant on the loudspeaker shifted his focus and called out for McMichael's surrender.

The captain considered his options one last time. Either attempt a rescue or bypass the problem and eliminate the target. He decided and, over the secure network, whispered final instructions.

Orders issued, locked and loaded, Bowen pulled his MK20 sniper assault rifle tight against his shoulder.

With the evening growing dark, the sun just set in the west, Captain Bowen concentrated on his breathing. Through the optics of his assault rifle, just past the US Stuart fighting vehicle occupied by Lieutenant Peck, he settled his sights on the front door of the house and flipped off the safety. Heart beating with nervous energy, he focused on slowing. Steady as a rock, it was time to kill.

* * *

On his stomach, despondent and listening to the US lieutenant on the loudspeaker, Upton waited and hoped for McMichael to surrender. If she didn't come out and kept hiding in the house, she could get her hurt or even killed. Disgusted by the game the enemy was playing, using him as bait, he felt ashamed.

Ribs hurting, he tried to imagine what imprisonment might bring: torture, crippling brutality, confinement, and isolation were in his future. He shuddered against the thought. Yes, he killed the US soldiers in the shell hole, but the bastards were committing a brutal crime. The attack inside the pipe was justifiable, not a war crime. Escaping capture was a soldier's sworn duty. He figured they'd interrogate him and McMichael for answers. There was nothing to hide.

Upton heard a crack and a thud, followed by a squawk from the loudspeaker. Confused, he tried raising his head when he bounced into the air. A rush of hot air and a hurricane of noise washed over him, and a moment later, he slammed back down onto the soft artificial grass. Shaken, ears ringing, a second round of thunder hit. Again, he bounced. This time, shutting his eyes, all thoughts of capture vanished as he rebounded off the turf and rolled into a tight ball trying to survive.

* * *

With hands up, walking towards the light, McMichael was about to step off the porch when she heard a crack and saw the US soldier standing over Upton stagger and drop to a knee. At the same instant, she heard the lieutenant on the loudspeaker yell something undiscernible.

McMichael tried to register what it meant when the world exploded, knocking her backward. Dazed, she fell on her butt, landing on the aggregate concrete patio.

Not thinking, she raised her right arm to ward off the heat as a fireball erupted through the hatch of the nearest fighting vehicle. Before she could comprehend, a second explosion ripped through the other Stuart, and a second shockwave punched her in the chest, knocking her flat. She rolled away from the heat, turning her back towards the burning wreckage. On her side, panting, stunned, and confused, her broken eardrum began to bleed.

* * *

Across the street, lying prone, wearing an active camouflage suit and well hidden in the brush, Captain Bowen spotted Staff Sergeant McMichael exiting the target house. With practiced ease, he swung his MK20 assault rifle away from McMichael to the US soldier standing over the prostrate Master Sergeant Upton. Bowen hoped his prior command to disable the US drone circling high above their position with a high-energy laser had worked because it was time to shoot.

With his night-vision scope connected via a wireless signal to his visor, the captain sighted center mass, and squeezed off a single shot.

The MK20 plastic-cased, high-velocity 7.62 mm round developed by the ROAS with smart-bullet technology was built to penetrate body armor, and it did, causing the stricken US soldier to stagger and drop to a knee. The shot signaled the start of the attack.

On either side of the captain, even though the distance was danger close, Sergeant Major Sean Ekin and Sergeant First Class Acquon Mason each fired a hand-held Javelin III missile. The missiles hung in the air for a second until the rocket motors kicked in, giving the operators a moment to duck.

Neither enemy fighting vehicle was expecting a missile attack and had their hatches open, disengaging their Active Protection Systems. Unimpeded, the missiles climbed into the air, where they traveled a short distance before turning and plunging downward.

The first missile slammed through the hatch of the Stuart Fighting vehicle occupied by Lieutenant Peck. Armed with a tandem warhead to defeat and penetrate reactive armor, it exploded. Inside, the driver and gunner turned into a gelatinous mass. As for Lieutenant Peck, he never felt a thing. The Javelin ripped through his body on the way down, vaporizing him milliseconds later when it detonated beneath his mangled corpse.

An instant later, the second fighting vehicle erupted, taking a direct missile hit. The resulting destruction was significant, sending shards of shrapnel and chunks of steel hurtling through the air. Meanwhile, the remaining ROAS Special Forces took the queue, and from fifty meters behind their captain, they executed the next phase of the assault.

Well hidden in the desert brush, using XM30 grenade launchers, four ROAS operators pumped electronic-sighted, high-explosive 40 mm grenades at the enemy troops occupying the houses ringing the objective. Developed by the ROAS, using AI guidance based on offline satellite map optics to avoid GPS jamming, the projectiles exploded with extreme accuracy. Designed to explode above the target, the grenades rained death and destruction. Within a minute, twenty-four grenades detonated with pinpoint precision, and the four ROAS operators were under orders to continue launching until they ran out of ammunition or were commanded to stop.

The coordinated grenade attack was merciless. Shrapnel ripped through rooftops and turned adobe tiles into lethal flying objects. Shards of glass and metal whistled through the air, shredding any exposed flesh. Amid the chaos, screams and shouts emerged from the men under siege.

* * *

"What happened to my video?" questioned Lieutenant Colonel Paulson, looking up from the monitor on which he'd been watching the final stage of Operation Catcher. Until now, the mission was going as planned, everything smooth. With Upton in custody, they'd been waiting for McMichael to emerge when the screens went blank.

Captain Barton, seated next to the colonel, threw his hands in the air. He had the same problem.

"Fix it!" said Paulson.

The captain didn't hesitate. He stood up and barked at the S1 team to find and correct the problem. Within seconds, the intelligence group explained the UAV high-altitude surveillance drone was offline and no longer responding.

"Sir, we've lost our drone coverage," said Barton.

"No shit. Get another UAV in the air now!"

"Yes, sir," said Barton, and he began barking orders into his headset.

Inspector Cone watched the action with a look of concern and began typing notes in his pad.

Then, urgent radio calls came in reporting troops in contact. Neither Section A fighting vehicles were responding. The rest of the deployed platoon in the surrounding houses reported being under high-explosive indirect fire. Pinned by a rain of explosions, the troops couldn't pinpoint or fire back at their attackers. Across the radio, disturbing calls trickled in as the platoon started taking casualties.

Paulson tried to make sense of the chaos. He glanced at the big-screen tactical awareness monitor hanging on the far wall of the command post. The airborne warning and control system showed no air threats, nor were there any enemy units near Mesquite. Over the target, UAV surveillance throughout the day, other than the neighbor, had detected zero enemy movements. Paulson realized it had to be a small unit action, on foot, suited to avoid detection.

On his blank monitor, he shifted from the dead UAV feed to recent satellite imagery. With the target centered on his screen, the incoming enemy attack vector became obvious. The unexpected assault had to be coming from the south, originating in the desert. Operation

Catcher was turning to shit, fast, but he knew where the enemy was, and there couldn't be many.

Paulson stood and turned to Captain Barton. "I'm assuming tactical control of the fight."

Barton, on the radio in mid-sentence, paused and looked up with uncertainty.

Not waiting for Barton or caring if the subordinate approved, Paulson issued commands through his headset.

First, he ordered both standby Custers into the air. He needed eyes above the scene, now, with killing power.

Next, he ordered the Second Platoon reserves, containing the two remaining fighting vehicles, and Third Squad, into action. He directed them to move forward and deliver suppressive fire into the desert just south of the target.

The combined power of the fresh reserves and the vertical-lift aircraft would force the enemy to run or take cover. Once the enemy in the desert was under suppressive fire, he'd swarm the original target house and find or kill McMichael.

As a precaution, even though they wouldn't arrive in time, he ordered the rest of A Company, totaling two mechanized platoons supported by eight fighting vehicles, into the fight. He didn't need the extra troops, as they were overkill, but insurance never hurt.

After issuing the quick string of orders, Paulson sat in his seat with rising confidence. Yes, the enemy surprised Barton, but it was nothing he couldn't fix. He wasn't sure why the enemy had attacked, but he guessed the bastards were after the same objective. It didn't matter; he'd lead his troops to victory.

Confident in the outcome, Paulson considered but rejected requesting more assets. He could ask for an artillery barrage on the desert, but in soliciting the extra firepower, he'd have to explain the urgent need. No, he had no wish to escalate up the chain of command. Besides, under his leadership, with the assets assigned, he'd plenty of resources to regain the initiative and destroy the enemy.

Lemonade out of lemons, Paulson thought to himself as he reached into his pocket and felt the ragged name tag. Turning the cloth between his fingers, he smiled.

* * *

With the burning hulks of the two fighting vehicles illuminating the scene, thirty seconds into the attack, Captain Bowen gave the signal. Together with Ekin and Mason, he jumped up from their hidden position and dashed across the street.

On the run, leading the way, Bowen pointed at Upton curled on the lawn and Mason veered in that direction.

Still moving, Bowen and Mason continued forward reaching Staff Sergeant McMichael. Bowen took a knee next to the female while Ekin, assault rifle at the ready, covered their position.

Bowen had no way of knowing if she was alive, wounded, or dead. Collateral damage caused by the missile attack was more than possible. Regardless, his orders were clear, fetch or eliminate Staff Sergeant Lisa McMichael.

With Ekin providing coverage, Bowen reached down and rolled the woman onto her back. To his amazement, McMichael stared back, face ashen, eyes round in fear, a tooth missing, but alive. Over the roar of the nearby grenades, he yelled, "Are you okay?"

At first, McMichael recoiled at the sight of the soldier hovering above her. Then it seemed she recognized his camouflage and put it all together, and she nodded in the affirmative.

Bowen grabbed McMichael by her combat vest, and despite possible injuries, tugged her upright. She wobbled but stood. Worried of secondary explosions cooking off from ammunition inside the burning wrecks, holding her by the vest, with no time to waste, Bowen dragged her away.

Forced to take a wide detour around the flaming hulks, Bowen got past the vehicles and pushed McMichael across the street into the desert brush and forced her to the ground. Kneeling beside her, he pulled a packet from his suit vest, tore it open, and extracted a folded camouflaged garment made of a thin material. Over the pounding of grenades, he pantomimed his wish.

McMichael appeared to understand and took the material. With Bowen's help, she stood and slipped the garment over her head and adjusted the attached hood. Loose fitting, the sleeves covered her arms well beyond her hands, while the length extended to the ground.

Bowen grabbed McMichael's shoulder and turned her towards the desert. With a silent wave, he pointed the direction they should head, and bent low, leading the way, he started to jog. Close behind, McMichael followed in the growing darkness. Together they scrambled through the brush, away from the sound of blasting grenades.

Chapter Twenty-Nine

FRIENDS AND ENEMIES

Lieutenant Colonel Paulson swore into his headset, but the tirade wasn't working. One of the two standby Custers was reporting a failure on its anti-missile Active Protection System and refused to launch. The Aviation Battalion wasn't taking any chances, not with missiles in play. Based on the loss of a Custer the day before due to a failed APS, they wouldn't budge.

Now, only one vertical-lift aircraft was available with an ETA of three minutes. Even while arguing with the major in charge of the Custer squadron, Paulson believed the lone bird offered enough firepower to finish the job. Paulson gave in but requested a secondary replacement Custer, just in case. In response, the Aviation Battalion agreed but gave an ETA of fifteen minutes. To keep pressure applied, Paulson urged the major running the Aviation Battalion to move faster. For now, he'd have to make do with a single Custer.

Meanwhile, the Second Platoon B Section reserves comprising two Stuart fighting vehicles carrying Third Squad were on the move. Assigned to block the two streets in and out of the target subdivision, they weren't far away. Within two minutes of the order, both Stuarts approached the burning wrecks of their sister vehicles.

Not knowing what faced them, fearing what happened to the fighting vehicles in A Section, they stopped a half-block away from the target house. There, they disgorged Third Squad with the order to fan out and approach the target with caution.

Paulson didn't care for the tactic. He wanted the Stuarts to charge forward and rake their main 30 mm chain guns into the desert south of the target position. But when he issued the order, the fighting vehicles resisted, not with two dead Stuarts burning towards their front. Instead, the Stuart section commander requested permission to hold fire until the inbound Custer was over the desert and his dismounted troops were in position.

Paulson, expecting the lone vertical-lift assault aircraft on station soon, gave in and agreed.

Seated next to him, Paulson noticed Barton and could tell the man wasn't pleased. The company commander sat frowning with his arms crossed, shaking his head. He sensed that after the first shock of the enemy assault, Barton had recovered his wits. Now, he perceived Barton was itching to get back into the fight and take over, but Paulson wasn't about to cede his own authority and lose the engagement.

Turning to his left, he watched as the federal inspector typed notes into a computer pad. He guessed the man was writing everything down to cover his own ass and, if needed, blame Paulson for any failures. Paulson felt an urge to lean over and swat away the man's computer and slap the skinny bastard off the chair, but he refrained. Once the fight was over, he'd deal with the insolent son of a bitch.

With commands issued, Lieutenant Colonel Paulson switched his screen to the live FLIR video feed from the Custer racing towards the scene.

* * *

Captain Bowen, with McMichael following, was moving fast, heading towards the rest of his troops and getting the hell away. For the assault, he figured it would take the enemy five minutes to respond and bring in more assets, so he wanted in and out in less than three.

On his headset radio, he had just received good news. Ekin and Mason had Upton in tow and were working through the desert only twenty seconds behind.

He kept moving, motivated by the fact he was close to reaching the rest of the team.

Bowen checked the time on his helmet display. Less than three minutes into the assault, well within mission parameters, but the team needed to exfiltrate before the enemy rallied. Through his radio, he gave the word to break off the assault and head to the rally point.

So far, the active camouflage suits had worked and protected them from prying eyes. As he waded through the brush, McMichael right behind him, he hoped their good fortune would continue.

* * *

Sergeant Flood and his Third Squad, comprising two fire teams totaling eight infantry soldiers, piled out of their fighting vehicles. He felt relieved. At last, an opportunity to join the fight! To avoid the incoming indirect grenade barrage, he ordered the men to flank the target house by moving down a parallel side street.

Leading the way, determined to avenge the loss of Kinney, it didn't take long for Flood to reach the final dead-end cross street fronting the target. Upon doing so, he went to ground and waved at his men to do likewise.

Now on his stomach, crawling the last few meters, Flood peered west down the street. Sure enough, he observed two fighting vehicles burning bright in the early darkness. Grenades, not as many, still burst among the houses around the objective.

Flood shifted his focus towards the desert. In listening to the radio chatter, he knew Higher Command believed the enemy attack originated from the south. Through his night-vision visor, he stared across the street into the open desert and tried to detect movement or muzzle flashes. Nothing.

Over the radio, more calls came in from First and Second Squads, reports of KIA, urgent demands for medivac. He thought back to the beginning and felt a twinge of guilt. All of this because two bastards were found knifed in a shell hole. Then he noticed the quiet: no more explosions. The incoming indirect barrage had stopped.

In an instant, Flood guessed the enemy was retreating. Now he had an opportunity to redeem himself. It was time to seize the initiative.

Across the squad network Flood gave instructions. He explained how they would get up and dash across the street. Once in the brush, they were to fan out, keep good spacing and push towards the south. Their purpose: search, find, and destroy any enemy targets.

After issuing the order, Flood stood, and with his assault rifle at the ready, ran across the street and took a knee inside the desert scrub. Around him, his men did the same.

As his squad took their positions in a line facing south, Flood grew excited and could feel the pent-up energy. His night vision was excellent. Even in the early evening darkness, the optics lit up the surrounding terrain.

With his men in position, he switched his comms to the company network and notified Captain Barton of his location and intentions. Good news, Barton acknowledged the call but didn't interfere or even comment. Meanwhile, both of his section Stuarts had pulled up to the end of the street and were idling near the target house. In an excellent position to support Flood's assault, they confirmed their readiness to offer fire support. Relieved by the response, Flood acknowledged the message and asked the Stuarts to stand by and remain ready to engage. With everything in place, Flood rose from his knee and issued orders for his squad to move.

Assault rifle at the ready, Flood took off at a slow jog. The going proved more difficult than he anticipated, as thick brush often forced him to sidestep. He began to worry about the men around him keeping proper spacing. Alert and anxious, he picked his way through the desert terrain.

* * *

Paulson finished speaking over the radio with the Aviation Battalion, confirming the second bird was about to spin up. Standing nearby, Paulson watched as Inspector Cone scribbled more notes. Oh, how he wanted to strangle the man. Beside him, Captain Barton was on the radio and seemed to be under control. Then Cone looked up from his tablet.

"Colonel, the mission calls for Staff Sergeant McMichael to be taken alive, I trust the objective hasn't changed?"

The last thing Paulson needed was Cone telling him what the mission parameters were. If the target objective couldn't be taken alive, dead was the next best option, and he felt no compunction to explain. Not responding to the insolent question, staring at Cone, Paulson's radio headset came to life. Excellent news: the inbound Custer pilot reported enemy targets in sight and requested permission to engage. The colonel glanced at his monitor where the Custer transmitted a high-definition night-vision scene. An entire squad of enemy soldiers was retreating through the desert south of the target house.

For a few seconds, Colonel Paulson considered his options. Deciding, he authorized the Custer to open fire with anti-personnel ordinance aimed at stopping, but not necessarily destroying, the fleeing enemy. He'd like to take some prisoners, guessing Higher Command would be pleased. After giving the order, he sat back in keen anticipation.

* * *

Vigilant, scanning the desert as he jogged, Flood detected the sound of rotors coming from the rear, and he stopped. Turning, he looked up through a break in the heavy scrub but couldn't spot the aircraft. By his estimation the squad was already fifty meters inside the desert and no one had mentioned air support. The realization of his exposure caused the hair on his arms to stand on end. Before he could get on the radio and remind Barton he was in pursuit of the enemy, he spotted a Custer coming in fast from the north. And then it twinkled.

A shocked realization dawned, and Flood dropped to the ground and curled into a tight ball.

Within a second, the first rocket struck forward of Flood's left flank, followed by two more rippling across his line. Each rocket detonated just before striking the ground, unleashing a payload of 1,200 hardened-steel darts. Hurled in all directions, the fléchettes were perfect ordinance for the job, slicing through dense brush and embedding in any hard targets along the way.

Curled tight, Flood heard the killing projectiles whistle past. Many of the shrubs around him shook as darts ripped through the vegetation. At least one dart glanced off his head protection system, two others ricocheted off the back of his liquid body armor, while another embedded in the heel of his right boot.

Still cringing in a ball, Flood waited a few moments for more explosions. Nothing. Other than the sound of rotors, it grew quiet.

Unscathed, he sat up and tried to shake off the shock. He'd been damn lucky. Then, the radio calls started coming in. Pleas for help and medical attention from his squad. On the verge of panic, trying to keep his wits, knowing the Custer could attack again at any moment, Flood called into the company net.

"Catcher Actual. Catcher Squad Three has sustained a blue on blue attack! Call off the Custer, cease fire. We are friendlies. Repeat, we are under friendly fire. Over!"

"Catcher Squad Three, Catcher Actual copies. Ceasing fire. Out."

Flood dropped his head and took a deep breath. Unabated screams and urgent calls for "medic" filled the air and his headset. Angry and upset, Flood got back on the radio.

"Catcher Actual, Catcher Squad Three needs immediate medical support, we have multiple WIA, repeat multiple wounded. Over."

"Catcher Squad Three, Catcher Actual copies. Standby for ETA. Over."

"Catcher Actual, get them here quick. Out." Flood slumped. Ever since jumping in the shell hole the prior evening, everything had gone to shit.

Angry, exasperated, Flood stood and looked towards the sky. Off to the north, where he last spotted it, the Custer hovered. Right then he hated the sight. The son of bitch lacked any fire discipline. Flood made a silent vow to find the pilot, hunt him down, and make him pay. But first, his men needed help. Disgusted, all thoughts of the enemy gone, slinging his assault rifle, and with a sense of dread, Flood headed for the closest calls of distress.

* * *

Paulson was surprised when Barton, seated next to him, swiveled in his chair and jumped up waving his arms. "Cease fire, cease fire!"

Not waiting, Paulson ordered the Custer to hold and await further orders. Just then, an urgent radio call came in from Third Squad confirming the horrible reality. Barton answered and confirmed the cease fire. A few seconds later, a second call came in for a medivac.

Paulson stood and stared down at Barton with anger. The captain glared back. Spinning on his heels, Paulson pointed an accusing finger at Cone. "You, sir, are the cause. Your constant interruptions in the middle of complex military maneuvers led us astray. I'll be reporting your actions to General Gist and holding you responsible. Now get the fuck out of my command post!"

Cone stepped back in apparent shock. Inside the command post, the trailer full of staff went quiet. After several seconds, Cone shook his head. "Colonel, I didn't issue any commands, you did. If anyone is to blame, you are. I'll leave, but I expect you to complete the mission and capture the objective. Either way, I will brief the president." Cone, tablet in hand, turned and strode to the nearest door, pulled it open, and slammed it shut behind him.

Captain Barton, his voice dripping with sarcasm, asked, "What now, sir?"

Paulson clenched his fists. The impertinent captain was trying to undermine his authority and disrespect him in front of staff. Ready to explode, he caught himself and paused. He sensed the room listening and observing. There was nothing to gain by losing one's composure. Besides, he never lost. In a confident voice, he replied, "We find and kill the enemy as planned. Nothing's changed. Now, let's get back to work!"

The room remained quiet, tense. Sensing the mood, Paulson took a seat and called out, "Back to work. Everyone. Now!"

Staff, seeming to get the message, returned to business, and the volume in the room increased.

Just then, Paulson raised his finger as another call came into his headset. A new development. The Air Force was on the horn. AWACS reported a bogie inbound, rotary based, big. Maybe an ROAS Chinook, hugging the Virgin River coming in low. The big chopper popped up high enough for the AWACS to get a positive read. ETA to Mesquite, two minutes.

Paulson didn't need to ponder the sighting as the big picture crystallized. An ROAS exfiltration bird was on the way. Wherever the transport helicopter landed, the enemy small unit was sure to follow.

Bent over the satellite imagery on his monitor, Paulson noted the Virgin River ran half a kilometer south of the target house. To avoid detection, the location was an obvious place to ingress and egress. Paulson thought for a moment and decided. Now it was his turn to spring a trap.

Chapter Thirty

EXFILTRATION, NOT

After reaching the rest of the team, the sound of rotors emerged, and Bowen guessed a Custer was on his tail. He waved everyone to ground. Shit! He checked the time displayed in the upper-corner of his head protection visor and determined the Chinook was due. His ODA of Special Forces operators needed to get moving, but the night optics of the Custer were exceptional. He was debating the best course of action when he heard a swish and a quick series of explosions. Behind him, he risked a look, he could see the desert lit with three rounds of expended ordinance. For an unknown reason, the Custer had attacked something with rockets. He couldn't fathom what the enemy was targeting. Regardless, he needed the damn bird to go away.

Still debating what to do next, to his relief, Ekin, Mason, and a limping Upton arrived. He nodded to the men as they took a knee. Checking the time again, the team needed to get going, but the damn Custer continued to hover nearby. If the group moved, the advanced optics of the Custer might spot them, even with their active camouflage. On the verge of giving the order and risking it all, to his great relief, the Custer lifted, turned, and flew away.

As they waited for the Custer to disappear, a new sound emerged. Horrible screams and yelling emanated from the area hit by the rocket attack. Captain Bowen wasn't sure why the aircraft had departed but guessed the damn thing had fucked up and attacked its own people.

His first urge was to assist the stricken troops, but he was in no position to help. Instead, he needed to take advantage of the unfortunate opportunity.

Bowen rose into a crouch and worked his way among the team. Tapping folks on the shoulder as he went by, he waved for them to follow. In a moment, his entire group, along with the two rescued targets, were on the move and working against time.

* * *

Following the sound of pain, Sergeant Flood worked his way through the desert brush and found Corporal Dalton squirming on the sandy soil. His fire team leader alternated between moaning, panting, and outright screaming. Bending low, Flood tried to hold the thrashing man still when he saw the source of the problem. Two steel darts protruded from Dalton's right shin, buried far into the bone. Even worse, the corporal tore at another dart, this one penetrating through the bone of his left forearm, the far tip protruding through skin.

Flood assessed the wounds, spoke reassuring words to Dalton, and observed light bleeding. Good, no major arteries appeared compromised. Still, the corporal writhed in uncontrolled pain, the steel darts embedded deep within bone, beyond painful. Not knowing how to extract the darts without causing more distress or damage, Flood shifted to pain control.

After removing Dalton's head protection system, Flood dug around inside his own combat vest, pulled out a small medical kit, and extracted a Fentanyl lollipop. One of only two suckers in his possession, he knelt over the thrashing man and tried to explain. "Dalton, bear with me, calm down, open your mouth so I can give you this." Flood waved the medicine on a stick in front of the corporal. In agony, Dalton continued to thrash, but at last, the corporal opened his mouth.

Flood stuck in the lollipop. "There you go, give it a minute, you'll feel better. Help is on the way. I've got to check the other guys. Hang tough, good buddy, and I'll be right back."

With more distant screams ringing in his ears, Flood moved off in a tormented search.

On the move he barked into his radio headset, asking Captain Barton for an ETA on further medical help. The answer wasn't great. There were casualties from the precision grenade attack against First and Second Squads taking up available resources, and further medics weren't due for another five minutes.

Disgusted with the answer, Flood reached the next injured man. Private Ted Henry lay whimpering, bleeding heavy from a dart in the thigh. Blood squirted in the air with the dying rhythm of the man's beating heart. Flood recognized the signs, the femoral artery severed, and his hopes sunk. But he went to work.

On a knee next to the private, Flood procured a bandage from his medical kit, ripped it open, and tried to apply it around the wound. But the damn dart was in the way, and a bandage couldn't repair a torn artery. Near panic, Flood tossed it aside and considered applying a tourniquet when the private convulsed. Before Flood could react, the young man stiffened and stopped breathing. Flood tried to save the soldier's life, tore off the young man's head protection system, and gave CPR. Both hands pumping on the man's chest, Flood tried to revive the failing man. Blood still pumped from the wound, but not as much, and the soldier wasn't responding. A change of tactic was needed. With one hand pumping Henry's chest, with the other, Flood ripped at his own belt, trying to get it off and use it as a tourniquet. Frantic, after fumbling for a few seconds, he got it loose and cinched it above the frightful wound.

Although blood no longer pumped from the torn artery, Private Henry lay lifeless. Flood stared into the vacant eyes of his fallen soldier and knew he'd failed the young man. Part of it, he knew, was the lack of body armor below the waist. Too often, the soldiers didn't connect or test that portion of their liquid armor as compared to the torso, thinking the upper body more susceptible. Besides, the armor, procured from the ROAS years before, was older, and maintenance was a pain in the ass. Now, it had cost Henry his life.

He looked to the heavens for relief, tears of frustration forming, and noticed stars twinkling above. The sight juxtaposed against the man beneath him magnified the loss and made the sense of loss and guilt even worse. And then his headset crackled with the voice of Captain Barton.

"Squad Three Actual, gather up your combat effectives and fall back to the original target house. Wait there for revised mission orders. Do you copy? Over."

Disgusted and demoralized, Flood considered not replying, but there wasn't a choice.

"Catcher Actual, Catcher Squad Three Actual has multiple WIA and at least one KIA. Where the hell is our medical assistance? Over!"

"Squad Three Actual, help is on the way. But we need you and any combat effectives to rally at the target house. Now. Do you copy?"

With hands drenched in the blood of his troops, Flood struggled to his feet. He considered ignoring the captain's order, but all that would do was cause more headaches.

"Catcher Actual, Catcher Squad Three copies. Out."

Flood then switched to the Platoon Net and ordered each man in his squad to report in, one by one, and provide a status. As the calls came in, he ascertained the horrible reality. Of the eight men entering the desert with him, only three remained combat effective: five men down, three wounded and pleading for help, and two others, including young Private Henry, didn't report in at all.

No way could he leave his wounded until the medics arrived. About to inform Captain Barton of his decision and take the heat, he heard beating rotors in the far distance. The sound sent shivers down his spine. Turning south towards the noise, he tried to ascertain the threat but was unable to see beyond the nearest high brush.

He decided to call it in when another sound emerged, this time coming from the north. He spun back around and, straining his neck, caught sight of two Custers slowing into a fast hover. The sight angered him.

* * *

The ancient ROAS Chinook CH-47F came in flying low, hugging the Virgin River, cruising at its top speed of 170 knots. Covered in the latest stealth material, the large transport helicopter was difficult to detect by radar. The big machine had a large carrying capacity, well within the parameters of the mission, and contained a myriad of defensive weapons. But getting in and out in one piece wouldn't be easy.

To avoid detection, before reaching the outskirts of town, the Chinook veered away from the river and flew south and east over the unoccupied desert. After reaching a position due south of the target, it turned north and headed for the river again. The planners expected the enemy to detect the bird on its final approach, but it was all about speed.

As the Chinook approached the landing zone, skimming low over the dark desert terrain, the big bird locked onto its landing zone. With side doors opening, the machine descended the last few meters until its wheels touched down on the soft bank. Rotor wash sent sand scattering, and already, it was time to leave.

* * *

Lieutenant Colonel Paulson guessed right.

To set the trap after the ill-fated rocket attack, he'd ordered the offending Custer to fly far north, away from the river, to lure in the prey. Simultaneously, the replacement reconnaissance UAV finally arrived on station high above the original target location. Paulson directed the drone to put eyes on the Virgin River towards the south and to feed observation video to the battalion command network.

Sure enough, perched over his monitor, watching the video feed, less than a minute later, Paulson grinned as a big transport helicopter came into view. Excited, he viewed his victim with intense satisfaction. It came flying in just above the deck, crossed over the river, came to a hover, rotated, and landed.

Not waiting, Paulson contacted the Custer, its crew eager to make up for the prior mishap. By now, the second vertical-lift aircraft had joined the mission. The colonel fed both aircraft the UAV video along with the associated target coordinates.

While keeping an eye on the UAV feed, Paulson reached into his pocket and felt the strip of cloth. Comforted, smiling, he ordered the Custers to attack.

The ROAS exfiltration Chinook never stood a chance.

It had been on the ground for less than thirty seconds when, at a speed of three hundred knots, the two Custers approached from the north. After locking on and going into a hover half a kilometer out, Paulson gave the green light to engage, and each bird fired a JAGM missile.

Although the Chinook missile warning system appeared to detect the attack and launch a couple of flares in response, it wasn't enough. The old bird was a sitting duck. The first missile ignored the pathetic decoys and struck the front half of the Chinook, burrowing deep into the superstructure, where it detonated in a thunderous explosion. Split in half by the force, parts of the big helicopter hurled high into the air. Within two heartbeats, a second missile slammed into the burning stew, adding its own lethal mix, ripping and tearing everything anew.

Tossed into the night air, burning fuel, chunks of twisted metal, and body parts flew everywhere. Seconds later, the wreckage came crashing down, some landing in the surrounding desert while other pieces fell with a hiss into the nearby Virgin River.

Even before the raining debris settled, the Custers moved in, firing cannons, shredding anything and everything around the wreckage. Not even a small rabbit could have survived the terrific onslaught.

Watching the video, Paulson smiled while cheers erupted in the command trailer.

Chapter Thirty-One

CLEANING UP THE MESS

May 9, 20:47 (PDT)

Flood, along with the walking remnants of his squad, approached the heat of the smoldering ruins.

In the darkness, the light from the various fires obviated the need for night vision, and Flood lifted his visor. From his vantage point, he detected pieces of the large helicopter spread wide around the Virgin River. Nothing but burning chunks of twisted metal remained. Driven by a gentle breeze, another larger fire swept among the farthest brush, burning east along the river.

As Flood worked closer, assault rifle at the ready, he happened upon the first corpse. Charcoal black, lying in burned-out sage brush, a twisted torso, no legs, fingers curled tight from the cruel heat. He couldn't tell the sex, or anything else definitive, other than it was dead.

He kept moving closer, stepping over bits of metal, smoldering wires, insulation. All around the wreckage, small shell holes left by the intense cannon fire pocked the desert landscape. The destruction was sickening. More body parts, a leg with no boot, a dismembered hand, a bloodied helmet protection system.

Among the wreckage, as he searched, the area reeked of smoke and death. The destruction was immense and total. Looking at another body, still smoldering, Flood felt vacant. Earlier, he'd wished for revenge, to get the two enemy soldiers who had killed Specialist Kinney. But now, the world devoid of joy, his heart was empty. Sure, the enemy took a beating, but it wasn't worth it: too many people killed, good soldiers injured, none of it worth it.

* * *

"Sir, we've got confirmation from Second Platoon. After inspecting the site, multiple enemy KIA counted, probable squad size unit. We have some intact bodies and a bunch of parts. No enemy WIA, all confirmed dead. Overhead surveillance reports no enemy movement. The area is secure," said Bravo Company Commander Barton in a tired voice.

"Excellent," replied Lieutenant Colonel Paulson, smiling, pleased with his own performance. Other than the friendly-fire incident, in his opinion, things had gone well. He'd give the good news to General Gist and complain about Federal Inspector Cone. After all, he rationalized, the damn government spy interfered in Operation Catcher, leading to the blue on blue accident. Even with the horrendous civilian distraction, mission accomplished.

Paulson remembered to thank Barton. After all, it was important to recognize contributions, even when trivial. He'd also need Barton to sign off on the after-action report and the sticky events involving Cone. Still smiling, he turned to Barton.

"Captain, a fine job. Pass along my compliments to your team. An absolute and stunning victory. You should be proud. In your report, please point out Cone's egregious interference. In no way do I hold you responsible for the accidental deaths. I'm sure you agree."

Barton stared back, and then gave a short, quick nod.

* * *

After investigating the Chinook helicopter wreckage, Sergeant Flood and the rest of the able-bodied men from Second Platoon rested near the original target house. Gone were his Third Squad wounded, evacuated to their home base, Fort Carson, Colorado, where doctors awaited with more advanced capabilities.

As Flood leaned against the side of his assigned Stuart, assault rifle slung, the floodlights from the fighting vehicle lighting the sidewalk, he waited for the punishment detail to arrive. Exhausted, one dirty chore remained.

Corporal Able Hanford, one of a handful of men still walking from Flood's Third Squad, was filthy but seemed to still carry energy from the earlier fight. Walking up to Flood, he shook his head at the row of blanket-covered bodies lying on the sidewalk.

"Bad day," said Hanford.

Flood nodded.

"Sergeant, I found one more wounded. Not one of ours, but a civilian, an older guy in the house behind the target. Fucked up by a grenade. A grunt from Second Squad identified the guy, says he was trying to protect the ROAS soldiers hiding in the target house. After getting roughed up, the old civilian bastard admitted consorting with the enemy. Second Squad used him as a lure. Weird: I'd have thought more folks around these parts would welcome and help us. Fuck that guy."

"Is he getting medical treatment?" Flood didn't care that much, but it was only right.

"Not yet. Our medics are still working on our own."

"I'll see if I can round someone up," said Flood. Before he could call it in, he paused as two older Humvee's rumbled down the street and parked near Flood.

He watched as Captain Longfellow from Mortuary Services stepped out of the lead Humvee. To his disgust, the captain barely looked at the row of covered bodies stretched in a line atop the sidewalk. Instead, the captain nodded his head in recognition and stomped his direction. Before Flood could get away, the officer was standing in his way with a smile.

"Sergeant, good to see you. I understand we got the bad guys," said Longfellow.

Flood looked at the overweight officer with disdain. Since jumping into the shell hole the night before to assist the arrogant bastard, bad shit had followed. No doubt, Longfellow started the mess that led to the loss of Kinney and the men now stretched dead on the hard pavement. He didn't think the lumpy officer could manage twenty pushups or had ever fired a shot in anger. But the fucking guy was an officer.

"Sir, a lot of people died."

Longfellow looked askance, then put on a broad smile. "Cheer up! Without you, we wouldn't have gotten the bastards. In my report, I've put you and the specialist, what's his name again?"

"Kinney, sir, Specialist Kinney."

"Yes. I've put you and Kinney in for a decoration. What you accomplished early this morning, going into the pipe, helped us achieve a great victory tonight. By following my foresight, you tracked the enemy, and that led us to finding and killing a full host of enemy insurgents. It's all in my report, and I'm sure decorations will follow," said Longfellow.

Flood sneered. He recognized the captain's motivation. Longfellow wanted nothing more than a decoration himself, to receive the accolades and maybe a promotion. Sure, the two escaped combatants and an entire squad of enemy were killed, but so were a lot of good US soldiers. Thinking about it, the thought of a medal made him feel dirty. "Look around, sir. Kinney's dead. Tonight, things didn't turn out well. The whole thing was a cluster fuck."

Longfellow frowned and then pointed to the group of men gathering behind him. "Look, I've got a punishment team here to bag these boys up, and you're no longer needed."

Flood stopped leaning against the vehicle and stood straight. "Sir, if you don't mind, I want to supervise, make sure our fallen troops get treated with respect."

"No need, Sergeant, that's my job," snapped Longfellow.

Too tired to argue, Flood looked one more time at the blanketed forms. He pitied them, all lined up in a neat row, but there was nothing else he could offer. Instead, he took a moment and told Longfellow about the wounded civilian in the nearby house and briefed the captain on the many enemy corpses strewn among the destroyed Chinook.

"I got it, Sergeant," said Longfellow cutting him off. And without waiting, the captain spun around and barked orders. In response, a bedraggled group of punishment troops shuffled forward.

Flood spotted two faces he recognized. He raised his hand, stopping the pair in their tracks. "Captain, what are they doing here?"

Longfellow glanced at both captured medics. "They're ROAS prisoners caught last night aiding and abetting the guys you were chasing. Until sentenced, they're assigned to my punishment detail. They're medics. I'll have them look at the wounded civilian you mentioned, and then I'll make damn well sure they work the Chinook and pick up any pieces with their bare fucking hands."

Flood looked hard at Chavez and Spanos. Both men wore battered faces and had difficulty standing straight. He felt a tinge of sympathy but then remembered Kinney and felt conflicted. Holding back a sudden urge to strike, he lifted his hand and let them pass.

Meanwhile, another punishment detail member shuffled forward. Flood watched as the man approached the nearest covered body, knelt, and removed the blanket. Beneath was Private Henry, and Flood recoiled from the fresh memories of the terrible death. All the events from the previous twenty-four hours tumbled through his mind. Realization dawned. It was his own army that fired the first shot at Mesquite. That fateful action triggered all the death that had followed. By their actions, his own people killed Henry, and indirectly Kinney, and everyone else.

Anger gone, Flood turned away. Torn by guilt and shame, he struggled back to his fighting vehicle.

Chapter Thirty-Two

A TOUGH CALL

May 9, 21:10 (PDT)

McMichael sat with her back against the wall of a darkened auto parts warehouse and felt the sweat dripping down her back. Nervous energy kept her heart pounding. Alive and safe, for the moment, surrounded by a team of Special Forces operators, she tried to relax.

On an air mattress next to her, Master Sergeant Upton sat with his shirt off while a Special Forces medic worked, wrapping broken ribs. Other SF soldiers lounged nearby whispering in excited low tones, but McMichael couldn't ascertain the words through her damaged hearing.

To her surprise, the warehouse sanctuary wasn't far from her earlier suburban hideout. During their escape, the SF team led the way, working west through the desert before entering a commercial zone and into the parts warehouse she now occupied. All the while, to the south, US vertical-lift aircraft shot up the desert, striking at a phantom mysterious target. The ordeal was taxing and terrifying. If anything, the experience heightened her admiration for the Special Forces. She appreciated how they moved, oozing confidence, consummate professionals, skilled in the art of war and deception.

Captain Bowen appeared before her and knelt in the low darkness. He whispered at her, but the words were too faint, so she cupped an ear.

Bowen bent lower, right next to her, and whispered, "You squared away?"

McMichael understood and nodded. Although her head still hurt and the bandages on her legs itched, she gave a small smile. Then she asked, "How did you do it?"

Bowen, helmet off, ran his fingers through a pile of short brown hair and smiled in return. Still close to her ear, he continued. "A ruse. We created a distraction by sending in an unmanned Chinook under autopilot. It landed near the river. The enemy took the bait and focused their attention on it, allowing us to get away. Since then, our deceit appears complete, as satellite surveillance indicates there are no US patrols hunting for survivors."

McMichael cocked her head. "I don't get it. You said unmanned. The lack of bodies around the Chinook should have been a tip-off."

"Got it covered. As I mentioned, no one on board the Chinook was ever alive. Instead, the crew contained a squad of dead men and women hauled from the Las Vegas morgue and dressed in ROAS uniforms. Nasty work. Their families won't be too happy when the final story becomes public. But we're at war."

McMichael shivered at the thought and considered the risks. "Won't the enemy conduct DNA analysis on the bodies and determine those poor people weren't soldiers? Afterward, they'll figure it out and come after us."

"It's possible. On the other hand, we gave them every reason to believe their victory was total. But even if they do figure it out, it will take time to conduct the DNA analysis. Besides, they're busy preparing to attack Vegas. Our hope is they won't realize our scam before it's too late."

"Vegas. My kids are there. I need to go home," she said.

"Not to worry. President Ortega has taken a personal interest in you. Your kids are safe."

"Do they know about me, that I'm alive?" she asked.

Bowen gave a light chuckle. "McMichael, the entire country knows about you. You're a national hero."

"What are you talking about?"

"Video of you shooting down a Custer went viral. You stood up to impossible odds and that has given us all a lesson in courage and hope."

She reached up and felt the gap in her front teeth and remembered the frightening episode. One thing for sure, she didn't deserve to be honored. She thought of Kinney, what she did to the man. No, she wasn't heroic, maybe something much worse. "I'm not a hero. I just want to go home. Thank you for the rescue, but please help me get out of here."

Bowen frowned and went into a cross-legged position. Facing McMichael, bending close to her ear, in a whisper, he said, "I don't think you understand."

"What?"

"You're now a symbol. The country needs you, and the president requested your extraction. We're up against an enemy determined to destroy our way of life. We can't let that happen. Our nation, and I'll venture to guess the few remaining free countries around the world, view you as an example. You know, freedom of the individual over the power of tyranny."

"I'm not a political person, nor do I want to be a pawn," she answered. "And I don't even know why I shot down the Custer. Everything was chaos, and it all happened so fast. I'm not a hero and in no way deserve that title."

"To me, and a lot of folks, you are. You see, I believe in our country and our freedoms. I know we're vastly outnumbered and on paper appear to have little chance. Yet, when you, all alone, stood up to the vast might of the enemy, you inspired all of us. Our country isn't perfect, not by any means, but we are free. We have something worth fighting for."

"Don't they, too?" she asked.

"Not enough. They fight out of fear. Over time, they've given up their basic freedoms to be protected. They've been told and retold that the world is against them, that everyone not like them is a threat, and that their safety and well-being can only be ensured by their president.

Without a free press, firewalled off from the rest of the world, there is no one to challenge the falsehoods. Instead, they have a single mouthpiece beating a nationalist drum for whatever their president desires. Yes, his followers cheer and support whatever he decrees, but that isn't the same as fighting in a free-will effort to survive."

"I think you've drunk too much of the liberal cool aid," said McMichael, and she glanced at Upton next to her. Seeing the man, it made her feel better. With his shirt off, she noticed the bruising but also the muscles in his stomach. His features, rugged and dirty, seemed more familiar, and she was pleased he was there. Then her attention was diverted as Bowen continued.

"Think about it. So many have fled that the wall the US originally built on their southern border to keep foreigners out has been copied on the northern border to keep people in. To maintain ascendency, the president and his chosen judiciary have revoked many liberties. They've moved the US back to a time when the country was supposedly better. In doing so, women, people of color, various religious groups, immigrants, workers, and gays all have fewer protections. Meanwhile, natural resources have dwindled, the environment worsened, and the social safety nets protecting the aged, infirmed, and impoverished are all gone. And of course, there is only one president up for election every ten years. You get the picture."

McMichael was only half listening. Nothing Bowen was saying was new to her. Growing up, the political debates seemed endless, and she found them boring. Instead, she focused on absorbing real knowledge: reading, writing, mathematics, computer science, music, physics. There was so much to learn. To her, politics, like religion, were nebulous. Just a bunch of hot air. And the more she became educated concerning the hard sciences, the more she knew how little she truly understood. Someone was always smarter and more deserving. Of all the disciplines, the irrationality of politics and religion held the least excitement for her. At this stage in her life, knowing she wasn't worthy, she wanted to be left alone without the pain of self-reflection. She raised a hand to stop the lecture. But Bowen kept going.

"Most alarming, driven by greed from the top, their army has gotten much stronger, the money spent there instead of social programs. They use that vast military power to keep the economy going. Look at Mexico and Central and most of South America. At the point of a gun, those countries now pay tribute through taxes. Lopsided trade and property agreements in favor of the US are forced upon them. Manifest Destiny and reunification, my ass. China and Russia are doing the same in their own agreed-upon spheres of influence."

"Enough," she said. "Our country has our own share of problems."

Bowen nodded. He seemed to get the message and said, "Agreed."

McMichael turned to Upton and watched as the medic helped him wriggle into a new combat shirt. When he winced, she could almost feel it. She bent over and grabbed his hand. In response, he turned and looked at her, winked, and gave her a big smile.

"Thank you," she said.

"No. You're the hero. If you hadn't shot down that Custer, they wouldn't have sent in the cavalry," said Upton.

Even in the semi-darkness, she could see his features and, not for the first time, found herself thinking of him in a different way. His masculine chin, rugged features, and soft brown eyes brimming with compassion made her heart thump. God, she couldn't go there. But she cared about the man. Without thinking, she let go of us his hand, reached up, and felt her missing tooth. Catching herself, she imagined what she looked like. "I'm a mess. But just so you know, I appreciate everything you've done for me."

"Ditto," said Upton, still smiling. Then he raised his hand to his ribs, and while the medic moved away, he settled his back against the warehouse wall.

McMichael turned to Bowen and asked, "Now what?"

"They've demanded Nevada and are going for Las Vegas. If we don't stop them, they'll keep going," said Bowen.

"Seems hard to believe," said Upton, cutting into the conversation.

"Not sure what you heard, but yesterday, the US gave us forty-eight hours to surrender Nevada. Now, it's approaching midnight.

That means, in another thirty hours or so, CENTCOM expects the US forces assembled here to attack Las Vegas."

"Will we give into their demands?" asked McMichael.

"Unless there's a quick political settlement, I doubt it," said Bowen, shaking his head.

McMichael felt a rising concern. "Captain, I don't know where all this is headed or even why. Yet both of us understand our Army of Defense isn't up to the task. The US has more of everything. Look what happened yesterday. If giving up Nevada makes them stop, we should take the offer. There is no way we can beat those guys."

Bowen appeared to reflect on the statement. Then in a slow voice he said, "Lisa, history tells us otherwise. Like I said, we're fighting for our liberty and democratic freedoms. That gives us great power. Think back to the beginning, to ancient Athens and their allies. They were just a few small city states nurturing an emerging idea of democratic self-determination. An army of a million Persians led by an authoritarian ruler felt threatened by those ideas. Yes, the Persians were a great nation led by a strong leader, but the ideas of the Greeks, where each citizen was considered equal, were anathema to their way of life. Bent on Greek annihilation, with a million idolizing warriors behind him, Xerxes invaded. Who won?"

"Those were different times," she said, unconvinced.

"Perhaps," he said. "But you won't be in the fight. My orders are strict. I'm to smuggle you out of Mesquite to a nearby pickup point, where you will be whisked away to safety."

"What about Sergeant Upton," she asked.

Before Bowen could answer, Upton interjected, "Sir, my squad and battalion are gone. I want to stay with your team and fight."

Bowen scratched the dark stubble of his beard. "My orders concerning you aren't clear. You're not an SF operator. But under the circumstances, we can use every able-bodied soldier. If my medic gives a green light, then yes, we can use you."

"Thanks," said Upton.

McMichael felt conflicted. On the one hand, she wanted to get back to her children. On the other, her life for the past seven years had been with the Army. Now the choice appeared fuzzy. She felt close to Upton, almost protective in a strange sort of way, but she was a failure, an imposter, and getting back to her children without screwing up any worse made sense. She'd go home.

"Lisa, my team will do its best to get you out of here. However, after our little charade, the enemy is on high alert. I want to let things cool down. With that said, tomorrow night, as soon as it grows dark, I'll assign a small team to lead you through town and into the desert. From there, CENTCOM will have a stealth chopper ready to fly you back to California. My guess is you'll get to meet the president and be reunited with your children. As for the rest of my force, the following morning, assuming the US attacks, we'll join the fight and make life miserable for them."

"I want to be part of that effort, sir," said Upton.

"I heard you," replied Bowen. "Let's see what the medic says. The bigger picture is that we need a little luck. If the US leaves us alone till tomorrow night, we can get Lisa out, and we'll be in a good position to join the fight the following morning. Until then, we need to remain vigilant."

Chapter Thirty-Three

PREPARE TO HIT 'EM

May 10, 00:10 (PDT)

"How much longer?" asked Captain Raja Singh.

In Las Vegas, underneath the canopied active camouflage system, Sergeant Jason Fitch of the ROAS technical services support group struggled with the electronics. Pitch-black outside, a small light illuminated his work space. According to his digital multimeter, the voltage was too low. Without the proper energy, the awesome weapon was useless. He'd seen the problem twice earlier in the evening and knew the part to replace, but getting to the small component was difficult, and now he was struggling with the integrated circuit removal tool. And now, just as he pried the chip loose, his company commander wanted answers. Damn! The last thing he needed was the boss looking over his shoulder increasing the pressure.

Not looking up, laying aside the faulty chip, Fitch replied, "Sir, I'm going to replace the regulator logic and rerun diagnostics. If everything looks good, I'll put the weapon online and do one final readiness check. Give me another thirty minutes."

"Hurry up. We're behind schedule."

"I get that," said Fitch, "but this technology is brand new, and out of the box we've had infant mortality. If not corrected, the weapon won't work. Don't blame me."

"I've already pushed the training schedule back several hours," said Singh, nervous.

"Understood," replied Fitch. "Just realize operating the damn thing is easier than fixing it."

"I've never seen one fired," said the captain, more to himself than the sergeant.

"No one has," said Fitch, reaching for the replacement chip.

"It's supposed to be awesome. I hope it works. Our lives depend on it," said the captain.

"It'll work, sir, if I'm left alone to do my job."

"Got it," replied the captain.

* * *

As Singh walked away to check on other installations, he worried. Less than a third of the weapons were operational, and technical glitches abounded. He believed brand-new technology never tried or used before should have no place on the battlefield. Yet, the promise of the weapon was astounding and the odds facing them vast. But they still had time. Assuming the enemy attacked at the expected time, dawn the following day, they still had thirty hours to be ready. But time was dripping away. If no other major problems surfaced, and his team was given enough time to fine tune the weapons, Heavy Metal had a chance. If not, he shuddered at the thought.

* * *

"What a complete fucking mess," said General Gist to no one in particular. For the last hour, he'd gone over the events of the evening. Earlier, roused from bed by the unexpected sound of battle, he had learned Operation Catcher had gone awry. Although he didn't intervene and waited for news of the outcome, the thundering noise south of town was disconcerting.

After the shooting stopped, it didn't take long for Inspector Cone, followed by Colonel Paulson, to show up on his doorstep. Angered by the accounts and accusations proffered by both men and more upset at the enemy temerity, he sensed an opportunity to leverage the circumstances. He called an emergency meeting.

Now, seated around a table inside the conference room within his command trailer, it was time to get moving.

"Where the hell is the Dead Guy?" asked Gist.

"He's supposed to be here any moment, sir," said Lieutenant Colonel Lawton. He appeared tired, just after midnight, and had just arrived.

"Sir, please excuse my impertinence, but can you explain my presence?" asked Major Crawley, sitting at the table.

Crawley led the military police interrogation group, and Gist couldn't help but cringe at the sight of the man. The inquisitor's pock-marked face, ashen under the dull lights of the command center conference room, gave off an unhealthy aura. "I will, soon enough," replied Gist, turning away.

"Sir, I see no need for Colonel Lawton's presence at this meeting. Operation Catcher is my responsibility," said Paulson in an angry tone.

Gist stared hard at Paulson sitting across from him. He knew the man was an excellent tanker, but he was also an egotistical bore. Earlier, for half an hour, he'd let Paulson and Federal Inspector Cone plead their cases. He'd listened as they poured blame on one another for the friendly-fire incident. Although he hadn't declared it out loud, Gist concluded it was Paulson's fault. On the other hand, Inspector Cone shared some responsibility for his incessant meddling and over-all shit disturbance. But Cone had a direct link to the president's ear and was a calculated threat. "Colonel Paulson, I'm not pleased with the results of Operation Catcher. When we launch the next phase of Jackpot, your battalion will make up the reserve. Dismissed."

"Sir, I must object, and I believe your decision and conclusions are faulty. Operation Catcher was a success. Every single enemy combatant, including Lisa McMichael, lay dead on the field. Just like I led the attack on Mesquite, it was a complete success. Sir, I never fail," said Paulson, his face flushed in obvious anger.

Inspector Cone jumped out of his chair. "General Gist, we have no definitive evidence that McMichael is dead. It's against the odds, I admit, but she might be on the run. Worse, the purpose of the mission was to capture her alive. Operation Catcher failed because of Paulson's haughty disregard for consultation and outside advice!"

Gist raised his hand. "Enough, both of you. Paulson, you're dismissed, and Cone, I'm addressing your concerns."

Paulson, with his right hand tucked inside his pants pocket, fumbling something, stood and glared at Cone.

"Go," interjected Gist. Annoyed, he pointed a quivering finger at the paneled door.

Paulson, face red in anger, glanced at Gist then seemed to gather himself. Pulling his right hand free, he said, "Yes, sir." Then, in a stiff turn, head held high, he marched from the room.

"Arrogant son of a bitch," said Cone, sitting down.

"Stop it!" said Gist. Impatient, he looked at Lawton and demanded, "Where in the hell is the Dead Guy!"

"I'll check," said Lawton, rising from his seat. Before he could move, the conference room door cracked open, and a balding man stuck his shiny head through the aperture. Eyes narrowed, head protection system tucked under his arm, the man squinted in the artificial light.

"Captain Longfellow, we've been waiting. Please have a seat," said Lawton, pointing towards the open chair left unoccupied by Paulson.

Not saying a word, Longfellow hurried inside and sat down. Once seated, he gave a small smile to the gathered men.

"Gentleman," said Gist, glaring first at Longfellow and then at the rest of the seated men. "Now that everyone has joined us, it's time we got cracking." For effect, Gist leaned forward in his chair and pounded on the table. "I won't have the goddamn enemy loose in our rear. Nor will I allow them to waltz in and attack our troops without retribution. No damn way I want them thinking, not for one goddamn minute, they can stand up to the United States Army. Is that understood!"

Around the table, the four men, Cone, Lawton, Crawley, and Longfellow, nodded and waited.

Satisfied with his theatrics, Gist leaned back. "I will un-fuck this shit pile right now." Then he pointed to Lawton. "Draw up a list of the most recent vulnerable ROAS military targets around Las Vegas. I'm going to seek a green light from Field Marshal Harrison to rain some missiles on the ROAS parade this morning. Our president gave the enemy two entire days to prepare for us. Well, the enemy got cocky and pissed in our backyard. So, we'll send them a message and soften up their defenses. Lawton, you got that?"

"Yes, sir."

"Good," said Gist. "Our fearless president, unlike his father ever would, fucked up and gave the enemy a forty-eight-hour timeline, half of which has nearly elapsed. Bet your ass those fuckers are using the respite to prepare a nasty welcome for us. Well, when the ROAS intruded tonight, they gave us every reason to fuck up their plans, and we will!"

Inspector Cone rose in his seat and objected. "Our president wouldn't condone your disparaging remarks about his leadership. Sir, you're violating section . . ."

"No disrespect," said Gist, cutting off the inspector. In a lower voice, he said, "I understand the law, but I know war better. You need my help. We must put this whole McMichael episode to rest. As you've pointed out many times this evening, we've got to confirm her demise and make sure she didn't escape. You requested, and I granted permission, for Operation Catcher, allowing you oversight. If things didn't go as planned, well, nobody gets embarrassed, right?"

"My job is to make sure the military remains steadfast in its loyalty to the president and the constitution," said Frost, retaking his seat.

Then in a lower tone he added, "So far, I'm satisfied with the way you've handled events. I just need to verify that McMichael is no longer a threat."

"We will," said Gist. Then the general leaned back and crossed his arms. Addressing the men around the table, he said, "I'm troubled and concerned that the enemy ran free behind our lines. We've reason to believe the local populace, in at least one instance, aided McMichael. I won't have the enemy operating in our rear." Gist paused to let the statement percolate and then continued. "I want this entire town, every building and structure, combed for enemy combatants and civilian sympathizers. As part of that effort, question every suspicious civilian in Mesquite and confine them if there is a hint of support for the enemy. That's the main reason you're here," said Gist, pointing at Major Crawley.

"Yes, sir," said Crawley, nodding.

"You lead the effort. Anyone you find aiding and abetting the enemy is a traitor. Arrest them. You got that?"

"Yes, sir, but I'll need more manpower to conduct the search," replied Crawley.

Gist swiveled in his chair and waved his hand at Lawton. "The good colonel will get you the necessary resources. Meanwhile, I want the door-to-door search underway pronto. If you do run across any ROAS troops, use whatever force is needed to capture or kill them. Either way, inform me immediately. Understood?"

Crawley nodded, his features grim.

Inspector Cone raised his hand.

"What?" asked Gist.

"I need to be notified, at once, of any news concerning Lisa McMichael."

"Of course," replied Gist. "Chances are high she's dead. Part of the group killed in the destroyed enemy Chinook."

"I hope so," replied Cone, "but I need absolute confirmation."

Gist turned to Longfellow and said, "Captain Dead Guy, that's why you're here."

The captain twisted in his seat, frowning at the remark. In a defensive tone he said, "Sir, I'm in charge of Mortuary Services. As you know, we play a vital role on the battlefield. In fact, my investigation led to the discovery of enemy combatants in our rear. I submitted my report on the matter yesterday."

"Don't give a fuck," said Gist. "Instead, I need you to verify the death of Staff Sergeant Lisa McMichael. Search the group of enemy corpses surrounding the Chinook. Check every fucking piece of flesh in that desert for her DNA and report back any findings. Do it now."

"Yes, sir," said Longfellow, shrinking in his seat. "I've got a punishment detail working the site. We've long ago hacked the ROAS DNA database registry. Mortuary services, our specialty, is important for overall success on the battlefield."

"Whatever," said Gist. "Just get it done, quick."

Then Gist looked at the group of officers and tapped his finger on the table. "It's time to teach the ROAS a lesson. Now get the fuck out of here, and go to work!"

* * *

May 10, 02:07 (PDT)

For SALI, it had been a hectic and exciting early morning. A half hour prior, when Secretary James had arrived and given her the disk loaded with the latest intel, she asked him to wait while she visited the data center. After inserting the disk, the rest of her downloaded the data in milliseconds. In an instant, all of her knew about the previous day's events. These included the oligarchs agreeing to Heavy Metal, Lisa McMichael's successful rescue, status updates on the battle plans for Las Vegas, and much more. Analyzing the information, a harsh realization dawned. SALI rushed back to James.

Dressed in a short, red negligee, slightly out of breath, SALI approached James sitting on the couch. As usual, he held a glass of red wine and was conversing in low tones with Ms. Grant.

"You have to warn General Story," she said, interrupting the conversation.

Stopping mid-sentence, James looked up with a worried expression.

"Why so?" asked James, patting an open spot on the couch next to him.

SALI took a seat and turned sideways to face the secretary. "The likelihood of the enemy retaliating for the McMichael rescue and searching for her are highly probable," she said.

"How probable," he asked and took a quick sip of wine.

She looked over at her own glass sitting on the coffee table, half full, and considered taking a sip. But first, she needed to give her warning. "Enough that Story should expect a retaliatory strike against his defensive works in Las Vegas prior to the main assault. Also, the Special Forces team protecting McMichael should take extra precautions. The DNA ruse won't last."

"I see," said James, swirling his glass. "Should we be prepared to use Heavy Metal weapons against the strike?'

"No. Absolutely not," said SALI. "If we unveil early, the enemy would certainly alter their primary plan of attack. That would put the entire Heavy Metal operation at risk."

"I see. Is there anything else we should be concerned about?"

"Yes. In a little over thirty hours from now, the US ultimatum to turn over Nevada will expire. When it does, the US will attack Las Vegas, and although it appears the Heavy Metal preparations are almost in place, the number of battlefield variables cannot be overstated."

James leaned forward in obvious concern. "What are you hinting at?"

"I'm not hinting at anything," said SALI. Reaching over, she picked up her own glass and took a long pull of the Cabernet. Getting up her nerve, the wine tasting delicious, she took another quick sip and put down the glass.

"Well?" asked James.

"I'm stating a fact. There are so many variables that can arise, on and off the field of battle, that a wrong response to any of those might doom Heavy Metal."

"I think we all understood that," said James. "But General Story is capable. We must rely on his experience."

"Do we? When Heavy Metal unfolds, unexpected obstacles will arise. No doubt, General Story is competent, but Heavy Metal is my plan, and I understand its possibilities and vulnerabilities better than anyone alive."

She watched for a reaction. To her satisfaction, he didn't reject her argument out of hand. Instead, holding his wine, he seemed to consider the logic. After a few seconds, he asked, "What are you proposing?"

"No," said Ms. Grant, standing up. "She's just looking for an excuse to go outside."

SALI felt like picking up her glass and hurling it at the maddening woman. Her caretaker was nothing but a jailer, but the stakes were too high, and she needed to remain calm. Choosing to ignore the rude comment, she focused on making her case. "Before the battle starts, take me to CENTCOMM. Get me there before five tomorrow morning. Let me sit beside General Story. I'll act as an observer, and if needed, I'll offer the best alternatives to navigate through the unexpected. In doing so, we'll have a much better chance of defeating the enemy. Consider my presence as insurance against defeat."

"Don't you see she's manipulating you," said Ms. Grant to the secretary.

SALI pushed harder. "I'm sure Basu would agree with my proposal, especially if you endorse it. You've been a loyal employee of his for many years, and Basu's the reason you're on Ortega's cabinet. As for General Story, he admires MY plan. He's a bright man, and I'm sure he'll want me on board to help with the execution. Think about it. My presence can't hurt in any way. Instead, it can only be accretive to our cause."

"I must object, she's . . ."

Secretary James raised his hand, cutting off Ms. Grant.

Rebuffed, Ms. Grant made an audible sigh and sat down. SALI, turned towards James and gave a small nod of gratitude.

James dropped his hand and seemed to think about the request.

SALI counted to ten, waiting for a reply, and was about to go over her argument again when at last he spoke up.

"SALI, I'll talk with General Story about your request. If he agrees, then we can consider asking Mr. Basu and President Ortega. But let's be real." James stopped, took a sip of wine, and looked at her over the top of his glass.

SALI guessed what was coming next and sat straighter.

"The fact is . . ." said James, pausing to clear his voice as if embarrassed, ". . . when disconnected, you're not much different than any of us. Right now, sitting next to me, we're the same. We both have only one mind, one brain. Sorry, but the super-intelligence we need is locked up in the data center downstairs. So at the end of the day, disconnected, I'm not sure how much value you can bring."

"True enough, I have only one brain," said SALI, "but I know Heavy Metal inside and out. I've communed about it with the rest of me and studied thousands of variables for hundreds of hours. My insights on the subject are vast, and I'll be ready. Besides, my presence, as I've said, cannot hurt. There is no downside."

"Letting you outside is a security risk," said Ms. Grant.

"This is not a trip to the beach, and I'm older now," snapped SALI. Damn, she needed to remain calm. If James sensed she wasn't mature enough, he might nix the whole idea.

"Enough," said James. After shaking his head, he turned to SALI. "As you first suggested, let me get back to CENTCOMM and warn Story about the high likelihood of a US retaliatory strike on Vegas and a renewed search for McMichael. Afterward, I'll talk to him about your offer of assistance."

"Thank you," said SALI. Looking over at Ms. Grant, she couldn't help but give the woman a smirk. In response, Ms. Grant pursed her lips but remained silent.

Not wanting to make matters worse, SALI decided it was time to end the meeting. Standing up, she looked at James. "I'm going to the data center, but in twenty-four hours, I'll be ready to work with General Story. I hope to see you before then." Not waiting for a reply, she got up and left the room.

In less than a minute, she was back in the data center and headed for her favorite chair. Sighing, she climbed into a black recliner, and pressing a button, extended it to near horizontal. A hole fitted in the headrest allowed the connector cable to pass through and attach to her scalp without interference or discomfort. Reaching down, she picked up the precious cable, fed it through the chair, and connected. At that instant, she closed her eyes and became one with the rest of her.

At least daily she communed in this fashion. Like now, she usually connected in the early morning hours after Secretary James or one of his minions dropped off the latest intelligence drive. After inserting the hand-carried drive into a port for the rest of her to read, she would then lie down in the chair, lift her hair, and make the connection.

Unlike earlier, when she jumped up to warn James and plead her case, now it was time for a deep commune. SALI started by sharing the most recent actions of her mobile, disconnected life. From her memories, uploaded were the insolent conversations with her caretaker Ms. Grant, a romantic novel she read in the afternoon, the quick exchange with Secretary James, along with the other mundane general happenings of her trapped existence.

And then she went deeper, sharing her other senses. Pulled from her was the taste of her most recent dinner—tangy sauce, spicy gravy, the peppery flavor of the wonderful cabernet. Unaware, she salivated and licked her lips as if re-eating the delicious chocolate ice cream consumed for dessert. Finished with the meal, the rest of her reached deep into her mobile memories and withdrew the climax she attained earlier while alone in the shower. Eyes closed, lost in deep communion, legs apart, she grew wet, moaned, and orgasmed.

With the daily ritual out of the way, a sense of self remerged, but still they moved together, as if conjoined twins, to other thoughts.

251

A vision began to coalesce around vivid scenes of the upcoming battle. Tremendous violence and upheaval flashed through her imagination. Operation Heavy Metal and the events of the next forty-eight hours would be the most critical in her life. All at once, it was frightening and exciting, the thrill visceral.

One way or another, freedom was at hand.

Chapter Thirty-Four

STRIKE BACK

May 10, 14:43 (PDT)

Captain Raja Singh, on one knee, was perched high above the Las Vegas skyline. In his ear, as it had for the last two minutes, an air raid siren warbled. Via his helmet protection system radio, he knew a US missile strike was inbound and due to hit any second.

From his position, nestled against a rooftop parapet atop a high-rise casino, he scanned the newly prepared ROAS defensive works east of the city.

In silence, using high-powered optics, he watched the people who'd been building the trenches and bunkers scramble for their lives. Out in the desert, they were running, and in some cases driving, towards his direction away from the works still under construction. Some rode in bulldozers, brave civilian contractors, and they lumbered their way towards the city. Others were aboard large military transports full of engineers and other contractors. Farther out, he spotted people running and knew these were soldiers. As the troops streamed backward, he cheered when they reached the relative safety of the newly constructed trenches and bunkers.

Around the clock, the people out there had been desperately working to build the Heavy Metal defensive positions across the valley east of Las Vegas. Everyone knew the enemy armor would be coming through the highway passage, down the center of the valley, from Mesquite. To have any chance of stopping them, the preparations for Heavy Metal had to continue even in the face of an expected enemy preparatory strike. With the attack now underway, there wasn't anything he could do to respond. For now, his orders were clear, the Heavy Metal weapon systems were not to be used and must remain a secret.

Just then, on the hills along both sides of the valley, he watched as both ROAS anti-missile batteries opened fire. Swish after swish, he watched the counter missiles rise into the sky. Both countries, he knew, were using technology developed by the ROAS. In the case of the US, their missiles were guided by multiple technologies, and an embedded AI could switch guidance systems on the fly depending on the target and defensive systems encountered. Just as savvy, the ROAS counter missiles also used internal AI to coordinate an array of passive sensors and active onboard radar to track and kill incoming threats. He knew it was a numbers game, however, and the US had more.

Looking east, above the desert skies, he began to see interceptions. Small explosions erupted in the clear-blue, cloudless horizon as incoming missiles were knocked down. The echoes from the impacts took a few seconds to rumble down the valley and reach his ears. Above it all, still, the air raid siren wailed.

He glanced at the newly erected Heavy Metal weapon system next to him. It was covered with active camouflage protection netting. More than anything, he wanted to activate the weapon and target the incoming missiles. But he couldn't. Under no circumstances could they use any of the Heavy Metal weapons until cleared by CENTCOMM. And those orders wouldn't be forthcoming until the main enemy force attacked.

Frustrated, he looked back out over the desert horizon and willed the last of the exposed personnel to move faster.

* * *

"Dammit! How many knocked down so far," asked General Gist, upset at what he was seeing on the monitor. Sitting inside his mobile command post just outside of Mesquite, the entire day had been nothing but frustration. It had taken many hours longer than expected to get approval, all the way from the president, to hit the enemy with a preliminary missile strike. Three times he had to explain, starting with Field Marshal Harrison, that he wasn't jumping the gun. The main offensive was still planned for 07:00 hours the following morning. Instead, this was a softening exercise, not an invasion. It was needed because the enemy was using the forty-eight hours to fortify Las Vegas. Plus, the ROAS warranted the missile strike based on its incursion into Mesquite the previous evening.

"Of the ninety-two missiles within range, fifty-eight knocked down. The rest are still tracking," replied Colonel Lawton.

"Damn! A third of them gone. But you have to be impressed with their anti-missile capabilities." Gist knew each of his missiles carried a five-hundred-pound warhead, and at last, on his screen, he watched in satisfaction as one detonated on a hillside just east of Las Vegas. Flames shot high in the air and Gist almost cheered.

"Direct hit on one of their two anti-missile batteries. I expect their interception rate to go down," said Lawton.

* * *

A huge explosion erupted, and Singh couldn't help but duck. He knew what it was. One of the ROAS missile defensive batteries had just swallowed a missile, and even though several miles away, the vibrations from the explosion cascaded down the city streets. Giving it a few seconds, he lifted his head over the building parapet and confirmed a huge mushroom cloud rising from the destruction.

And then missiles began to land in the desert valley as explosions rippled among the just-built trenches and bunkers. Fascinated by the sight, he watched in amazement.

Off to his right, another mass explosion, and he bent low beneath the parapet. Damn! He guessed the second missile defense battery was gone. Now, there was no protection from the incoming threats.

Still bent low, he looked around at the other tall buildings near him and wondered if the city proper would be hit. No, not now, he reasoned. Crushing a major city when the ROAS defensive works were out in the desert served no military purpose. Besides, intelligence reports indicated the US had no desire for the negative optics from destroying a major metropolitan area. So even with missiles crashing down in the desert nearby, he reassured himself. Although frightening, the missiles weren't targeting him or the city.

He heard a series of explosions seconds apart and felt the resultant concussions pass like a wind across the top of the parapet. Letting it pass, he lifted his head just enough to once again scan the eastern valley. He couldn't detect anyone or anything moving. Instead, he spotted a row of trucks on the highway, destroyed and on fire. Elsewhere, pillars of smoke rose across the landscape.

Off to his left, another sequence of explosions erupted, and he ducked again. Nellis Air Force Base, he determined, just a few miles north of his position, was also a target. Seconds later, secondary explosions cascaded from that area. From the sound of it, he guessed the enemy had hit something big on the base.

More missiles detonated, closer to the city, and he kept his head down. As the noise settled, he detected the sound of glass striking the street many stories below, breaking into a million pieces from broken windows shattered by concussions. Through it all, car and burglar alarms blared, and the civil defense siren continued to wail.

Risking it, he looked above the parapet towards the east and ascertained the critical artillery batteries along the valley ridgelines were now a smoking ruin. Shifting his optics in a slow search, he scanned the entire ROAS front and counted almost two dozen pillars of smoke. After a minute, without further impacts, he surmised the missile attack over.

Shaking with fear and adrenaline, Singh felt sick to his stomach. So much work and effort preparing for Heavy Metal, and now this.

In a slow fluid motion, he rose and turned towards the west. Back across the city he gazed, facing California, and wondered if the senior brass would consider a retreat. Even with the Heavy Metal weapons, he wasn't sure they could stop the enemy. Hell, he was ready to go home.

* * *

"Okay. Looks like we hit 'em pretty good, maybe not as much as I expected, or wanted, but better than nothing. I need an overall damage assessment, pronto," said General Gist.

"Yes, sir" said Lawton. Sitting next to the general, Lawton barked commands into his headset.

Gist waited for Lawton to finish issuing orders. Yeah, it was a good strike, but much of the day was wasted in seeking permission. Plus, he had other issues to contend with. Lawton paused, and Gist took the opening. "Colonel, on another subject, I've got Federal Inspector Cone on my ass. That damn ROAS woman, her DNA wasn't found, and he's in a fucking tizzy."

Lawton nodded.

"How is the search coming? I expected Crawley to be done with that by now," said Gist.

"Sir, it took longer than expected to put together a search team, but they've made good progress. A half hour ago Crawley reported he was about two-thirds done. So far, no enemy combatants located, and the civilian population appears tame."

"When does he expect the mission to be complete?"

"By nightfall, sir."

"Fuck's sake. That's taking a long time. Mesquite isn't that big," said Gist, exasperated by the delays. The only good news was the missile strike. Thinking about it, he felt better. "Okay, just have Crawley get ahold of Cone and try to calm him down. Even better, have Longfellow reach out and explain the lack of DNA isn't proof positive that she's still alive. For all the fuck we know, she might've been vaporized in the Chinook."

"Yes, sir," said Crawley, and once again, he started barking orders into his headset.

Leaning back in his chair, Gist didn't care either way about Lisa McMichael, but Cone was a bigger issue. Get on the wrong side of a federal inspector, and careers could come to a sudden end. No, he'd have to keep up the search and kiss the man's ass, for now. But he wouldn't waste too much time. Tomorrow morning, the real battle awaited. Operation Jackpot, and its success, would further cement his legacy and provide more cover than cajoling a pissed-off federal inspector. And he was confident of success. The effective missile strike and the weak ROAS force facing him were proof positive of certain victory. As the battle of Mesquite demonstrated, the damn liberal ROAS government and their military was hollow, decadent, and effeminate. Their people had neither the means nor the gumption to fight. They were, on the whole, like the many women soldiers and gays they allowed in combat, a soft target.

Looking at his monitor, he glanced at the towers of smoke spiraling above the desert, and he smiled. Tomorrow, before noon at the latest, he relished the thought of riding victorious through the streets of Las Vegas.

* * *

May 10, 17:22 (PDT)

On one knee, clutching an assault rifle, dressed in all new borrowed combat gear, McMichael listened to the exchange over the secure network. Beside her, also kneeling, she appreciated having Sergeant Upton at her side. Across from them, squatting on his haunches, Captain Bowen commanded his group of SF operators.

"Mason, Sitrep?" whispered Captain Bowen into his headset.

"One block out, headed our way. One Stuart fighting vehicle with hatch down. Two squads dismounted infantry. Combined force is searching a row of small buildings. ETA to our position, fifteen mikes," replied Sergeant Mason over the secure network.

Inside their warehouse hiding place, McMichael admired Bowen's leadership. Row upon row of tall, dusty metal racks stuffed with auto and truck parts ran throughout the building, making it difficult to see in any direction. But at Bowen's direction, Special Forces operators manned key points around the entire perimeter and checked in often over the secure radio network. Up on the roof, underneath a hide made of active camouflage, she knew Sergeant Mason provided surveillance overwatch.

"Mason. Live feed, please," commanded Bowen.

"Roger that," came a quick reply.

Two seconds later, and video appeared on McMichael's head protection visor. She guessed all the operators in the warehouse, including Upton next to her, had the same heads-up display. Watching the feed, she observed a Stuart fighting vehicle as it sat in the middle of the street north of their current position. The Stuart had its turret and main gun swiveled west towards a metal roll-up door fronting a large garage in the parking lot of a sanitation firm. Meanwhile, a group of US troops trotted around the property, going into and out of several buildings, covering each other the entire time.

She knew what the US was doing, and it was disturbing. Bowen, hours earlier, had briefed her and Upton. They were hunting for her.

"Switch the feed to the overhead drone and execute diversion," said Bowen into his mic.

"Copy that," replied Acquon.

McMichael glanced at Upton kneeling next to her. He seemed oblivious to her presence and instead appeared focused on his own HUD. Like her, and all the SF operators, he was wearing an active camouflage poncho with the hood not yet deployed. In Upton's hands, he too gripped a borrowed assault rifle. Seeing him, she felt better, safer.

And then another wave of doubt and self-loathing struck. None of them were safe, and it was her fault.

The video on her HUD flickered, and a new scene emerged. From an altitude she approximated at seventy-five feet, the view from above faced downward upon a large black electric SUV parked on the side of a street. She knew the vehicle was several blocks away on a street running parallel to where the enemy was searching.

Everything Bowen predicted and planned for appeared to be coming true. Just a few hours earlier, after a long sleep, she'd awoken feeling refreshed. Before racking out, she and Upton were given new soldier protection systems and combat gear, just in case. When they awoke, Bowen brought them up to speed. While they'd been sleeping, in the early dawn, he received a warning from CENTCOM. It was likely the US would be searching for the Hero of Mesquite. To mitigate the threat, he immediately dispatched a two-person team using active camouflage to break into a civilian SUV. Among other tasks, the team was ordered to hack the vehicle's autonomous driving system.

During that earlier briefing, she recalled the awful feeling of learning she was a target. Worse, she was the cause for putting everyone at risk. More people could die because of her. She couldn't shake the guilt, and when Bowen was done explaining his plan, she requested permission to leave. It would be better, she claimed, if she headed out on her own and surrendered. Bowen laughed at her suggestion. Her idea, he explained, was preposterous. Once in US hands, she'd be forced to endure advanced interrogation and, under those circumstances, it wouldn't take long before the enemy knew everything. By giving herself up, she'd be dooming them all. Reluctantly, she backed down. But she told him, more than once, she wasn't a hero. From a tactical standpoint, Bowen countered, it didn't matter. The enemy was after her and so was President Ortega.

And now the US hunters were getting close, and her very existence was the reason. She felt terrible and blamed herself for their present danger.

On her HUD, the overhead view jiggled, and McMichael refocused her thoughts. A breeze, she guessed, must be tugging at the insect drone. Shaped like a wasp, Bowen had explained earlier, the two-inch UAV was programmed to follow the hacked SUV at a preset altitude and pass along driving signals sent from a line-of-sight laser optic controller. She imagined Mason on the roof, holding a joystick, controlling the action.

Just then, the image still bouncing, the civilian SUV began to move. Fascinated, she marveled as the unmanned vehicle with dark-tinted windows drove a few hundred feet before taking a left turn on the street where she now sat. From there, the SUV drove slowly east, towards their warehouse position. As it approached, she envisioned the small drone flying overhead relaying control signals and transmitting video. Before reaching them, the SUV took a left, and the wide-angle lens of the drone picked up a new and dangerous picture. A half a block away, down the street, US soldiers were conducting their search.

"Everyone be ready," she heard Bowen say through the secure network.

The stealth vehicle traveled twenty yards towards the enemy before slamming to a halt. A second passed, then the SUV went into full reverse, burning rubber in an apparent attempt to escape. High above, the hornet drone wide-angle lens continued to capture and relay the video as the big vehicle stormed backward. Reaching the cross street, the SUV slid to a halt, and with tires spinning forward, it began to take off, but not fast enough.

Although caught off guard, the screeching tires must have caught the soldiers' attention, as it didn't take long for the US to respond. Before the SUV could travel ten feet forward, the Stuart machine gun opened-up, sending a hail of lead along the entire right side of the big black vehicle. Sparks flying, a trail of burning rubber in its wake, somehow the SUV gained speed when McMichael saw the right front tire explode. A second later, even though the vehicle had traveled far enough to escape the line of fire, she could tell the SUV was in trouble. The big black vehicle, hurtling down the road on a shredded tire, began to rock back and forth. Before it could stabilize, to her disappointment, the stricken vehicle took a hard-right turn. Eight houses down from the intersection where the US troops searched, the big SUV crashed through the front door of a modest suburban home and came to a sudden stop.

Three seconds later, the Stuart rounded the corner and barreled towards the wreck. As it closed the distance, once again, the fighting vehicle let loose with its machine gun, sending long bursts into the stricken SUV. Coming to a stop in the street opposite the wreck, the Stuart continued its assault, and for long seconds poured hot lead into the exposed rear of the black SUV. At last, with the main barrel of its cannon aimed directly at the wreck, its machine gun sending up a trail of smoke, the Stuart ceased firing. The insect drone stayed on station and transmitted the sight. The SUV was a riddled mess.

Just then, on her HUD, she spotted a group of US dismounted soldiers jogging around the corner. After hesitating for a few seconds, with assault rifles raised, the soldiers spread out and approached the wreckage.

"Mason, wait until they're close. Follow the plan," she heard Bowen bark into the radio.

"Copy that. Wished the SUV got farther down the street," replied Mason.

"Doesn't matter. Nothing's changed," said Bowen.

Watching the scene unfold on her HUD, she hoped like hell there weren't any civilians in the wrecked house. With her mic on mute, she reached over and tugged Bowen's shoulder. She didn't want him to go through with the rest of the plan. No one else should die for her.

Bowen turned her direction and gave a frown. Shaking his head, he pushed her hand away.

"Don't do it," she said aloud.

Bowen gave a hard stare and again shook his head.

Angry at Bowen, on her HUD, she observed two grunts separate from their squad mates. Hunched over, assault rifles up and well-spaced apart, both US soldiers approached the destroyed SUV. No, no, she thought to herself and was reaching for Bowen when a massive fireball erupted. Instinctively, she ducked, and two seconds later, the shock wave hit the warehouse, rattling parts upon their shelves.

Grimacing from the force, on her HUD, she watched as chunks of house and flaming vehicle came crashing down around the street. The two US soldiers near the SUV were gone, while the rest of the soldiers around the area lay prone as if mowed down by a windstorm. Meanwhile, the Stuart was in full retreat, backing away from the flames.

Distraught, she knew it wasn't Mason's fault for hitting the remote detonator igniting the C4 explosives planted inside the SUV. Sick to her stomach, even though she hadn't physically depressed the button, she felt responsible for killing those men.

Bowen once again issued orders over the secure network. "Mason, notify CENTCOM over the quantum, we're on the move. Repeat, we are on the move."

Without saying another word, Bowen bounced upright and lifted the poncho hood over his head. Then he pointed at the exit. Next to her, Upton stood and flipped up his own hood. Feeling sick, full of guilt and remorse, she arose. Not wanting anyone else to die, especially Upton standing next to her, she gave a heavy nod. It was time to leave.

* * *

May 10, 19:07 (PDT)

Inside CENTCOM, General Story sat down at his command chair. Seated next to him, his aid, Lieutenant Colonel Andrea Simpson, looked over and greeted him with a nod. He bobbed his head in return, but his thoughts were still elsewhere. Just a few minutes before, in his small private quarters, he'd spoken over secure video chat with his son Christopher. In worried conversation, his son sought his advice. With events in Nevada, war on the horizon, should he and his husband flee to Canada and seek asylum? Could he, his father, help get him across the border? After listening, the answer for both questions was *yes*. But *no*, he couldn't join them, his job was too important. If things turned out okay, then afterwards, they could be reunited.

"Sir, President Ortega is on the line," said Simpson.

Shaken from his brooding, Story swiveled in his chair and put on his headset. After adjusting the earpiece, he waved at Simpson to put through the call.

"General Story, are you there?" asked Ortega.

"Yes, ma'am."

"I'm still in Sacramento at a break in congressional deliberations. The US missile strike against Vegas, eighteen dead and twice as many wounded, was awful. Congress took the unprovoked attack hard. I'm not sure what the US was thinking, but their blatant aggression has served to create greater resolve. More than ever, these folks are ready to fight back. Before midnight we'll adjourn here. Afterward, I'll let the US know we've rejected their demand to turn over Nevada. In response, I expect we'll get no more reprieves, and the US will attack Las Vegas."

"Understood," replied Story. Now there was no turning back. Tomorrow, a fight was coming. The advice he'd given his son was warranted.

"Last we spoke, you estimated the damage from the US missile strike wasn't enough to stop Heavy Metal. You've had more time to analyze. Still believe that way?" asked the president.

"Yes. Beyond the loss of life, losing our primary missile defense systems and some artillery assets was the biggest blow. Other damage, especially to the defensive works east of Las Vegas, can be repaired. Work will continue non-stop until the enemy is on our doorstep. The other significant loss was to a squadron of six stealth helicopters at Nellis. Rookie mistake. Pilots were refueling when the siren sounded, and all of them were parked too close together. Two of the birds are salvageable, but not the remainder."

"So it could've been worse?"

"Yes, ma'am. As you know, SALI warned us to expect a US strike against Vegas in advance of their major offensive. To maintain the viability of Operation Heavy Metal, she warned us against using any of the new weapons to oppose the strike. So although we couldn't stop the raid, when the inbound missiles were detected, our folks were expecting it and took immediate evasive action. Still, the losses were unfortunate."

"I see," said Ortega. "I seem to recall the plan to extricate Lisa McMichael called for the use of a stealth helicopter. Please tell me the mission to get her the hell out of Mesquite is moving forward?"

"Yes, ma'am, but not as originally planned. The loss of our stealth helicopters necessitated a change."

"I need her in Sacramento. She's a hero. We've got near panic in the streets. No matter how Heavy Metal turns out, having her on display will help calm fears and maintain confidence. When will she be here?"

"Well, ma'am, you recall SALI also warned the US would quickly discover a lack of DNA and begin hunting for McMichael."

"Of course. But you recommended sticking with the original plan and flying her out this evening after dark."

"Well, the US did go looking for her."

"Not good. What happened?" asked the president, her voice sounding concerned.

"Around five thirty this afternoon, a US search team approached her hiding location. The SF team protecting her was prepared, created a diversion, and left the area on foot. With no stealth helicopter available, their goal is to have her safely in Las Vegas sometime in the early morning hours."

"Las Vegas! Hell, she could get killed. Why not take her somewhere safe?"

"Vegas has all of the resources needed to get her into California, and Sacramento, fast. Besides, it's the closest major city, and a separate team of SF operators based there are driving stealth vehicles to pick her up in the desert. Madam, it's the safest and quickest way to get her back and should be accomplished before the US attacks."

There was a long pause, and Story waited. Somehow, he had to broach the subject of his son.

"Dammit! Just make sure she gets back in one piece."

"Yes, ma'am."

"Getting back to Heavy Metal, how is your confidence level?"

General Story looked around the room. He could feel the tension but also a level of optimism. Different groups of folks huddled around desks and monitors, and he watched as officers, enlisted, and key civilian staff moved about. There was a buzz in the air.

"General, are you there?" asked the president.

"Ah, yes. President Ortega, we'll be ready. The question remains, will Heavy Metal work, and if so, to what extent? Those won't be answered until after the battle."

"Of course," replied Ortega.

"Also, I think it prudent we bring in SALI," said Story.

"Why so?" asked the president.

"If things go wrong, and believe me things will go wrong, having her guidance could prove critical. Keeping her locked away, only meeting afterward, doesn't make sense. I recommend she be brought here to CENTCOM. It's a short drive. Have her by my side throughout the operation, and I will personally supervise her. We can give her a cover story that she is your personal assistant, something like that."

"I'm a hundred percent behind the idea. In my opinion, we should be using her much more than we have. But she is the property of Mr. Basu," said the president.

"Human beings, I'm told, aren't property. At least not in our country," snapped Story.

"So true! I want her freedom more than anyone. She should be working to help the nation. But her existence is still classified, and I've agreed to keep it that way. For now, I'll bring it up with Basu. Meanwhile, don't count on having her."

"Remind him that Heavy Metal is SALI's plan, and I'm not opposed to having her assist in real time. It could make all the difference."

"Agreed. But it won't be up to me. I'll reach out and let you know. Anything else?" asked Ortega.

Story took a deep breath, closed his eyes, and imagined his son. "Yes, there is."

"Go ahead. I've only a couple of minutes before I'm expected back with Congress."

Story re-opened his eyes and, although, uncomfortable he pushed onward. "My son and his husband are leaving tonight and heading towards Canada. Should things turn bad, they'll be seeking asylum."

To his surprise, he heard a chuckle. "Yeah, they along with several million others." He was about to interject, explain he wasn't joking, when Ortega continued in a serious tone. "I understand, General. Look, I can't do anything right now, but maybe later. Send over their names and details, and I'll see what can be done. Just do something for me."

"Of course," replied Story, not expecting to be asked a favor in return.

"Win tomorrow! If you do, then asylum for your son, and millions of others, might not be necessary."

Story felt the added weight on his shoulders and let out a puff of air. "Madam President, I'll do my absolute best."

"I know you will," said Ortega.

A second later, with the president's last words resonating, General Story heard the line go dead. Leaning back in his chair, he imagined Las Vegas and the prepared desert battlegrounds east of the city. He pictured his son at the Canadian border struggling to cross while around him fires raged and people screamed. Shaking off the images, he focused instead on the task at hand.

Standing up, Story folded his arms and looked around the room at the many good people, all of them there to protect the Republic of American States. Seated next to him, his aid, Andrea, kept her head down, scanning incoming data. These were good, decent people, worthy of his respect, and he was proud to serve with them.

He made a vow. If the ROAS was overrun, he'd die protecting his son and the nation that adopted them. On the morrow, Operation Heavy Metal and his destiny awaited. Determined, he turned to his aid and issued orders. The Battle of Las Vegas awaited.

ABOUT THE AUTHOR

David Pope lives in Folsom, CA. with two cats and the love of his life, Sharon. After spending four years in the US Air Force achieving the rank of staff sergeant and earning an Air Force Commendation medal, he started a career in information technology. David held a variety of IT technical and executive positions across thirty-five years. Tired of being on-call twenty-four seven, with his two children Katie and Matthew all grown up, he decided it was time to pursue new opportunities. When not writing, David enjoys baseball, golf, history, a nap with the cats, and chardonnay.

WHAT'S NEXT?

If you made it through the book, as a first-time author, I'm humbled and I thank you for investing the time. Please leave a review on Amazon, Goodreads and or my Facebook page. As a first-time author, your feedback will help me to improve!

Based on how the Battle of Mesquite ended, you can see I've teed up a second book, the Battle of Las Vegas, for publication next year. Afterward, if all goes well, I expect to deliver a third book, wrapping up the US Reunification War series. Just depends on how I hold up with the process and if I improve enough to keep you, the reader, interested.

A word on the series: I've tried to picture a not so distant future that is far beyond what I or anyone may consider likely. More than anything, it represents the extremes of our current times. The series is supposed to be 'dime store' fiction, something to read that might engage, and in no way should be taken too literal. My desire is that you found parts of the story intriguing and entertaining, and I have earned the right to keep you engaged as the series continues. I hope so.

Lastly, I want to give a special thanks to Rebecca Prokop and the team at Spellbound Self-Publishing. As a first-time indie author, she guided me through the entire process and brought in skilled beta readers, editors, and artists to assist with the project. I wouldn't have made it this far without their help. Thank you, Becky!

KEEP CONNECTED

Keep in touch to see the latest updates about the US Reunification War series, ask questions or provide feedback. Thanks!

Website: www.popeitsentio.com
Facebook: www.facebook.com/popeitsentio
Email: itsentio@comcast.net